Soul

TRINITY  TRILOGY
BOOK THREE

PRAISE FOR SOUL

"Reading Soul felt like I was at the theater watching a thriller because the thrill of this book is exactly that....a thriller. So much going on and it just kept you wanting more, more and more! It was so hard to put down and I just needed to find out how it was going to end."
~ Brittany's Book Blog

"I am so sad to see this trilogy, or should I say trinity, come to an end. It is one of the best romantic suspense series I have read and I don't say that lightly."
~ Give Me Books

"I don't think Ms. Carlan missed a thing in her presentation of Soul. We have been given her no holds barred hot, erotic tension, evidence of true love and need, bone-chilling terror and a peek into the minds of her characters, as she has proven, once again, that she is a literary force to be reckoned with who has a huge future ahead of her!"
~ Tome Tender Book Blog

Soul

TRINITY TRILOGY
BOOK THREE

WATERHOUSE
PRESS

To my husband Eric,
You will always be my past, present, and future.
You are my one true soulmate.
I give you my body, mind, and soul.
Forever.

CHASE

CHAPTER ONE

She's gone, but I can still feel her. My soul aches to be with its mate. If Gillian were dead, I would know it, for I too would cease to exist. One cannot live with only half a soul. I'm so tired, but I can't sleep, not with her still out there. It's been three days and very few leads. Austin is still out. He barely survived the lethal dose of the Etorphine plunged into his neck, but he hasn't woken up. Every day that passes is another day my love is with a madman.

The resort performed a forced lockdown at my insistence. Every hotel guest was offered a free night off their stay for their inconvenience, and each person was questioned. One couple gave the best lead. Right around the time that Gillian was kidnapped, they were walking the path behind the bride's room. Said they saw a man wearing a uniform pushing a laundry cart. The staff confirmed that the laundry service is far more discreet and doesn't wear the gray utility uniforms. They wear the standard black and white, connoting the housekeeping service. And the staff knew not to be anywhere near the location of the wedding at the time unless specifically requested by my assistant, Dana.

The two only remembered that the individual was a

white male and built. Meaning, he was either overweight or worked out a lot. They couldn't recall any descriptive features aside from that he was very tall, a few inches over six feet. Unfortunately, that didn't narrow things down at all. We are at a complete dead end until Austin wakes up. He's the only person who has seen the kidnapper face-to-face, and he's unconscious in a hospital bed in Cancun, Mexico. The city where I was supposed to marry the only woman for me. Also the place where my mother took her last breath.

Deep gut-wrenching pain tears through me, twisting and swirling. For the umpteenth time, I swallow and convulsively grip my stomach. I cannot lose it. Staying strong is the only thing I can give to Gillian. As it is, I can't keep any food down. Coffee is my only salvation. Reflexively, I clench both hands into fists, stare unseeingly at Austin's prone form, and close my eyes. Once again she comes to me.

Red hair spills over porcelain skin. The towel is covering her lower half as she dips a toe into the steaming water. My gaze caresses the skin of her rounded shoulder, the slight curve of her spine where her back arcs and her waists slopes in. The small indents at her lower back catch the light and I salivate, wanting nothing more than to press my lips against those smooth patches, maybe even bite down until she purrs.

With one hand, she sweeps the fiery locks over one shoulder, exposing her entire bare back to my view. It calls to me like a homing beacon. A halo of light sparkles around her as she turns her head slightly. I can now see the swanlike column of her neck, except something's not right, but my gaze shifts and my focus changes when she drops the towel. Her heart-shaped ass is glorious. My love turns just the side of her face, but her eyes, are dark, hollow, tortured. They're not the stunning green of the most perfect emerald like usual.

I gasp and cannot move toward her, but still I watch my love as something red trails down her smooth back like paint dripping down a canvas. Her head tips back, and a gnarled gaping black hole stretches along the front of her neck. As I watch her turn her head around completely, giant purple bruises mar every surface of her face. It's swollen, bloated, and splotched with dried rusty-colored blood.

"No! Gillian!" I scream, but nothing comes out.

Her eyes close, and when she turns around fully, her body can be seen in all its hideous glory. Dark black-and-blue bruises cover her breasts, her ribs, and stomach as blood pours down her chest and sternum from the wide cavernous hole at her throat.

I yell and shout and battle with my unmoving limbs, trying desperately to get to her, but I can't move.

With everything I have and through sheer force of will alone, I send her love. All that I have to give, the grief, the sadness, the ache of not being with her. I need to be with her.

I open my eyes, and she finally speaks. "Wake up, Chase."

My love's body shimmers and disappears as white light pierces my eyes and a hand is at my chest.

"Chase!" Dana shakes my chest, and I push her away forcefully, jump out of the chair, and back up until I hit the wall, still stuck in the gnawing clutches of the sick and twisted dream. Three sets of eyes are staring at me. Dana's, Jack's, and Austin's.

"You were dreaming, you're okay," Dana whispers, eyes brimming with tears.

I suck in a breath and clasp Austin's arm. "Can you speak?" I swallow down the bile stuck in my throat.

Austin blinks and licks his dry lips. Dana rushes over a cup with a straw. Austin takes it between his lips and sucks the water down. I can hardly breathe as I watch him take one, two, three, gulps before looking back to me.

His eyes water. "He got her," he croaks.

I close my eyes and breathe in slowly, tamping down the desire to shake him, yell, or pound my fists into every surface within a mile radius of me. Instead, I nod.

"I've seen him before."

Jack comes close to the other side of the bed. "Where?"

Austin swallows, and his voice comes out sounding pained. "Pictures, you have them." He sucks in another breath, grits his teeth, and then closes his eyes. "She knows him."

Jack pulls out his phone and pulls up something. "From the pictures I showed you?" Jack asks, his own voice tight but holding on.

Austin shakes his head. "The penthouse. Her stuff that we moved in." The tone turns into a scratchy roll of words. Dana brings him the water, and he sucks down more. Then pushes it away, clearly frustrated. He tries to sit up. "Have to go there. He's in the pictures in her stuff. Blond, blue eyes. Big fucker. Huge."

I push him back against the hospital bed with both hands as Jack grabs his wrist before he can rip out the lifesaving meds being pumped into his arms. The doctor said once he woke up he'd be in the hospital for a while, and right now he's still getting the antidote that's helping to stabilize his vitals.

Blaring alarms start in the room from the multitude of equipment. "I have to get to her!" he roars. "It's my fault.

He's going to hurt her!" Austin's eyes look wild, completely black, like a man about to lose it.

Several doctors rush in. One holding a needle. "Everyone out!"

"No, no! He knows who took Gillian! We need him awake!" I press through the doctors, trying to get to Austin. I make it to his bed as random arms claw and grab at me.

Austin holds my arm. "Scar, scar on his hand like a burn," he says, winded right before the doctors stick a needle into the port for his meds.

I sink to my knees. The tears finally come and rip down my face. I grip my hair and pull on it.

A heavy set of arms lifts me up and drags me out of the room before slamming me against the wall. "Chase, pull yourself together! We have a lead on him now!" Jack holds me against the white hospital hallway wall outside of Austin's room. His eyes are focused and his mouth held tight. "We need to move, call the girls. See if they know him."

Instant calm melts over my form like stepping inside a perfectly heated hot tub. I pull out my phone and dial Maria.

"Chase?" Her voice is strained when she answers. They are all beside themselves with worry, waiting for any shred of information about Gillian.

"Maria, did Gillian know a man who was blond, blue eyes, and big?" She gasps into the receiver, and I hold it tight against my ear. "Had a scar on his hand, like a burn?"

"*Dios Mio.* That could be Danny."

I bite my lip so hard I taste blood as that tingling sensation skids down my spine. The warning that we were close to something. "Danny who?"

The line was scratchy. "Danny Mc…uh…Mc something. Bree, Kat? What was Danny's last name?"

At the same time that Maria says McBride, so does Jack who is already lifting his phone.

"Daniel McBride, get there now! His work, his house, his gym, now!" he growls into the phone. "I want everything you have on him. I want to know who his parents are, his childhood friends, what he fucking had for breakfast this morning! Now! Every man on it."

For the first time, I am able to breathe. We have a lead. A solid one. She is closer. Has to be, because I can feel her essence now more now than before.

"Daniel McBride," Dana croaks, her face pale. She leans against the wall as tears slip down her cheeks. "No." She shakes her head. "No, it can't be!" she whispers.

"I'll call soon," I say into the phone and drop it into my pocket before taking the few steps to Dana and cup her cheeks. "You know him?"

Dana's eyes flash and her face contorts into a pained expression. "He's my…my boyfriend."

Three days. He's had me for three days in this room with no light, no warmth, and no way out. A cinderblock room that has no windows and is incredibly cold. The deep chill makes me think it might be underground, possibly a basement. He's kept me in and out of a semiconscious state since he took me. All I know for sure is that we were in a car for a long time before I woke up here. He admitted last night that we are back in the States. Even laughed when he told the story that he set me up like a sleeping bride in the car when crossing border. Makes more sense as to why he was in a tux when I woke the first night. At the time it didn't dawn on me, as I was drugged to the gills. Then Danny proceeded to tell me how he is going to use that tux for our wedding when the time is right. He went so far as to share that Austin was likely dead based on the horse-sized dose of tranquilizer he gave him and that Chase's mom was definitely dead. That I remember. It plays on a constant loop in my mind. Danny even lamented how excited he was that he was leaving that present for Chase to find along with a missing bride.

The doorknob jiggles and then opens. I cower into the corner where a mattress is lying on the floor. He moved from ropes to chains and a pulley system. Now, I can walk over to the pot in the corner that he left for me to use as a bathroom.

"Been three days, princess. You ready to be nice?" Danny grins, his lip curling sadistically at the edge. His blond hair is cropped tight to the scalp, the long layers he had yesterday now gone. Maybe another attempt at looking different in case Chase and his men figure out who took me. God, I hope they've figured it out by now.

Instead of responding to him, I stay silent. The first day I spoke. Since then, I've kept quiet, not knowing what to do. My stomach growls violently. I haven't had any sustenance for the past three days.

"I can hear you're hungry." He sets down a tray with a sandwich, an apple, and what looks like a glass of milk on the lone side table near the mattress. "If you eat, I'll reward you. Give you a blanket. How's that?" he offers.

I shiver. My revealing wedding dress is the only thing I have on. No shoes, no bra, just a slip of lace and the dress. The bare back is lovely, and the sheer overlay on the sleeves beautiful, but it isn't meant for warmth. It takes me but a moment to realize I'm going to need food if I'm going to survive until Chase finds me, and I'm frightfully cold. My teeth have been on a permanent chatter since Danny not so gently tossed me into the cinderblock room. Danny points to the food, and I make my way over to it and sit on the mattress. The chains rattle and shriek as I move like a hundred-year-old woman toward the mattress. My limbs and joints no longer have full mobility.

Danny waits, leaning against the opposite wall. He watches while I lift the apple and take a bite, figuring this is the least likely item to be laced with more drugs. The entire time I've been here, I've felt lethargic, with a sour stomach and fuzzy head. Either I've got a cold or some twisted fuck is drugging me. I am pretty certain the latter is the culprit.

"Good girl," he says condescendingly. "Now, we're going to get right to the point today. I'm going to keep you here until I believe that you've seen the errors of your ways, have forgotten about the rich fucker, and are ready to see that we're meant to be together."

The apple starts to roll and churn, like acid in my gut, ready to shoot up my throat in a volcanic burst of vomit.

"That is not going to happen, and you can't hold me forever, Danny. This is crazy. Y-Y-You killed a woman!" I finally allow the fear to tear from my lungs.

He ruffles a hand through his short blond hair. Back in the day, I loved his long blond layers. They were so soft and shiny, especially for a man. Women would kill to have hair like that. Now it just makes me wish I could run my fingers through Chase's dark, thick cappuccino-colored locks. God, he must be so worried. The ache and need to be with him is devastating. I choke back a sob, not wanting Danny to see how frightened I am.

Danny pinches his lips together. "Killing Mrs. Davis was nothing. I'm actually getting good at it; although recently, I found out that your stupid fucking friend is alive. I gotta hand it to you, princess, that was a sneaky trick. Posting an imposter like that. The girl was a dead ringer for Bree. Well," he chuckles, "now she's just dead." He shrugs with absolutely no remorse or respect for human life.

"Who are you?" I whisper.

In two steps, he's in front of me, his hand around my throat, squeezing tight, cutting off any airflow. "I'm your worst fucking nightmare if you don't wake the fuck up and start doing what I say!" he yells in my face, spittle hitting my cheeks.

Cringing, I press my face as far back as I can. He grips my neck, pulls it forward, and slams my head onto the concrete, hard. Lights flicker across my eyes, and I slump down the wall to the mattress below. His body straddles mine, his knees pressing into my biceps keeping me from moving my arms. "See, I can do whatever the hell I want to you. Why?" He trails a finger down between my breasts and cups both of them roughly. "Because. You. Are. Mine. Get it now?" He grabs the top of my wedding gown and rips the fabric down to my breasts. "You always did have a great fucking rack." He leans down and kisses my neck, lower between my breasts, and the top swells peeking out. Tears fall down the sides of my face, wetting the mattress beneath me. I stop fighting and look up at the ceiling where I imagine Chase's face, his bottomless blue eyes.

Before I know what's happening, I'm being lifted up and smacked hard. The split in my lip from when he punched me in the bridal room busts back open, and the metallic taste of blood fills my mouth. "What the fuck are you doing? You think you can close your eyes and think of someone else while I love on you?" Danny smacks me again. This time, my left eye starts to throb from the blow. "You stupid bitch! You whispered *his* name!"

Danny stands and paces from one side of the room to the other, talking to himself and tugging at his hair. It's only a ten by ten space, so he doesn't go far. I lift my hand and feel around my eye to see if he gave me another wound. He didn't. Just adding to the bruising already there. I lick my lip and hold my finger to the cut, hoping to stop the flow of blood, as my other arm holds the fabric of the front of my dress together. At least he didn't remove the dress. I fear that if he does that, it's over. He'll rape me.

Finally, after a few minutes of him brooding and me cowering in the corner, he stops and turns to me. "You'll learn. You'll forget him." He points at me, and I shake my head. Wrong thing to do. He roars and rushes at me, grips my head, and slams it into the concrete blocks again and again, until the world around me goes black.

X

Why, why, why can't she just fucking listen to me? Christ, that bastard brainwashed her. What the fuck happened to my perfect princess? I slam the door of her cell, clamp it shut, and set the lock, shoving the key into my pocket before walking halfway up the steep concrete steps where I plant my ass on the cold ground. "Fuck!"

Okay, think, Danny, think. I've wanted her since she left over a year ago. Since then, I've spent a lot of time thinking how different things were going to be when I got her back. She wants to be fucked like a whore. I'll give her that, and soon. Over the years, I've fucked everything that walked every way under the sun, but not my Gillian. My perfect princess. She deserved better. Until the day she sat up naked, turned around, and presented her perfect ass as she held herself up on all fours. Something in me just snapped, and the rage I'd been holding back from her came to the surface. It reminded me of all the other stupid cunts I'd fucked. The weeping holes ready to take any dick without seeing the face of the man fucking her.

Not my Gillian. No, I never wanted to defile her like those other whores. She was different, perfect, and broken when we met. Finally, I got it out of her what that bastard before me did to her. And I spent the better part of a year making her mine. Treating her like the queen I wanted her to be. Even seeing her in that room, in her wedding dress, sent all kinds of ideas rushing to the surface. My princess standing there in her white wedding dress, waiting to marry me.

Well, if she thinks she's getting out of here and going back to *him*, she's sorely mistaken. I'll break her—again. I don't care how long it takes. She was broken in before by Justin. I'll just rip a few pages of notes from his book of hard knocks. Eventually, she'll come around. There's really no other option, because if I can't have her, no one will.

Standing, I figure it's time I get some bandages and shit for her head and lip. Stupid bitch. If she'd just start listening, I wouldn't have to knock some sense into her. Once at the top of the stairs, I lift the latch to the rotten wooden door and open it to a blue, sunny California sky. The trees around the property are thick. My parents didn't like having too many neighbors. Probably because they spent their time smacking me around, and normal folks didn't take too kindly to people beating the shit out of their kid.

At the edge of the property though, way in the back of my old childhood yard, I found my perfect getaway. My idiot parents didn't even know it existed. The house was built at least a hundred years ago, and with it was an old bomb shelter. A room built into the ground that would probably survive a nuclear attack. These things are not common in California, but I was glad that whoever built the property had thought to add it. Over the years, it's been a genius hideout. It even has a closet off the stairs where I keep my guns, additional explosives, a safe with my legal paperwork—basically anything important to me.

The original house is gone, of course, since I burned it down when I was fourteen with my parents' bodies still inside, but in its place, I put a motor home I got for cheap. It doesn't look like much, but it works well enough. I paid to tap into the waterlines but use a generator for everything else. Even though my old house isn't here, I can lie down at night and still hear the ghosts of when I killed my biological parents. We need to get out of here and soon. When I get Gillian to see the light, we'll move on and live somewhere pretty. I saved most of the money I got from my parents' life insurance policies when I was eighteen and all the money I was paid for serving my country. When you don't have a place to hang your hat, you don't have any bills, so I pocketed everything. Even now, working as an accountant in San Francisco, I make a mint but live small. All to get to this moment—when I found the perfect girl. I knew when we dated that she was the one for me. Even if she never said she loved me, I knew it was because of Justin and what he'd done to her. It will take time, and I have a lot of that—the rest of my life—to make her see how good it will be between us.

Still, something made me come back here to this shithole, and I'm glad I did. No one can hear my girl scream, and no one will ever find her as I work on making her mine again. She's lying on a bed in the room, still in her fancy white wedding dress. It excites me to see the dirt, grime, and blood all over the fabric.

The soiled gown reminds me that I probably should get her some clothes. Of course that thought leads to thoughts of me removing that gown. Just holding onto her full breasts, kissing her skin, made my dick painfully hard earlier. I need to be inside my woman and soon. It's only a matter of time. Smelling her vanilla-cherry scent, tasting the saltiness of her skin... It's like coming home. And now I am home, back where I grew up.

Soon she'll feel the same love and affection too. I'll make sure of it. In the meantime, I need to get some provisions to clean her up. I am not going to fuck a dirty cunt. I'll pick up some baby wipes until I can trust her to come into the motor home and take a decent shower. Yeah, I'll take care of my girl. Slowly remove every inch of clothing and wipe her down. Get her ready for me. Then, when I'm done caressing her skin the way I remember she likes, she'll be begging me to fuck her. There's no way she won't remember how it was between us. How good it felt to have me buried inside. That's the only time for me when everything goes away. The screaming in my head, the demons on my shoulders telling me to do things, hurt people, get her back. All of it. Gone.

All I need is to make love to my princess, and all the bad, the rage, the anger will go away. Just disappear. As long as I have her, I can be the real me. That's what I need back. The calm after the storm. Gillian has always been that for me, since the first day we met at the gym. There was something different about her, more special. Maybe it was seeing that broken little girl inside, the one I think spoke to the broken boy inside me. When we were together, it was right. My mind stilled. I could sleep, work, take showers, and not remember. Not think about what my parents put me through, how everyone ignored the signs, the bruises, the pain they must have seen behind my eyes. Then after I killed them, their bodies went away, along with their fists, but never their voices. I can always hear them. Calling me names, screaming at me, demeaning me, telling me I'm ugly, a bad son, a horrible person.

All that shit went away when I was with my girl. That's why I needed her. Had to have her. She was my salvation, and once I get inside her, she'll remember I was hers. That I was the one who secured a restraining order against Justin and kept him away from her for so long. Until he fucking touched her again. Then, of course, it was nothing, breaking into his parents' home while he was on house arrest recuperating from his pansy-ass beating and strangling him in his sleep. Then I simply set everything up to look like a suicide. Easy enough because I strangled him with his own belt. Only fingerprints that'll be found are Justin's. It was nothing to hook two belts together, one over the beam running along the ceiling, another for his neck. Then I placed his lifeless body in it, measured the chair distance to make sure I had the loop at the right measurement, and softly kicked the chair over. I walked out of the room with his dead body still swaying. Even took a picture of it with my phone so I could share it with Gillian. I want to give that to her as a present. Perhaps when we're living the easy life on a beach somewhere far, far away.

CHASE

CHAPTER TWO

I dream of her again. Only this time she is alive, glorious in her beauty. Mahogany-colored hair as soft as silk slides through my fingers and fans out in a burst of color across the white sheets. "Baby," I mumble, and then my eyes come open with a start. The scent of vanilla fills the air, and I look around, panicking, searching for her. The flight attendant offers Jack a beverage and walks past me. Vanilla clings to the air around her. Gillian smells of vanilla. It clings to her like a second skin. Only this time it isn't her. Just another dream. Always a godforsaken dream. Either she is being tortured and her body a mess of gaping wounds, or she is lovely, and I am being tortured by the gift of her image. I prefer it that way. I'd rather see her perfect and whole than broken and dying.

Jack alerted Dr. Madison to what happened to Gillian and requested a script for a sleep aid. He knows me well. Even still, the only time I'm able to choke down those two little pills is the moment I sit down in one of my jets. We're heading home. It feels right. Being back in San Francisco is where we need to be. That might not be where Daniel McBride took Gillian, but it's the ideal location to bring all the forces together. The FBI is involved now due to the abduction crossing state and international lines. Thomas Redding, Maria's boyfriend, is still one of the leads on the case, though that took a lot of rubbing elbows with some serious folks in Washington to maneuver. Whatever. I'll donate to whatever campaign those bloodsuckers want to get my fiancée back.

Fuck. My fiancée. She should be my *wife* right now. Mrs. Gillian Davis. Four days ago, we were to marry, until that bastard took her and slit my mother's throat. The knot in my gut squeezes painfully, and I lean over, clutching at my stomach.

"Sir, you all right?" Jack asks, his tone expressing worry as he grips my shoulder.

I shove his arm off. "Fine. What the fuck do you have? Anything?"

"Chase, it's only been a few hours. We're about to touch down at SFO now. I'll know more when we land."

He'll know more. Those three words do nothing to resolve the constant ache permeating every cell within me. Where is she? It goes round and round in my overly tired brain. She is *not* gone. That sadistic bastard has her hidden away somewhere, and I have every intention of finding her whole and alive.

We exit the plane and a town car is waiting on the tarmac. "Take me to the FBI headquarters," I tell Jack.

His jaw tightens. "Sir, we'll be meeting with Detective Redding and Agent Brennen at a secure location close to the strip. In the event that we need to shuttle off, I thought you'd rather be close," Jack says.

"Yes, thank you, Jack. Good thinking." Again, thank God someone is thinking straight. My mind is a jumble of emotions. Something I've only recently tapped into. Gillian has brought out many new sides in me, the emotional one being the most uncomfortable. Prior to her, I wasn't worried about what people thought, how I spent my money, what the media said, and I most certainly didn't give a damn about making important friendships. Her influence has taught me how shallow and empty my life was until she filled it with light and love. She makes me *want* to be the kind of man she can be proud of.

Right now, though, I'm about to become the shrewd businessman, the demanding and controlling billionaire who has no qualms about throwing his money around to get what he wants. As long as the end result is Gillian back in my arms and my bed, making my life complete, I'll burn every last bridge, fuck over anyone who gets in the way of the investigation, and throw as much weight and money around as it takes. My eye is on the prize, and she's one petite, curvy redhead who owns my body, mind, and soul.

Jack brings us to an airport hotel. The moment we walk in, the hotel manager walks us straight past check-in to the elevator. "Mr. Davis, thank you for visiting our establishment. When your representative called early today, we made sure everything was in order as specified." I narrow my eyebrows, not knowing anything about specifications. The man's eyes flick to Jack and then back to me. "Uh, the computers, the secure Internet connections, and round-the-clock access to a Detective Thomas Redding and an Agent Brennen to the penthouse suite."

I nod and look up at the number. Once we reach number thirty-five, it stops. The doors open to a small hallway. To the left is one set of double doors, to the right another. "We reserved both rooms as requested. You will have no disturbances. Here are your keys, sir." He holds out the cards after opening one of the doors.

The room is wide with a spectacular view. Only I don't care to look out. *Can Gillian see out of her cage? Is she locked in a tower high above the clouds or a dirty filthy dungeon with no light?* Pinpricks skitter along my spine as I toss my blazer over the armchair and head to the bar where I pour two fingers of Macallan, toss it back, and promptly pour two more in a second glass. I look up at Jack and gesture to the glass. He walks over, grabs the glass, and gulps the drink back. He sucks in a breath and hands me the tumbler.

"Another?" I ask, knowing I'm going to need several more of these to get through the night. Jack shakes his head. If I am being honest, it took me by surprise that he accepted the first. He doesn't usually drink when he's working, but as it stands, he's on point until she's found. I know Jack very well, and he won't dare leave me until Gillian is safe. He is my bodyguard and driver, but I've also known the man since I was a child.

Three raps at the door, and Jack leaves the living space. Moments later, Thomas, Maria, and the individual I assume to be Agent Brennen enter. The agent is nondescript, wearing a brownish-gray suit that hangs off his form instead of one that actually fits. He has a white mustache, and his beard covers the bottom half of his face, making him look more like Colonel Sanders than a serious federal agent with years of military experience. I close my eyes and pray that he has the mind of a Samurai warrior hiding behind that granddaddy face.

Maria rushes past the two men and flings her arms

around my neck, pulling me into a hug. I hold her, but don't reciprocate. I feel dead inside. There is no woman I would take comfort in right now other than my woman, Gillian.

Maria pulls back and her ice-blue gaze holds mine. "She's alive," she says in a voice so low only I can hear.

"I agree."

She nods and then takes in a breath.

Jack narrows his brows at the Italian Spanish firecracker. "Why is she here?"

He asks exactly what I'm thinking.

Maria turns around on a toe, cocks a hip, and plants a hand on it. Her black hair flies around her like it had a static charge. "That there is my man." She points to Thomas. "And he"—she points to me—"is my best friend's fiancé. My best friend is missing. I have every right to be here. You're just lucky I was able to escape without the other two knowing about it. Now *cállate*. We have some news." She sits down, leans forward, and clasps her hands together. "Go ahead, Tommy."

Thomas lets out a long breath. "Chase Davis, meet Agent David Brennen."

I shake the man's hand and find he has quite the grip. Strong man, strong mind...hopefully.

"Take a seat. Let's go over the information." The four of us sit down in the living room. Two couches face one another with a table in between. Jack stands behind the couch but within sight, a habit he formed in the service. Says he likes being able to move at any given time. The man saw his fair share of sneak attacks during his time in Iraq during Desert Storm, so I never question him.

"With the information you provided us this morning,

we were able to ascertain that Daniel McBride is actually Daniel Humphrey," Agent Brennen speaks loud, clear, and precise. Everything that his wardrobe and physical attributes contradict. "He was adopted as a teen after his parents died in a house fire."

"But he got out?" I ask. The way he spoke made it seem as if there were more to the story.

He nods. "Yes, the sole survivor. At the time, the local police just saw it as a tragedy. The wood burning stove had been left open, a spark flew out, caught the rug, and so on. The boy, Daniel Humphrey, suspect Daniel McBride, narrowly escaped by jumping out his bedroom window. That's how he claims he obtained the burn to his hand. In the reports, he reiterated that he grabbed the handle of his bedroom door, and it burned his hand. Only look at these pictures." He lays out a picture of a pale, dirty hand. "See the burn."

I focus on that hand. The same hand that cut my mother's throat and kidnapped Gillian. "The burn isn't shaped like a circle."

Agent Brennen smiles wide like he's won the lottery. "Exactly. If he had grabbed the handle, the burn would be circular or shaped like a handle. This burn covers most of the *top* of the hand as if he were holding something really hot and burned the outer layers of skin."

"So what are you saying?" I'm no longer in the mood for charades. "Get to the point, Agent Brennan. My future wife is in the hands of this man as we speak."

"I think he received those burns when he set the fire, and whatever he was holding, a torch of some sort, burned his hand in the process."

"You think he killed his parents?" Maria gasps, eyes bulging.

Agent Brennen nods. "Yes, I do. I think he killed them, just as he killed that poor girl in the yoga studio, your mother, and attempted to kill Mr. Parks. This man is highly skilled, extremely intelligent, and very patient. According to our profiler, he likely has some type of fascination with Gillian." I swear under my breath. "No, Mr. Davis that could very well work in her favor. The fact that he believes she's his means he's formed a deep attachment to her and probably thinks he loves her. The odds are in her favor that he won't kill her right away because of this."

"Then you think she's safe for the time being."

His brown eyes crinkle at the edges and go flat. "No, I don't. Unless she reciprocates that fascination or love, he will hurt her. He will try to break her of her connection to you and the outside world so that all paths lead back to him."

I close my eyes, suck in a strong breath, stand, and start pacing. "What are our next steps?" The energy around me feels charged, zipping with focus. It's the same feeling I get when I'm about to acquire a failing company. The hunt is on. We will find her.

Thomas logs in on one of the laptops Jack has on the coffee table. "Well, we've already checked his apartment." I look into his eyes. "He wasn't there. He lived very sparse, though we did find all the makings for his bombing of the gym." I give a hand gesture to speed it up. "He left his work over a week ago, and they haven't seen him since. His boss reports that he took a month-long sabbatical. Destination…" He tightens a fist. "Mexico."

Of course it was. *My fucking wedding.* "Well, we know that. What don't we know?" My tone is harsh, unrelenting.

"The place where he was raised, he still owns the land. According to Google Earth, there aren't any houses on the property. Seems abandoned."

"Where is it?"

"San Diego."

I turn to Jack, but he's already in motion. Calmly, I walk over to my coat and throw it on.

"What are you doing?" Thomas asks.

I look at him as if he is ignorant and insignificant. In that moment, I hate myself, but I hold onto that version of myself. The one who doesn't sob over his abducted fiancée or murdered mother. The man who does whatever it takes to get what he needs and wants.

Jack barks into his cell phone as everyone moves to follow us out of the suite. "Have the jet fueled and file the flight plans for a nonstop route to San Diego International. Have two cars waiting on the tarmac there. We'll be at the hangar in fifteen minutes."

"We're coming with you," Thomas says, anger making his words sound gritty.

"I expected that."

"It's a vacant lot. We might not find anything. We are going to head there first thing in the morning."

I know he wants me to see that he is making every effort, and I do see that. Only now is not the time for pats on the back. It's crunch time, and only the relentless will find what they are looking for in time.

"Gillian may be dead by morning."

"Chase! Chase, it's me!" I scream out. The wind carries my voice to the single man standing on a cliff out over the horizon. He's in a sharp black tux, his dark hair blowing in the breeze as the waves crash against the cliff. "Chase!" I yell again, but he doesn't hear me. The sand is thick and muddy as I run barefoot, trudging step by step. My wedding dress catches sand, rocks, and shells, slowing me down. I tug on the dress, and pieces fall off the back. Strips of satin instantly get swept up into the air and float on a cloud, swirling around magically.

I pick up my pace, but he starts to walk away. His head hangs low, shoulders slumping.

"Chase!" I yell at the top of my lungs. My man stops, finally turns around, and sees me. He *sees* me. Even from this distance, his smile is splendid. The damn dress pulls at my waist now, the train filled with muck and mud. I rip at the bodice, trying to yank it off, pulling at the satin. The sound of fabric shredding—no, being cut—enters my subconscious. The beach shakes, and I grapple to hold my footing. Chase's arms reach out. I'm closer but still not close enough. The dress yanks me back, and I fall to the sand—only it's not sand. It's softer, bouncy. With all my might, I press up, only this time, it seems as if I am pressing against the wind and it's pushing me back down. I clutch and push, trying to get to my feet. Chase stands still in the distance. He doesn't come for me. He's close enough to see me struggling, yet he doesn't come.

I push my arms out, trying once more to pull at the dress. Finally, it breaks free, and I slam into a hard body. My eyes flutter open, and I'm no longer on the beach. The dank smell of must and mold along with sweat and man enters my senses, demolishing the ocean air and beach where Chase was in my dream. The sound of my breath is loud against the slick neck of a man. Not a man. My captor.

"Thank God you've come to your senses," Daniel says into my neck, kissing the column.

Nausea stirs in my belly. "What?" I heave against him, realizing that the top half of my dress has been alternately cut and ripped open. Danny's holding up a pair of scissors. They reflect the light of the single bulb above my head. Like a frightened animal, I skitter back, the pulley system above my head shrieking as metal grates across metal. My back hits the cold concrete. Instinctively, I cross my arms over my chest. The chill of the room seeps deep into my bones. With the top half of my dress ripped open, my breasts are exposed.

Daniel's eyes run all over my chest. I swallow reflexively, trying to push the vomit back down to where it came from. If he touches me, I may throw up on him.

"You've always been beautiful, princess, but seeing your body like this, bare for me, reminds me of so many good times. Do you remember how I loved on you?"

I shake my head. "Danny, no, you do not want to do this." I can hear the panic in my voice betraying fear and rejection.

He smiles wide. "Of course I want to. But you're too dirty. I brought you these." He sets a package of baby wipes, a white tank top, and a pair of booty shorts on the bed. They could almost classify as underwear. "I want you to remove that fucking disgusting dress, wipe off your entire body, even *there*"—he looks down to where my legs meet—"and get all clean for me. If you're real nice, maybe I'll take you up to my motor home and make love to you in a real bed instead of on this mattress."

I gulp and steady my breath, trying not to sound affronted. "When, Danny?"

"You just can't wait to get back between the sheets with me, can you?" He smiles wide and smarmy.

It's a smile I don't recall ever seeing on him before. This is not the man I was in a relationship with for almost a year. This guy is cold, scary, and calculating. The Danny I knew was sweet, kind, and treated me like a fragile, priceless artifact.

"Danny, why are you doing this?"

His eyes narrow, and his mouth purses into a tight bow. "You know why." His gaze is white-hot fire and ready to burn through flesh. My flesh. "Obviously, the rich fucker manipulated and blinded you. You had diamonds in your eyes and forgot what a real man is. What having someone love and take care of you the way you should be looks like." He takes a few steps, pulls me into his chest. The chains clang as I'm slammed into his large body. "You will remember. No matter how long it takes. You'll remember how good we are. How perfect it can be when it's just the two of us."

He yanks my head, and his lips are on mine. When he tries to push his tongue into my mouth, I bite down hard.

"Motherfucking cunt!" he roars and backhands me. I fall onto the mattress, the side of my face pounding anew. "Clean yourself, get that dress off, and wipe every ounce of your old life off of you. That is the last you're ever going to see of it again. Because if you don't learn real quick, Gillian, I'm going to get angry and be forced to teach you a lesson. Got it?" One of his knees hits the mattress as he forcibly drags my chin up to look into his eyes. The kindness I knew when we dated is gone. Hatred stares back. Daniel's fingertips dig painfully into the bruised skin of my jaw. "Well?" he roars.

"Okay, okay, I get it. Thank you, Danny. I'll get cleaned up," I croak out.

"That's a good girl. And eat your fucking food!" he spits, and then pushes me back onto the mattress.

He storms to the door, opens it, and slams it closed. I hear the lock clicking into place. The sound of that lock might as well be my death knell. Pain ripples through every surface of my face and down my chest. I block it out as much as possible and catch sight of a thin flannel blanket near the clothes. I grab it, toss the tank over my naked chest, and wrap my body in the blanket's warmth. It isn't much. Curling into a ball, I let the fear and shock swallow me whole.

Tomorrow, Daniel will rape me. I know it just as I know that Chase is doing everything in his power to find me. Believing that he will make it in time is useless. Today is day four. Daniel doesn't look scared or worried that we'll be found at all. As a matter of fact, he is rife with confidence. He believes beyond a shadow of a doubt that he is going to get me to fall in line. To be some ethereal representation of a relationship only he knows about within his mind.

The situation is bleak. I am dealing with a madman who not only wants me to love him, but also wants me to be this perfect vision he's made me out to be. Only I don't know what that is. I think hard. What would Dr. Madison say? It is possible he'd say that I should find a way to connect with the Danny I knew and the Daniel this man has become? Try to get him to remember the fun we had when we were together? Perhaps remind him what he is doing to me now goes against what we had in our relationship over a year ago? Might work. What else? Slowing my breathing, I close my eyes and let my thoughts wander.

Trying to find out why he's the way he is would probably get me killed. Playing his game, attempting to be the perfect woman he believes I am in his warped version of reality, would likely be the best possible means for survival. Of course that option will also cause the most lasting damaging effects. There is no way I can ever willingly let that man put any part of his body in me. Now that I know what he is, who he is, just the thought of his hands on me forces the nausea in my gut to roil.

My stomach shudders and quakes, a physical earthquake inside. It's too much. I barely make it up to heave over the side of the mattress before I'm spewing onto the concrete. It's mostly bile and water, and it burns like I've swallowed a handful of razor blades. Violent hacking coughs rack my frame. Gradually, I'm able to take small, slow breaths, bringing my heart rate back to something akin to normal. I can still taste the vile stomach acid on my tongue.

When I close my eyes, little flickers of the dream I had earlier come rushing to the forefront of my subconscious. Chase is back on the side of a cliff, wearing his tuxedo. But when I hold my arms out to him during that dream, he doesn't come for me.

Chase doesn't come for me.

Just that simple speck of doubt causes the tears to fall

down the sides of my battered cheeks. The salt burns the abrasions on my skin. He'll come for me. There's one thing I know for certain in this world, and it is that Chase loves me. Together we forge an unbreakable bond that no one can destroy. Besides, Chase reminds me over and over when we're faced with something challenging, or I feel the need to run away that no matter what, he'll always run after me, that he'll find me and bring me home. He's promised me this countless times over the past year.

I let thoughts of Chase and how our life could be when he finds me settle the fear and allow me a moment's reprieve from the filthy hell I'm in. With dry, cracked lips, I whisper a prayer again.

"Chase, please find me. Please find me, Chase."

CHASE

CHAPTER THREE

The flight to San Diego is just over an hour. Another hour without Gillian. Seventy more minutes that she is held against her will by a psycho. Both Agent Brennen and Thomas try to offer polite conversation. For the most part, I ignore them. Jack doesn't even try. What he does do is ensure I have a tumbler filled with the amber liquor of the gods. The whiskey goes down smoothly but twists and churns in my gut. At some point, probably when I'm staring out the window, a turkey sandwich is set in front of me.

Is Gillian being fed?

"If her stalker claims he loves her..." I issue the statement into the cabin, but my eyes are directly on Agent Brennen. "He'll feed her, right?"

The agent clasps his hands and leans back into his seat. "Yes, I do believe he will. He will want her alive. Unless, of course, she fights him."

Without responding, I stare out the window again. *Unless she fights him.* I smile, thinking about my feisty redhead kicking, screaming, and throwing punches every chance she gets. She will definitely fight him. The miniscule moment of elation passes when it sinks in what he said. "What will happen if she fights him?"

The agent licks his lips. I wait patiently, my body temperature heating from the inside out as real fear seeps deep into my bones. "Tell me," I grate through clenched teeth.

"He'll hurt her. Try to break her into submission."

I close my eyes and lay my head against the soft leather. *I'm coming for you, Gillian. I will find you and bring you home.*

The plane lands, and the four of us shuffle into the two vehicles. We could have taken the same car, but I need the space. With Jack, I can be myself. He doesn't judge or share his thoughts and opinions unless asked. Over the years, we've experienced a great deal together, forming a strong bond that goes beyond Jack's service to me. He's the only man I'll ever trust to protect my life and the one man whose opinion I trust above all others. I can always count on an honest, straightforward response, regardless of the circumstance.

"Do you think she's alive?" I ask him from the back seat of the SUV.

Jack's eyes meet mine in the review mirror. "I'm afraid I can't answer that. It would be speculation at best."

"I'm asking you if you *think* she's alive. Not whether or not you know it to be fact." My tone is harsh, cold.

"Chase…" he warns.

"Why don't you like her?"

Jack's shoulders stiffen and his jaw clamps down as he maneuvers the car through town to the outskirts where Daniel McBride's land is located. I wait, watching the subtle nuance of the man I've come to know better than any other. My one true confidant, aside from Gillian. He's considering how to respond to me, and something about it makes me angry. Around-the-bend, pull-out-a-gun, and shoot-somebody-type rage.

"You're delaying. Why?" I finally ask.

He clears his throat. "Because you are taken with her."

"Again. You're evading the question. I've been taken with people or things before."

His eyes find mine in the mirror, and he shakes his head. "Not like her."

"Dammit, Jack. Answer me? Why do you not like Gillian?" I'm exasperated and ready for a fight. My blood is pumping, heart pounding, and I feel better than I have in four days. Alive. I feel alive.

Jack's brows narrow. "It's not that I dislike her."

"Then what is it? God damn it! Admit it. She has felt it since day one. You have avoided all conversation when it comes to her over the past year. And when I told you I was going to marry her, you didn't congratulate me. You couldn't even spare a handshake. As a matter of fact, you've never said a kind word about her. So what the fuck is it about Gillian Callahan…?"

He cuts me off. His tone his tight, firm, and crackling with frustration. The only other time I've seen him break his titanium emotional exterior is when Megan fucked me over on our wedding night. "Gillian is perfect for you." The words come out of his mouth sounding sour and bitter. "Beautiful, smart, driven, and the type of woman every man with half a brain would bow down to secure."

I'm about to lose my fucking mind if he doesn't get to the point. "So what the fuck is the problem with her if she's so damned perfect?" I lean forward and grip the back of the passenger seat in front of me, digging my nails into the soft black leather.

"It's not *her*. It's what she does to *you* that I have a problem with." His voice is a dull growl when he finishes. "Chase, that woman makes *you* weak."

After that revelation, I sit back and let the scenery roll by in swaths of black and midnight blue, splotched by flickering streetlights. It is late, and down this path through the landscape, we haven't passed a soul.

"Where are we headed?" I look down at my watch and realize we've been in the car for an hour. Sixty additional minutes that she's been with him. I bite my tongue and hold in the desire to scream, roar, and destroy anything within a ten-mile radius.

Jack briefly looks into the rearview mirror. "The land is just outside of the Cuyamaca Mountains. Ideal place to hide if you ask me." I nod. "Should be there in ten minutes." Jack fiddles with the car and dials a number.

The buzz blasts through the silence followed by, "Agent Brennen," delivered through the car's surround sound.

"Agent Brennen, how do you want to handle this?"

Static crackles through the line as the agent fills us in on the plan. We're going to park about a half mile from the property and walk up. If he sees any activity, he'll call for reinforcements before we go in. Everything has to be by the book. Thank Christ he's not in the car with us. I want to reach through the line and strangle him. By the fucking book, my ass. If I see anything suspicious, I'll shoot first and ask questions later.

Jack ends the call and brings the SUV up to a covered area. "We're close enough. The land should be just up that path." He points through the window.

"You have your gun?" I ask.

"Guns? Yes." He turns around and hands me a 9 mm. It's the same gun I've shot a hundred times before. Jack has trained me well with this particular pistol, and at this moment, I've never been more grateful.

"Let's go then," I say while tucking the gun into the back of my jeans. I toss my suit coat on the seat, and Jack hands me a black zip-up sweatshirt and Kevlar vest. Not my usual fine threads, but they will do. Leave it to an ex-military sniper to know exactly what is needed.

We meet up with Agent Brennen and Thomas walking alongside the wooded edge. Eventually, we come to a clearing. It's massive, with woods surrounding the open space. A lone motor home sits in the middle of the wide enclosure. There are no lights on in the motor home.

"You two stay here. Detective Redding and I will go in first. Cover us from here. Stay hidden in that outcropping of trees. We'll wave you over when the time is right." Agent Brennen is efficient and tactical. He just earned a bit more respect from me.

Jack and I wait, guns drawn, and watch the two men creep onto the property. The moon is high and shines brightly on their exposed forms. A soft wind makes the leaves on the trees sway and sing a soft melody. Both Jack and I search for signs of movement. Thomas and Agent Brennen circle around the motor home, and I want nothing more than to storm the fucking place, open the door, and beat the shit out of the fucker who stole my woman, but I can't. Adrenaline thunders through my veins, making me hyperalert to every sound and subtle nuance of the woods surrounding our position. The snapping of a twig here, the rustling of an animal there, all coalesce into myriad sounds, making my trigger finger twitch.

Agent Brennen opens the door to the motor home and goes in, Thomas hot on his heels. Nothing moves. Jack and I are dead silent waiting for something—anything— to happen. I caress the trigger of my gun and lift it high, pointing directly at the motor home's door. A figure emerges. My heart feels like it's going to jackhammer out of my chest until the form enters the light of the moon. Thomas. His gun is down and he's shaking his head. I slump against the tree I was standing near and take a few deep breaths. Jack is already in motion, running across the overgrown grass.

When I meet up with them, Thomas's shoulders are slumped and he's pushing a shaky hand through his hair. "He's not here, but it looks as though he's been here recently. There's food in a cooler that's still on ice. Someone has definitely been here and may come back. We need to head out, set up a perimeter. It could be anyone. A squatter or someone he's renting the land to."

"Wouldn't there be records of that?" I ask.

"Not if he takes payment in cash. We need to look into this, notify the authorities in the area, find out if the motor home is in his name," Agent Brennen adds. "And the rest of you need to fucking sleep."

"Yeah, man, when was the last time you got some shut-eye?" Thomas asks.

"None of your goddamned business. Jack, let's get a hotel. We're coming back at first light to search this place."

Jack tips his chin up and follows me back out of the woods.

The closest hotel is a shithole, but I imagine it's a

hundred times better than what Gillian could be living in. Jack insists on connecting rooms. Says he has a bad feeling, and I've learned not to question those.

Jack enters the room and sets two pills on the sideboard along with a bottle of water and a sandwich wrapped in plastic. Looks like the same sandwich I didn't eat on the plane.

"I'm not hungry," I say, even though my stomach growls loudly.

His eyes narrow. "You need to eat, drink the water, and sleep."

"I told you, Jack, I'm not fucking hungry."

Jack grips my shoulders hard and brings his face closer to mine, closer than he's ever come at me before. "Look, you know I'm not usually the type to tell you what to do"—his mouth pinches tight and his lips turn white—"but if you have any hope of bringing her home, you need to take care of yourself. Eat, take the fucking pills, and sleep it off. At first light, we're back on that land and smoking out whoever has been staying in the motor home. Got it?" He shakes my shoulders as if he were shaking sense into me.

I grit my teeth and look hard into his eyes. They are ebony holes of anger, not at me but *for* me. I give a tight nod, pick up the pills, and chug back the water. In what feels like a minute, I've demolished the sandwich, never having tasted it.

X

She better be clean and dressed for me. I can't wait to burn that disgusting wedding gown. Today I'll build a bonfire, shackle her, and have her watch while it goes up in smoke, just like the memory of the rich fucker. Then, I'll bring her into my motor home and prove how much I've missed having her body under mine. It will be perfect. I'll kiss every bruise, cut, and scrape, showing her that I can worship her again. Just like before, only this time she'll know the real me. Maybe I'll even tell her my real name. She'd like that. Something no one else knows.

Kissing her yesterday was close to perfection until she bit me. Of course, that was because she was overtaken with lust. It has been well over a year since I've put my lips on her pretty pink ones. And her scent. Fucking hell, that vanilla lingers even after four days. Maybe she's just that sweet, her body naturally creating the nectar to drive me wild.

I wade through the backside of the woods from my property. I've got my car hidden in a dilapidated barn on the abandoned lot next to mine. You can never be too careful. And now that she's been missing for four full days, I'm sure all resources are being put to finding her. I smile to myself knowing they never will. If they didn't figure out who I was before the wedding, they most certainly wouldn't have since.

As I'm walking through the woods, the moisture from the early morning dew mists across my face, keeping me cool. The trees give the air a rich, natural woodsy scent. Reminds me of the good parts of my childhood. Running through the trees, climbing them, hiding from my father. The memories of him are always hiding just under the surface, and being here has not helped me to forget.

My father and I used to shoot paintball guns in these woods. At seven years old, I was a professional. My father was better and ruthless. He didn't allow me to wear protective gear. Said I needed to learn how to be a *real* man. After a session of paintball in the woods, I'd barely be able to crawl home. Mom wasn't much help. She'd clean me up, of course, or she'd end up getting smacked around, but she didn't care that her child was hurt. I'd stand there naked, embarrassed, my entire body covered in black-and-blue bruises, red welts, and open sores. My father liked to use the stronger bullets and higher air speed toward the end of our game. A game. Shooting your seven-year-old repeatedly with hundreds of paintballs was a game to him. One I lost every time, but not before getting in several of my own shots.

When I was ten, we stopped playing. I'd gotten as good as he was, and he ended up receiving as many hits as I did. One of the best days of my life was seeing my dad walking back to our home as if he were a cripple. Only my mother didn't fare so well that night. He beat the shit of her, which she then took out on me the next day. Back then, I'd never hit a woman. Now, I know what women are. All useless holes to fuck, to shoot your wad in as many times as a wet pussy can take. Not my princess though. Her skin is white like an angel's. Her pussy is soft, pink, and snug. I shake with desire, recalling the last time I was inside her tight sheath.

Thinking of my princess reminds me of the satchel on my back. Gillian's going to love the things I've brought her this morning. Fresh fruit—she seemed to like that apple yesterday—bakery bread, butter, and a decadent dessert. I remember how much she loves to end a meal with a sweet. I'll show her just how thoughtful I can be if she'll let me. Eventually, I'll have her back, wanting me, making love to me willingly. Tonight though, I'm going to have to take her even if I need to tie her down and make love to her struggling form. If she screams, I'll gag her. If it takes all night, I'll love on her, make her feel so good until she forgets any other man who came before me.

The rope in my bag will do just fine. My dick stirs in my pants, reminding me I haven't fucked a woman in a few days. That Dana bitch was a nice hole, pretty enough face when I opened my eyes. Most of the time I fucked her with her face pressed into the mattress and her ass in the air. The same way Gillian wanted me to fuck her that one time. No. I won't fuck my perfect girl like a whore. Only the empty holes of the faceless women can be fucked like that. Gillian deserves more, and tonight, I'll give it to her. One way or another, she is going to have her legs spread wide, her arms open in invitation, and her body bared to me. Only me.

I make it close to my home and hear voices. Silently, I set down the heavy weight of the pack I carried, leaning it against a tree. Slinking closer, I can see that pig cop Thomas Redding and a gray-haired man scanning the ground around my motor home.

Fuck, fuck, fuck!

I reach into the back of my pants and pull out my gun. I can take them out one by one without anyone being the wiser. Just as I get Thomas's head in my sights and my finger pressing ever so slightly on the trigger, I hear it. A voice. Scanning to the exact place I don't want anyone to go, I find

Jack Porter's large form. He is at least fifty yards from where I stand, but I know he's found it. The storm shelter. I watch, with a lethal shot pointed at his head, as he waves. Then the bane of my fucking existence is running toward him. Chase Motherfucking Davis.

Goddammit!

How the fuck did they find this place? Seething anger rips through my body and tears along the edges of my skin. I grind down on my teeth as I see Jack Porter scatter the leaves I have used to hide my storm shelter. They're going to find her. A gunshot rings out, the lock probably blasted into pieces. I watch in sick fascination as they open the latch and Jack's frame, followed by Chase's, disappears down the stairs. Seeing Thomas and the gray-haired guy running across the clearing, I run back down the opposite side of the mountain.

The sound of a gunshot pierces the silence of my tiny cell. I wake with a start, pull my knees into my chest, and press as far as I can against the cold cinderblock. There isn't anywhere else I can go.

"Get away from the door. We're coming in," a man's muffled voice says through the door. Then, another gunshot.

I scream and cower into the corner, my shackles cutting painfully into my wrists and ankles. I can hear sounds in the dark until the light blazes like the sun into the room. I shut my eyes and hide my face.

"Baby, oh my God, Gillian!" The voice is Chase's, but I don't believe it. He didn't come for me. It's a trick. My mind is playing tricks on me. I'll throw my arms around him, and I'll wake up, and it will be Danny all over again, groping me, touching me, kissing me. Violent sobs rack my frame as I hold onto my knees.

Hands are pulling at the blanket covering me, and then at my shackled hands. "No, no, don't touch me!" I scream at the top of my lungs. *Please, God, someone hear me. Get him off me.* "Chase!" I yell as loud as I can, hoping anyone, someone, will hear me.

"It's me, Gillian. Baby, it's Chase." Fingers are on my face, light caresses, much softer than Daniel has touched me. "I'm here. We got you." He presses his forehead against mine, and the scent of sandalwood and citrus enters my nostrils. I open my eyes and stare into the stunning Caribbean-blue eyes. Tears fill those ocean-colored orbs and fall down the sides of his cheeks.

"Chase," I croak, my gaze cataloging every feature, every nuance. "You came," I whisper, tears pouring down my cheeks. His hands gently clasp my battered face, his thumbs swiping along the apples of my cheekbones.

"What did he do to you?" His voice is hoarse, full of emotion.

I shake my head and watch as he does his own examination. His thumbs pet my busted lips, the bruises over my face. Based on the way his jaw gets tighter, I know it's bad. I can barely feel the pain anymore, due to being so cold, and I know I'm in a state of severe shock.

A man I don't recognize comes over to me. "I'm Agent Brennen, Mrs. Davis." *Mrs. Davis.* He called me Mrs. Davis. More tears slide down my cheeks. "I've got a medical chopper on its way. We have to get you out of these chains.

Can you stand?"

Chase stands close, helping me up. The chains shriek along the pulley system.

"What the fuck is this?" Chase traces a hand up the thick rusted iron chains attached to my wrists and feet. I stand barefoot in the pasty vomit, which hasn't even completely dried from last night, but I couldn't care less. He is here. Chase found me. "I want her out of here now." His tone is a deep protective growl.

Jack comes over and puts a hand on my shoulder. I cower into Chase. "Let me see your wrist." Chase grabs my hand and holds it out. "I found this in that closet at the top of the stairs." He pushes a heavy-looking metal key into the lock at my wrist and turns. The shackle drops to the ground with a bang. I jump at the noise but allow Chase to maneuver my other hand to get that bond off. Jack pushes aside the toile of the bottom half of my wedding dress and unhooks the remaining bands. I wince as each one is removed.

The big bodyguard breathes in deep. "She's bleeding around each ankle and wrist. The wounds on her ankles are showing signs of advanced infection," he says, but I can barely hear him. "Get her out of here."

Instantly, the world turns upside down. Lights and sounds move in a swirl of dizzying motion through my vision. The light gets brighter as I am carried up what I think are a set of stairs. Ice-cold air hits the bare arms of my skin, and I shiver, my teeth chattering automatically. A whirring sound gets louder and louder, and I'm bounced up and down. I hold on tight to Chase, focus on his scent, his heartbeat, and his warmth. Nothing can touch me if I am with him. Just him. Surrounded by his love.

Vaguely, I realize I am being laid down, and a woman and man are barking orders. The whirring sound is so loud, and I'm beyond freezing. So cold. Only one point on my body is warm, and that's my hand, because Chase holds it tight, never letting me go.

"You found me," I say, trying to get my eyes to stop rolling around.

"I'll always find you and bring you back to me," he promises, his lips pressing down against my cracked lips in a featherlight touch. For the first time in four days, I close my eyes and am blessedly free. Chase has me, and I know he will never let me go.

GILLIAN

CHAPTER FOUR

Beep. Beep. Beep.

"Chase, baby, turn off the alarm," I mumble. Turning my head, I feel scratchy linen against the tender skin of my cheek. "Ouch, burns." I turn my head to the other side and feel the same gritty fabric, only this time it's coupled with a zing of pain that makes me open my eyes. The room is fuzzy, hazy, even as I attempt to adjust to my surroundings. White. Everything is white. I scan the room while opening and closing my eyes. The process takes a great deal of effort because my eyelids feel like they have tiny chains weighing down each one, making it almost impossible to keep them open.

Finally, I turn my head all the way to the right and find the most beautiful face known to mankind. Eyes so blue I can swim in them, and I do, often. A slow, painful smile slips across my face as I take in every feature. His thick coffee-colored hair is a mess of layers falling along the sides of his temples and forehead—a testament to how many times he's likely brushed his fingers through it or given it a good tugging. He's sporting a few days' beard growth, more than I've ever seen. Makes him look more rugged and dangerous.

I quite like it. Instead of the ever-present tic in his jaw, he's sporting a huge, toothy grin.

It takes me a moment, but I notice that I'm holding his hand. The happiness I see in his eyes and the strength with which he holds my hand tells me everything I need to know. I'm safe and I'm home.

"How do you feel?" he asks and leans a hip on the bed. While I take stock of my body, he places kisses all over my palm. He closes his eyes, pressing my hand to his cheek. I push back, appreciating the gentle caress.

I point my toes, and rivers of tension and a burning sensation trail up my legs. Sucking in a breath, I let the air flow between my teeth until the pain subsides. Squeezing my hands into fists, I find I can barely lift my own arms. It's as if I'm lying in quicksand, my body having succumbed completely to the pressure and ache deep within my bones. "I'll survive. Seeing you, though, makes it better." His eyebrows furrow, but I look away. Scanning the room, I see all the flowers and cards. Three sets of perfect white daisies perch prettily along the window, proving my soul sisters have been here.

Seeing those flowers is when it all comes crashing down. "Oh my God, are the girls okay? Did he hurt them?"

Chase shakes his head and leans forward, cupping my cheeks so softly I can barely tell they are there. "No, baby, no. They're all fine. Phillip too."

His eyes search mine. Then it hits me. Tears fall unchecked down my cheeks.

"What's the matter? Gillian? Are you in pain?" His face twists into a grimace. "I'll get the doctor." He moves to stand, but I hold him in place.

"Chase, your mom. I'm so sorry…" I choke out the rest of what I need to say. "It's m–my f–fault." I shudder as tears fall in a deluge of sorrow.

"No, no, no, nuh–uh. Do not even start with that. You did nothing wrong. It's that sick fuck who did all of this." Chase kisses my forehead and whispers against it. "You've done nothing wrong. I'm just so thankful, so happy to have you home. Gillian, God…I'm nothing without you."

I hold his cheeks as he places kisses all over my face. I know it's bruised, but the meds they've got me on are masking any serious pain. "I thought I'd never see you again," I admit, the grief and residual fear cropping up to dig gnarly claws into my psyche.

"Baby, there's nothing that could ever keep me from you. Don't you know that by now?"

I smile, and he wipes away my tears. I do know that. He's proven more than once that he'll do anything, pay any price to take care of me. Only none of us were prepared for the stalker to be my ex-boyfriend Daniel McBride. It never once dawned on me that he could have a nefarious and demented side to him. During our relationship, he was nothing but kind, generous, and sweet. Treated me like a queen. Always. Even helped me get that restraining order against Justin when I needed one.

Justin. Another pawn in Danny's game. Makes me wonder if he did have something to do with Justin's death. I'd bet money on it. Justin was not the type of man to take his own life, especially without leaving some type of manifesto or legacy behind. Plus, the cops found no suicide note.

"How long have I been out?" I push into the mattress and try to sit up. My muscles ache and lock in protest.

"Two days." Chase's voice is heavy, as if he's been carrying around an anvil the last couple days.

I close my eyes and try not to let that destroy the warm feeling I have being here, safe, and with the man I love. The man I'm meant to love.

"You've been worried." It's a rhetorical statement. I can see the shadows underneath his eyes, the gray pallor to his usually tanned skin, and the weight he's lost. At least ten pounds in the past week. Though I'm absolutely certain I look no better. Before the wedding, I lost a lot of weight, worrying about Phillip, and then Bree, and the attack by Justin, and planning our wedding. Add abduction to that list, and you've got a woman who's normally a curvy size eight who's now probably a size two.

"I'm just elated you're back, that you're awake and on the mend."

I scooch as much as I can to the side, even though my limbs and muscles protest aggressively, sending lightning bolts of pain throughout my body. Clenching my teeth, I move to the side. "Get in. I can feel my eyes getting heavy, and you look dead on your feet."

"No, you need your space to rest."

"I need no such thing from you. Believe me, I'll rest far better if you're holding me." I quirk a brow, but the drugs they've got me on make me slur my words. I'm going down fast. Chase kicks off his shoes and, with great care, centers his body on the space I've offered. "I wish you had your shirt off," I mutter into his polo shirt. He chuckles and runs his fingers through my hair. It's heavenly. With measured movements, he massages my scalp with the pads of his fingers, avoiding the bumps that must surely be there, and then trails his hands out, allowing the curls to fall through his fingers. Chase does this over and over. Sandalwood and citrus fill my nostrils, reminding me of the safest place in the world. Chase's arms. I snuggle my face in and let out a deep sigh.

"I love you, Chase," I whisper.

"I love you, more," he says, my own words back to me, and I know from here on out, I'm going to be okay.

She's so beautiful, even with black eyes and swollen cheeks. I can hardly catch my breath looking at her. Little puffs of air slip from her split lips, and I want so badly to kiss her, ravage her, prove she's mine. That caveman inside, the one I try to curb for her sake, is roaring with the need to mark and possess. Only my marks wouldn't need bandages or medication. That piece of shit put his hands on her. Her chest was bruised...again by an attacker. Did he violate her?

The team did a rape kit when she was unconscious and didn't find semen or bruising, so I have to hope his abuse never got that far. Her body, though, is covered from head to toe in bruises. The shackles at her ankles and wrists cut deep grooves into the tender flesh. Dr. Dutera has her on a hoard of antibiotics, antifungals, and a host of other drugs. It's a miracle she didn't sustain any broken bones. I'm thankful beyond measure that she isn't more damaged. She will heal from this, and if he didn't violate her, the healing process will progress more smoothly.

I shift the blanket and scan her form from head to toe.

Aside from the bruises, cuts, and scrapes, she's thin. Sufferably so. I can feel every rib as I hold her close. The Gillian I met at my hotel bar in Chicago was filled to the brim with curves. She'll need a new wardrobe, although not for long. I plan to stuff her full of food. It's obvious from how much weight she lost she wasn't eating much if anything at all while abducted. Probably was afraid to. Can't blame her. If I'd been in her shoes, I wouldn't have either. A shiver runs through me, and I pull the blanket tighter around us both and allow her warmth to seep into me. Gillian is back. She's here, and I have her in my arms. There is nothing and no one who will get between us again. I'll hire a team of bodyguards to protect her. If I ever let her out of my sight.

I need to call Dana. She needs to get my second-in-command on point for the foreseeable future. I make a mental note to call her later. Right now, I'm perfectly content to hold my girl, feel her breath on my chest, the warmth of her body against mine.

Had anyone told me a year ago that I'd meet the woman I was meant to spend forever with, I'd have laughed in their face. When Megan fucked Coop on the night of our wedding over ten years ago, I never believed I'd get this second chance. No, second chance isn't right. Perhaps finding Gillian was the way it was always supposed to be. It certainly feels that way. When I'm with her, I can be me. She doesn't have any expectations other than to give her my time. The only thing she's ever wanted from me is *me*. And I want to give her everything in return, yet she seems to want nothing. That's why the bastard is obsessed with her. I can relate. He caught a glimpse of what it was like to be loved by this woman. Justin was sucked in, too. Only their volatile ways demolished any prospective life she could have had with them. Their loss is my gain.

My entire empire has been built on devastating losses and extraordinary gains. It's the way of the world. And in this, too, I profited at the highest possible return on investment. I won Gillian. She's mine. I'd willingly give my life for her, and I suspect she would for me in return. Above all else, it's her I need. Not money or material things, not the power that comes with doing what I do...just her. I'd give it all away to ensure our happiness. The truth is I do have considerable power and wealth. All of which I will use to ensure that nothing ever happens to her again. I close my eyes and let out a calming breath, pulling Gillian closer to my chest, burying my lips in the hair at the crown of her head.

I enter the bridal room at a full run and stop cold when I see the back of my mother's head. Her hair is pulled up tight into a bun, but she's not moving. Her hands lie limp along the sides of the wheelchair. Blood trickles down the slope of her hand. Drops fall from her index fingers into a puddle on the floor.

No. God, no.

The room has been tossed, the bed a jumble of sheets with no coverlet. Chairs are askew on the ground—makeup, hair accessories, jewelry all scattered on the ornate rug. There's been a mighty struggle. Gillian is not here. Step by step, I take a wide berth around my mother's still form. No movement, not even a twitch, a moan, groan, just silence. Absence of sound, deafening quiet.

I swallow the bile as the metallic scent of blood enters my nostrils. My mother's blood. It's as if time stops. I can hear the blood as it drip, drip, drips onto the floor. And that's when I see her. Her mouth is open in a scream, eyes rolled back into her head. A gaping hole at the front of her neck gives a glaring look into the back of her throat. Her dress is stained crimson like a disgusting bloody bib down the front of her body.

She's dead, and Gillian is gone.

"Baby, wake up." I feel a hand on my sternum. I jolt to a seated position, holding her body to me. Gillian tenses as I come back to the here and now. "It was a dream. You were dreaming." Her fiery hair comes into focus, and then her emerald eyes. Christ, I've missed those eyes. Without thinking, I crush her mouth to mine and take long draws from her lips. If she's in pain, she doesn't mention it or push away. If anything, she's pressing harder, taking the kiss further by licking the seam of my lips. I open for her. Always for her.

Gillian's little tongue enters my mouth, and I groan. I clasp her head in one hand, tip it to the side, and stake my claim. My fucking woman. Her lips are for me and me alone. She moans into my mouth and presses her body more fully into my chest. I can feel her pert nipples grate along my skin and my dick comes to life. It has been soft and unfeeling for days. With one press of her lips, she awakens my cock, as if it's been taking a week-long nap.

Rubbing my lips across hers, I share it all. The fear, the grief, the gut-wrenching need for her in my life. The fact that I spent four days without her, a piece of me dying every second that she was gone. She takes it all and gives back joy, love, and a bright future to rejoice in. And I do, rejoice in all that is her as her lips control mine. Gillian is not the type of woman who just kisses you. With every touch of her mouth, she shares her past. With every whisper of her breath, she claims the present. With every ounce of her being, she gives me her future. It's all in her kiss.

I pull away, gasping for air when the metallic taste of her blood registers. "Shit, I've busted open your lip." I press the pad of my thumb against the swollen tissue. Regret is harsh, a bucket of cold water thrown over me.

"Worth it." She licks my thumb and waggles her eyebrows.

"Saucy little vixen." I rub my forehead against hers, trying to express what I'm unable to with words.

"When can I go home?" she asks on a sigh.

"We're not going home. We're going to the Davis Mansion when you're sprung out of here, but I think it might be a couple more days." If I have anything to say about it, it will. I've got two fully armed guards at her door and another four patrolling the building and parking lots, looking for suspicious activity. McBride's still out there. The only thing we found when the area surrounding her shelter was searched was a brown satchel with provisions in it.

Her eyes turn a darker leafy green. "I don't know about you, but I'm going to be sleeping in our bed at the penthouse. I've been locked away in a goddamned cell for a week." Her voice shakes, and it sends my temper ablaze. "I need to be home. With you. Where I'm most comfortable."

I suck in a breath and try to control my anger. The fact that I have to worry about where my fiancée is going to be safest instead of comfortable after what she's gone through is infuriating. "We'll figure it out."

"Like I'm trying to figure out how you thought it best to crawl into bed with my patient, Mr. Davis," comes a grumbling voice from the door. Dr. Dutera enters, his rimless glasses perched on his bulbous nose.

Even with the well-mannered doctor, I'm not going to justify his remark by giving him a response. Gillian is my woman. I go where she goes. Period. And after being faced with her abduction the last few days, anyone who gets in my way will pay dearly.

"I sleep better next to my fiancé, Doctor." Gillian glances down to the wedding ring on the doctor's left hand. "I imagine your wife feels the same about you."

A slow smile fills the doctor's face. As with any man, his woman is the way to his heart. Not a meal, as the overused cliché suggests. Just the love of a good woman. Of course my woman would pick up on that. Gillian has always had a way with people. Most days I wish she didn't. I'd prefer to have her all to myself.

"Yes, well, we need to check your vitals and go over your injuries," he says while flipping through the pages on her chart.

I slowly remove myself from the bed. "I'll just speak to security and grab a cup of coffee…" I barely have my hand on the door handle before Gillian screams.

"Chase, no! Don't leave me!" she screeches. In less than a blink, I'm back at her side and she's in my arms. Tears pour down her cheeks and soak my shirt where she rubs her battered face into my sternum. "Just, please, don't leave me." She chokes back a sob and sniffles, wiping her face against my shirt. I don't care. The violent response to my leaving is enough for me.

"I'm not going anywhere. Shh, it's okay. I'm here." I hold her until her sobs become soft hiccups against my chest. When I look up, the doctor's mouth is set into a grim line.

"We're going to need to have psych come assist—" he starts, but I cut him off.

I point my finger at him, my tone menacing and firm. "Don't say a word. Not a *word*. She's fine. Just shaken up, which is understandable after what she's gone through." I pet Gillian's hair, and she shudders against me. The emotional waves tear through my own defenses, and the lion comes out, claws sharpened and incisors ready to tear flesh. "Now, we have a great psychologist named Dr. Madison that I'd like you to call. Give him a brief rundown of the situation, and I'm certain he will be happy to assist in Gillian's mental health. Do I make myself clear, Dr. Dutera?" My tone leaves no room for argument. If he does argue, we'll get another doctor within the hour.

The doctor sighs, and his mouth tightens. "I understand," he says, and proceeds to go through the laundry list of injuries she sustained. For the most part, the wrists, ankles, and face received the most damage. All will heal well as we continue her on the antibiotics and taper off the pain medications.

"According to my records, you've lost twenty-five pounds since your first visit with me when you got your stitches removed just under a year ago. That's a lot of weight for a slight woman. I'd like to see you put at least ten of those pounds back on," he suggests.

She nods but doesn't move her face from the position against my chest. If anything, she's made herself more comfortable there. Again, I can't complain. She needs me. Having this woman *need* me is everything I've ever wanted. I just didn't want it under these conditions or circumstances.

I settle Gillian back down on the bed but lean against her side. She clasps my hand, bringing it up to her lips, and holds it there. Just holds my hand against the abrasions on her chin and mouth as if it were a safety blanket. In that moment, I know we need Dr. Madison's expertise far more than I had imagined.

X

That rat bastard has had *my* princess for two fucking days now. The hospital they've taken her to is crawling with fibbies and hired rent-a-cops. I'll just bet all of them have my picture, too. Stupid fucks. Nothing a little brown hair dye, a pair of colored contacts, and a little facial hair won't fix.

The white walls of the hospital corridor remind me of a psych ward. Up ahead, I see one of the rent-a-cops. Perfect test. He moves to walk past me, and I stop him with a hand on his elbow.

"Excuse me, do you have the time?" I ask, looking him directly in the eye. He looks down at his watch.

"Sure, pal, it's ten to four," he says, and then adjusts his belt. Something I find that security guards do. Somehow they believe it makes them look more powerful. Like they have to go through any actual training to carry a baton and a walkie-talkie. I try hard not to roll my eyes.

I look around and catch the uniform of another fake first responder. "So what's with all the security? Is there someone famous here?" I ask in a hushed tone, making sure to use good voice inflection and prod his shoulder like we're old high school buddies.

He scans the space for a moment, places his hands on his belt once more, and leans forward. "You didn't hear this from me, but yeah. A billionaire is here, and his wife is being treated. She was kidnapped."

His wife. Not fucking possible. I grit my teeth and try not to correct the man. "Really? Is she okay?"

He nods. "Banged up pretty bad. The guy who took her was a real sicko if you know what I mean."

My head flies back at the offensive slam. "No, I don't. Tell me!" My voice turns harsh, and his eyebrows narrow. "I mean, you know, buddy, what did he do that was bad?"

"I don't know everything, but from what I heard, he had her shackled like a slave. Stole her on her wedding day, too. Still had the dress on when she arrived on the chopper half-dead."

"Half-dead?" I say far too loudly.

"You deaf? Yeah, guy almost killed her. Anyway, I need to do my rounds. Keep an eye out for this guy." He holds up a picture of me. It is one that Gillian had of us together, only someone cut her out of it.

Do they think they can cut me out of her life? That I'll go away so easily?

I study the photo for another moment. "Well, I hope you find the guy."

"Yeah, it would be great if I'm the one who gets to take him out. Would be a real service to mankind." The overweight man slaps me on the back. I clench my fist to prevent my natural inclination to wrap my hands around his beefy head and twist his neck until the bones snap, crackle, and pop.

He left to finish his rounds as I move to do the same.

Only I make it a point to walk past every security guard. I ask them a question or bump into them. None of them recognize me. Stupid idiots. This time tomorrow, I'll have my girl back.

GILLIAN

CHAPTER FIVE

Something tickles my nose, and I open my eyes. It's Maria. Her smile is huge.

"*Cara bonita*, you are a sight for very sore eyes." She sits in the chair next to me, clasps my hand in both of hers, and pulls them to her cheeks. The olive of her skin is a stark contrast to the pallor and bruises of my own. A long breath escapes her lips. Two tears fall delicately down her cheeks.

"No." I shake my head. "I'm okay, really." Those full lips of hers tip upward slightly but can't seem to hold onto a smile.

"Gigi, we almost lost you. *Ido*. Gone. I cannot lose you. You, the girls, you're all I have."

I frown. "That's not true. You have Tommy and Phil, and Chase."

She laughs before her ice-blue eyes focus on mine and she gets very close. Her nose touches mine and she nuzzles it and then rests her forehead against the crown of mine. "It's not the same, and you know that, *cara bonita*."

I do know that. No matter how many men come and go in our lives, the four of us—Maria, Bree, Kat, and I—have something no one else has. It's unconditional, sent down from the heavens above. It just is. Losing one would be like losing a limb or a piece of me. Completely, utterly unbearable.

Instead of responding, I nod and run my hand through her hair. The silky, dark waves are soft and shiny. She smells of coconut and a summer day. Maria brings that to my life. The sun—warm, enriching, a necessity to keep the dark at bay.

The door flings open, and Bree and Kat enter, each holding two Styrofoam cups. Bree sets down the cups and dashes to my side. "Thank God, Gigi." Tears instantly pour down her beautiful face as she tries to hug me around her belly but also holds herself back, her arms shaking with the strain. "I'm afraid to hurt you."

I pull her into a tight embrace. She slumps into me, returning the hug. "You could never hurt me with a hug." Her tears wet the shoulder of my hospital gown, and I pet her hair and wipe away her tears with one hand. "I'm on the mend. I'll be good as new in a couple weeks," I say while looking into Kat's and then Maria's eyes.

Kat grabs Bree's arm, hoisting her up and off the hospital bed. "Share the love, chick!" She scowls at Bree and takes her place, her arms wrapping around me like a warm blanket on a cold day. I snuggle in, and she runs her hands up and down my back. "I cannot tell you how happy we are to have you home safe. Those few days were torture. The not knowing..." Her voice catches, and I hold on tighter. "We're just really glad you're back..." She pulls away. Her lip is trembling, and those caramel-colored eyes fill to the brim with unshed tears. She looks up and presses at the corners of each eye, shakes her head, and then smiles as if she's just put herself in check. Kat has always been one of the strongest women I know. Of the four of us, she's usually able to keep it together in difficult situations. I hold her hand and Maria's. Bree sits at the foot and places her own on my ankle. I wince, sucking in a breath. She jumps back.

"Oh, I'm sorry. I didn't mean to hurt you. I mean, it's your ankle." Her face scrunches into a mask of worry and confusion.

Maria's eyebrows narrow. "What's wrong with your *tobillos*?" She brazenly clutches the blanket between her fingers and pulls it back. Bree chokes back a sob and covers her mouth with her hand. Kat looks away, the tears finally falling. I look down and see the bandages wrapped around each ankle are soaked through with blood. Looks like it's time for the nurse to change them. Maria's jaw tightens, and she speaks through her teeth, "Why are they like this?"

It's surprising that they act as though they haven't been informed of my injuries. Then again, Chase would spare them. "Uh, Danny. He had me shackled by the ankles and wrists. I was connected to this pulley system, but the shackles were too tight and rusted through. When I struggled, they dug in. At the time, I didn't notice. Really. It's just that the wounds got infected, so they're giving me oral and topical antibiotics. Doctor says I'll be fine. Really. In a couple weeks, it will be like nothing ever happened."

That's when Maria begins to pace, muttering obscenities under her breath. I can barely catch a few words. Something about *cerdo asqueroso,* which I recall meaning "disgusting pig," and then she says *martarlo,* which I know for a fact means "kill him" in Spanish.

Kat shakes her head, holds my hand, and smiles. "Well, with us around all the time, you're sure to heal quickly.

Right, ladies?"

I scrunch up my face, but that movement hurts. Really bad. I close my eyes to breathe through the jolts of pain spreading from my head down to my gut where nausea bubbles.

I will not throw up. I will not throw up. Breathe through it, Gigi. You've done this a million times before.

When the pain lessens and the nausea subsides, I fake a smile. Kat and Maria don't buy it, concern heavy in their gazes. Bree riffles through her giant patchwork purse. She pulls out a little brown bottle with a purple label.

"Here, sniff this. It's Valor, an essential oil. It will give you strength and something else to think about besides the pain."

I inhale deeply and am reminded of doing yoga. Taking classes with the girls, Bree calling out the cues in a serene tone. A happy place. As soon as I can move without pain, I'll be back to the practice.

"Reminds me of I Am Yoga," I say with a wistfulness I know she can feel. She tips her head and caresses the side of my face.

"Good times," she agrees.

"The best. I can't wait to go back. What's going on with the studio?"

Bree stiffens her shoulders and twists her lips. She clasps her four-and-a-half-month pregnant belly. I lift a hand out, and she holds mine over her stomach. I can almost feel a baby there. At least I'm able to convince myself I can.

"I don't know yet. Chase found a new location though. Says it's mine if I want it."

I press up trying to sit straighter. "Really? Where?"

One of her eyebrows rises into a point. "In your building," she snorts. I shake my head. My man's protective qualities know no bounds. "As if you didn't know."

I open and close my mouth. "I so didn't! I swear to God."

Her head pops back. "Huh. Well, when I mentioned it to Phil, he was all for it. We'd only be a few floors apart. And get this..." She laughs and I watch her pretty face as mirth takes over her features. "Chase has made the entire tenth floor a yoga studio, small gym, and wait for it..."—Maria, Kat, and I lean closer to her—"...a day care!"

"No way." A day care? Chase? I mull it over. "He did *not* mention that to me. I mean, I overheard him saying something to Dana about expanding the company on the tenth floor to a larger building across the street, but that's all I heard. A day care, really?"

Bree nods her head vigorously. "Says he wants to offer more benefits to his employees. The gym, the yoga studio, and the day care are going to be a benefit. During the evening hours, the day care can be used for those yogis who don't have anywhere to leave their kids. It will be part of a monthly fee they can tack onto their classes. The gym though, that's only going to be for staff and their families. He says I can run my business like usual only he'll pay me per employee per session, but at a severely discounted rate."

I narrow my eyes. "Why severely?" That's very unlike Chase. Usually he'd just give the studio to her.

"Because I'm not going to be paying rent or utilities. That's a huge expense. I'm actually going to triple my income, maybe even quadruple it."

Now that sounds like my Chase. I smile. He gave my

soul sister a new home for her studio and a day care for not only her new baby coming in a few months but also for Anabelle. Of course, I'm sure he'll play it off like it was for everyone. He is giving, but I know his ulterior motive. He knows it will make me happy knowing my friend is so close, and to have her yoga studio and day care in the same building as our penthouse? Perfection. He is so going to get laid. Just as soon as I break out of this medical jail.

"So what's the problem?" Kat asks. "Sounds like a dream come true to me. You have a new untainted location that's bigger, a safer location, a free day care for baby Bree and Anabelle, and you'll be close to Phil and Gigi. I'm not seeing the issue."

Bree shimmies from foot to foot. "I just don't want to take advantage, you know? Gigi, Chase is going to be your husband, but just because he's got more money than all of us combined doesn't mean we should abuse that. I want him to know that we're his family now, not just some moochers."

"You calling me a mooch, *senorita*? I live across the street rent-free in a building with cameras and a doorman. Initially, I had a problem with it, and then I realized Chase didn't do it for me."

"Sure he did!" I say, my words coming out with clear irritation.

Her eyes narrow right back as she shakes her head. "*Mierda!* He did it because he knows *you* will be worried and freaked out about my safety. Which is *ridículo* by the way. I can defend myself. Though I can't deny being able to afford the good vino and a few extra dance outfits has been nice." She grins, and I push at her shoulder.

"So you think I should take Chase's offer and move the

studio?"

Three sets of eyes focus on Bree. A simultaneous "Yes!" echoes throughout the room.

Bree holds up her hands in surrender. "Okay, fine, fine. I'll tell him when he comes back."

When he comes back?

I look around the room. He's not there. There is absolutely nothing in the room that shows he's been here. My heart starts to pound, thumping powerfully in my chest. The beeping of the machine instantly goes red and a little alarm sounds. I can see my blood pressure rising. Sweat beads on my forehead.

Where is he? He can't be gone.

"He can't be gone. Where is he?" The tone of my voice isn't mine. It's unrecognizable to even me. Maria's eyes go from blue to dark. Her face twists into a grimace. I squeeze her hand and ground down on my teeth.

"Gigi, what's the matter? You're hurting my hand, *chica*." She tries to tug it out of my grasp.

"Gigi, you're okay. We're right here," Kat says, but it doesn't really get through.

I close my eyes and then open them. Chase. He's not there. "Where is he?" I yell, the sound bouncing off the walls of the small white room. My entire body is hot, and my vision comes in and out. I shake my head, but instead of seeing clearly, I see colors. A rainbow of color everywhere forces me to blink furiously. "He's gone! He's not here!"

∞

I walk down the hall, whistling. The world is not perfect, but having Gillian back goes a long way toward making it possible for me to breathe a little easier. We'll find the fucker who did this to her, and I'll ruin him. One way or another, he'll be paying for what he's done to Gillian and her friends.

Dana is by my side, reading through the list of things that need handling at work. When Gillian fell asleep, I called the girls and told them they could come see her when she woke. When they arrived, I slipped out for my meeting with the second-in-command of Chase Industries. Knowing there are two bodyguards outside her door and a team still in the vicinity relieves a bit of the stress of leaving her. Plus, she has the three crazy sisters to keep her company. I feel relief for the first time in days...until I hear her blood-curdling scream.

"He's gone! He's not here!" Gillian is screaming into the face of a nurse who entered only moments before I did.

"Baby, Jesus Christ!" I rush over to her and pull her into my arms.

She sobs into my chest like earlier. "You weren't here. You left me! You promised you wouldn't fucking leave!" Tears track down her bruised face. Her nose runs, but that's not what gets to me. It's the eyes. Her beautiful emerald eyes show everything. Fear, anger, betrayal—three things I never want to see when she's looking at me. "How could you?" Her voice cracks with emotion.

I sit down on the bed, and she crawls into my lap like a frightened animal. Over and over she chants *you promised, you promised, you promised.* Every time she utters the words, it crushes my soul a little more.

With as much courage as I can muster, I pull her head from the cavern of my chest and look into her eyes once more. "I didn't leave you. I wasn't gone. I was down the hall speaking to a business associate and Dana." I look over at the door. Dana is standing in the doorway, holding the MacBook up against her chest as if she too needs to comfort something. Maria, Bree, and Kathleen are standing stock-still and staring unbelievingly at their friend. This woman— she's Gillian, but not the Gigi they know. "See." I gesture to the doorway. "Dana is right there. She came to meet me and to see you." I shoot for my most placating tone.

Dana clears her throat, and Gillian looks up at her. Then her eyes go to her friends' concerned ones. Her face crumbles, and tears rush down her face. She hiccups into my chest. "What the fuck is wrong with me?"

That's the question of the century, and one I fear only Dr. Madison is going to be able to answer.

Once I've soothed Gillian, the nurse gives her a dose of pain medication and a sedative, and after a short while, she falls back asleep. Leaving the door open enough that she can see me if she wakes up, I walk over to her friends.

"Ladies, I'm sorry you had to see that."

Maria's face contorts from concern to anger instantly. Fits with her fiery Italian Spanish heritage. I have many people working under me from similar ethnic backgrounds who can also go from cool as a cucumber to red-hot in mere seconds. Those are the most passionate, loyal, and dedicated of my employees but also the individuals who give me headaches.

Maria points to the room that Gillian is in. "What. The. Fuck. Was. That?" Her words are a short staccato sound.

I shake my head and let out a breath I've been holding. "She's going through something. It happened earlier when I was going to leave her side. Her psyche seems to be holding on to something that never occurred. It involves me leaving her, or somehow letting her go. I think I just need to work hard to let her know I'm with her. Always. That I'm not going anywhere."

Kathleen bites her lip, and Bree stays still, silently holding onto her protruding belly. Maria, on the other hand, has absolutely no problems voicing her opinion.

"Nuh-uh. What I saw in there, that was fear. Hard-core, absolute misery. She was fine, Chase. We laughed, we cried, we told her how happy we were she was home and it was good. Really good."

"Then what?" I ask, wondering how she went from being with her friends, women she's known and trusted for years, to a terrified, screaming mess.

"We spoke of Bree's new studio in the Davis Industries building. And then one of us mentioned something about talking to you when you got back, and she lost it. Her blood pressure rose, and a full-fledged panic attack overtook her. This was no normal panic attack either. *Escuchar esto,*" she says, *hear this* in Spanish. "I've seen Gillian have many panic attacks over the years dealing with the backlash of the Justin situation, but nothing like that. What I saw there was a woman who was literally destroyed over the thought that *you* were gone." She points an accusing finger at my chest.

My shoulders slump, and Kathleen brings me into her arms and hugs me. "It will be okay. She'll get through this."

I pull away and look into her brown eyes. Kind. So kind. I know now why Gillian is so taken with her. With all of them. Even though I'm not used to sharing my space, and the desire to lock Gillian away with me for years to come is tempting, I also know these women are good for her. They give her something I cannot. That thought alone sends a sizzle of irritation along every synapse. The three of them, hell even Phillip, love Gillian like a member of their family. They'd do anything for her, and because of that alone, I will make certain all of them are safe. For her.

"That's a great segue into what I need from the three of you. And Phillip." I lock my gaze onto Bree's.

"Anything," Bree says, holding my hand. She looks at her two friends and they nod. "Whatever it takes."

"You know McBride is still out there." Maria's hands go into fists at her sides. I gotta admit, I love how protective and physical she can be. "I need all of you to move back into the Davis Mansion." The three women respond with completely opposite reactions.

Kat shrugs and says okay. Bree groans, slumps her shoulders, and nods. Maria's eyes narrow and a hand comes up to her hip. "Do you really think that's necessary? I just started connecting with my apartment. The one that has security and a doorman, plus the three of us still have bodyguards." She points down the hall where three giant men in suits lean against a wall.

"And you'll keep those men, too, for as long as it takes to find McBride. He's dangerous. Really dangerous. And now he's going to be out for blood. All of ours. If anything happens to one of you, Gillian would be devastated. As it is, she's barely hanging on by a thread."

"Come on, Maria, what's another two, three weeks? Tommy's working with the FBI, and Chase has a horde of personal investigators and bounty hunters on his tail. They'll catch him really fast, but if this makes Gillian feel better, more at peace so she can heal, we have to be there for her," Kat says. I couldn't have given the speech better myself.

Maria rolls her eyes but nods.

I lock my gaze on Bree's concerned eyes. "Bree, please notify Phillip of the plan. I want him and his daughter at the mansion tonight."

"Okay." She looks to Gillian lying peacefully in her bed. "Do you think she'll be okay?"

I look at the woman I love more than anything, the one I'd give my last breath for. "We'll make certain of it. Right, ladies?"

"All right, *chicas*, let's go pack our bags." Maria turns, whistles at her bodyguard. "Hey, hot stuff, let's hit it."

I can't help but chuckle. The woman is incorrigible.

"You know, Tommy's not going to like you calling your bodyguard 'hot stuff,'" Bree says as she waves at the six-foot Viking guard I have assigned to her.

Maria lets out a sound that mimics a tire losing air rapidly. "I gotta keep my man on his toes." She clucks her tongue and sways her hips into a little dance.

Kathleen moves to turn away and then faces me once more. "What you're doing…" She swallows and starts again. "How you love her, it's special. Beautiful. I'm glad she found you." Then before I can respond, she's got me in her arms once again. This time I pull her against me and hug her tight. She hums, pulls back, and kisses my cheek. "It will all be okay. Very soon. I can feel it."

"I hope you're right, Kathleen."

"You know, you can call me Kat."

"Your name is lovely the way it is."

"Charmer. Now I see how she fell so quickly. It wasn't the physique, though since I'm bedding a member of your family, I can attest that's a factor." I chuckle. "It's your charm, and your belief that she is meant solely for you."

I look one of her best friends in the eyes. "I never believed in soul mates until I met her. Now I'm sorry for every schmuck out there who doesn't find theirs. Do you think you've found that in my cousin?"

Kathleen smiles wider and winks before turning and walking away, leaving my question unanswered.

On heavy feet, I make my way back into Gillian's room. She's mumbling in her sleep. Every so often she says my name, only she doesn't say it with happiness. It's said with desperation. Closing the door, I kick off my shoes, remove my pants, and pull off my shirt. Then I press the button to bring the bed flat. There's a chair that turns into a cot near the bed, but I can't be away from her tonight. Not tonight. She needs to know I'm here for her, even in sleep.

I slip in cautiously. Before I can lie back, she's cuddling into my chest. Medicated sleep doesn't prevent her body from knowing mine. Soul mates. I meant what I said to Kathleen a bit ago. Meeting Gillian almost a year ago at the hotel bar was like the universe opening up and delivering me a piece of heaven. It's something I never knew I wanted or needed, but it was there. And I took it and made it mine. I will continue to protect what is mine until my last breath.

Holding her warm body to mine, I close my eyes, enjoying the feel of her breath against my chest. Too many days have gone by since we've been skin to skin.

She snuffles against my chest and says in the most serene voice yet, "Chase…my Chase."

I swallow down the emotion, needing to be strong for her. The next few weeks, maybe even months, are not going to be easy ones. We have absolutely no leads on McBride. The only thing all of the investigators and my men can agree on is that he will strike again. He's going to come after Gillian or her friends in one way or another. We stole something he believes is his, from *his* property. To a psycho like Daniel McBride, that's worthy of a death sentence.

Thoughts of him, what he did to her, how he kept her locked up prevent me from easing into sleep. Eventually, I change my thoughts to the wedding we never had and the honeymoon we're currently missing. Right then and there I make a decision. We will be married and soon. I cannot let a madman keep me or Gillian from something that means more to us than anything else has in our relationship. The moment she's better, I'm taking her away. Away from it all. Just the two of us.

GILLIAN

CHAPTER SIX

The morning frost crunches, and the spikes of my low heels dig deep into the cold ground as we make our way up the incline. My healing ankles resist, but I tamp down any residual pain. Clenching my jaw and grinding my teeth works just fine. I've been out of the hospital a week, and it's been a total of two weeks since our wedding day. The day that never happened.

It's a sea of black everywhere you look when we arrive at our destination. Hundreds of people stand like a hill of ants, waiting to worship their queen, only their queen is dead. Ms. Colleen Davis is being laid to rest today. Chase held off on the services until I was found and out of the hospital. Now, he's finally dealing with his loss, though I'm not sure dealing with it would be the right term. More like avoiding it completely.

I clutch Chase's hand and look up at his profile. He's stoic. Hasn't smiled or moved a muscle in his sculpted face in the last hour. It's a cold day when the world isn't graced with one of his smiles. For a while, I got so used to seeing them, it became a welcome permanent fixture in my life. Lately, we've all been nothing but frowns. Today is no different.

Solemnly, we tread through the group of people. So

many stop him with a few kind words, a pat to the shoulder or back, people I've never met or seen providing small snippets of comfort in Chase's time of need. Except me. I have nothing to say. There's nothing I can say that will ever take away this hurt. Because the woman Chase loves is the reason his mother is dead. The one woman he trusted above all others is gone, and it's my fault.

I'm a realistic person. I get that I wasn't the one who murdered Colleen in cold blood, but I was the catalyst for Daniel even being there that day. I watched Chase's mother take her last breath. As much as that hurts, it's the topic of what we were fighting about before Daniel entered that bridal room that plagues my every breath. She never believed that I was the right woman for her son. Those thoughts and feelings were the last things she had on this Earth.

I haven't even been able to talk to Chase about it. How could I? *Oh, yeah, baby, your mom hated my guts, and on our wedding day, she was making it clear how wrong I was for you. Five minutes later, her neck was slit by my ex-boyfriend. Sorry.*

I let out a deep sigh, and Chase pulls me tighter against his side, leans down, and places a warm kiss on my head at the hairline. We're here to bury his mother, and he's comforting me. Things are so messed up. When we get to the graveside seating area, I see my six favorite people, aside from Chase, all sitting together like my own personal cheering section. Tommy is sitting next Maria, who's next to Bree, who's alongside Phil, who's next to Kat, who's sitting with Carson. All of our friends are in black, all wearing matching somber expressions. Chase leads me to them.

Carson gets up first. "Hey, man, I…uh…" He clears his throat and tries again. "This has to be hard, after what happened to your girl and all." Carson glances to me and then back to Chase. "Aunt Colleen, well, she loved you more than anything in this world. Everyone knew that." Carson pulls Chase into a man-hug, and surprisingly, Chase accepts, though his expression is still set in stone.

Maria clasps Chase's hand, looks into his eyes, and says, "*Voy a rezar por el alma de su madre para estar en paz.*" He nods and gives Ria a tight-lipped smile. I pick up a bit, something about his mother's soul and rest in her words, but not much else.

Bree stands, and her pregnant belly bumps him. Chase reaches out both hands to prevent her from tipping but ends up cradling her bump. He gasps, and his eyes get glassy. The first hint of real emotion I've seen since the hospital. She covers his hands with her own.

"She likes you. Feel her?"

Her. She said *her.* His eyes sparkle for the first time in what seems like forever. His hand cups a specific spot on her belly, and she presses it close.

"I do feel it. The kick. Your daughter is very strong," he says, and she nods, sniffing and rubbing her nose on her tissue.

Kat and Bree's eyes fill with tears that fall prettily down their cheeks. "We found out yesterday but with everything going on"—she looks to both sides, and Phil puts an arm around her shoulder, comforting her—"it just didn't seem important," Bree finishes.

Maria closes her eyes and shakes her head. Tommy pulls her into his side protectively. I hold a hand over my mouth and stifle a sob. She didn't feel it was important because of everything that's happened. My best friend is going to have a baby girl, and instead of shouting it from the rooftops like any one of us would in the same circumstance, she held her tongue and tried to not make a big deal of her news. Doesn't she know that news like this can heal us? That her baby, the life within her, gives us all hope?

"Congratulations." Chase pats her hand and proceeds to shake Phil's hand and Tommy's. "Gillian, want to stay with your friends while I check with Dana about the arrangements?"

"Uh, yeah. Okay, if that's what you want."

He gives another tight smile, the one I've seen him use in business meetings when things aren't going his way. Never with me. I'm not really sure how to take that. Leaving it alone is all I can do right now.

Maria pulls me into a big hug. "Hey, girl, how you holding up?" she asks, pushing back a lock of my hair that slipped out of the chignon.

I shake my head. "Doesn't matter. I'm fine."

"You don't look fine. You look... I don't know, different."

"Well, we are at a funeral. You know, sad day and all," I remind her, my tone coming across as a bit bitchy.

She purses her lips. "Have you seen Dr. Madison yet?"

"No." I stare off into the distance and bite my lip. "I will, soon actually. Couple days from now. Chase is forcing it."

Her icy eyes turn a warmer blue. "You know as well as I do that after everything you've been through, not seeing a therapist would be *estúpido*. This is not your first rodeo dealing with traumatic experiences."

"You're right. It isn't." I sigh a long soul-cleansing breath. "I don't know why I'm avoiding it. Regardless, I'm going on Wednesday."

"Chase too?"

The mere thought of Chase being anywhere I'm not sends a river of panic rushing down my spine. I straighten and look all around, trying to spot Chase. Instead, I see Megan "The Bitch" O'Brian holding onto Chase's arm and standing close...really close. "The nerve of that woman," I growl under my breath.

Maria's head snaps to where I'm looking. Kat and Bree stand and flank my sides, both having heard me.

"That the ex? The *puta*?" Ria asks, the words spilling out as if they have been shoved through a meat grinder.

Instead of responding, I focus my attention on sending a bushel of visual daggers in Megan's direction. When she pulls Chase into her arms, holds him close, and he doesn't instantly pull back, I actually sway on my feet. Bree and Kat hold me up.

"Easy there," Kat says, her voice a comforting whisper.

Maria looks at me, shrugs her man's hold off her shoulder, and beats feet to Chase and Megan. I can't move or go after her. I just can't physically defend myself or my man. It's like I'm a hollow statue that was once made of solid stone. My insides are so weak I can barely keep the outside from cracking and splitting at the seams with the deluge of emotions pressing against all sides.

I watch in sick fascination as Maria interrupts the lovefest that is my man holding onto his ex-fiancée. She pulls him aside and whispers in his ear. He immediately leaves The Bitch behind and heads in our direction. His eyes are cold, his face as hard as granite. The long black coat he wears flares out, making him look like he's just stepped out of photo shoot for London Fog outerwear. Maria, on the other hand, doesn't follow. Looks like my soul sister is having words with the redheaded siren. I can barely find the energy to care.

Chase reaches my side and pulls me into his arms. "What's wrong? Are you unwell?"

I clutch his back and drop my face into the crevice at his neck. That woodsy fruity scent that is solely Chase slams against my senses and tears slide down my face. And that's when the shaking starts. Tremors curl through my body uncontrollably while I hold onto Chase for dear life.

"I'm sorry, I'm sorry, I'm sorry. My fault, my fault, my fault," I whisper over and over against his neck, my tears soaking the collar of his shirt. He doesn't seem to be fazed by it. Instead, he just holds me, his own face pressing against my neck, finally taking the comfort I know he needs right now.

"Baby, you have nothing to be sorry for. This is not your fault. That's the truth." He pulls back, cups my cheeks in his hands, and swipes at my tears with his thumbs. The bruises on my face are almost gone. He leans forward and takes my lips in a soft kiss. "I can taste your fears. It's lovely that you cry for me, but unwarranted. You are not to blame for what happened to Mother. There's only one man who needs to come to justice for the crime he committed against my mother, our friends, and you. Please stop punishing yourself. It hurts me to think you're carrying this weight. Let it go, okay?" His gaze turns gray matching the sky and clouds overhead.

"Okay," I lie. He can say what he wants, but even though there is a lot of truth to his words, I can't let go.

Daniel would have never touched this family, that girl in the yoga studio, all those people at the gym, or my best friend Phillip if it weren't for me. That's a lot of collateral damage adding up, and each and every instance is digging a bigger hole into my heart where I fear no amount of happiness will be able to fill it again.

Maria comes walking back with pep in her step and a wicked grin. Seeing her with a grin like that means she's up to something, and it is most definitely bad, illegal, or perhaps both.

I narrow my gaze at her as she cuddles up to Tommy. "Ria, what did you say to her?" I gesture with a head tilt to where the redhead was.

Her eyes widen, and she places a hand to her chest. "Who me? Oh, nothing really. I just reminded her that this is a rough time in our friends' lives and to mind her manners."

Chase's eyebrows rise up to his hairline. "Well, that was very big of you, Ms. De La Torre," Chase says formally with a hint of jest.

She smiles widely. Uh-oh. Her tone is saccharine-sweet when she adds, "And then with the same tenderness and compassion she's given our Gigi in the past, I reminded her that if she ever laid one of her skanky-assed fingers on my best friend's man again, I'd take that finger and break it. Then I'd happily break her face for good measure, so that her face would match her finger and she'd never have to understand what jealousy felt like."

I look from Maria to Chase, completely horrified. Leave it to my best friend to offer a wallop of drama at a graveside. Even if it was one hundred percent justified.

"Oh, wow. Karma got evil on her ass," Bree says under

her breath, yet still loud enough for all of us to hear.

"Chase…" I try to smooth over the potential disaster this may have caused when he responds in the exact opposite way I would ever expect. He laughs. Literally drops his head back, put his arms out to the sky, and laughs. Loudly.

Eyes from every direction zero in on the hysterics that have overtaken my normally emotionally guarded business tycoon. I scowl at every person until they all look away and wait for Chase to come back to himself.

"Fuck, I needed that," Chase says after a long bout of laughter. So long that people are making a point to look everywhere but at the spectacle our little group has created.

"What?" Maria holds up her arms. "The *puta* deserved it. Besides, it's not like I hit her." She grins again. "I wanted to, but I thought that would get me in trouble with one of them." She points to a section of guys with earpieces, sunglasses, and black suits who look quite menacing. "Or those guys." She points to another section. "Maybe even them." Again she scans the perimeter. "Or perhaps those ones. They look downright jumpy for some action."

"Chase, that's a lot of guards."

"Honey, they think McBride will come today. The announcement of Mother's service was in the paper this week, along with the location so mourners could attend and pay respects. It stands to reason that he'd want to see you again. I can't take any chances. The FBI even has snipers in the trees watching for activity."

"You're kidding." I search his gaze.

He shakes his head slowly. "I wish I were."

X

When will they ever fucking learn? They think they can keep me from my girl? That the FBI and his rent-a-cops will prevent me from seeing her today? When I saw the announcement in the paper about the rich bitch's funeral, I could barely contain my excitement. Chase being in the hospital every second of the goddamned day did not give me the chance to reconnect with my girl. Originally, my plan was to take her from the hospital. Just shoot her full of the tranquilizer again and mosey on out of there with her on a stretcher.

I even had the guy and ambulance picked out. But no, the stupid dick had to screw up my plans. I mean, really, who stays with a woman every second while she is in the hospital? He never left to sleep, or eat, or anything. The couple times they had her sedated that I could see, he had those bitches watching over her. As much as it would have made me bust a nut to take out all three of them at once, the two guards posted at her door and the dick's presence ruined it.

Not for long. For the past two weeks they've been in hiding, but I suspect they are at the Davis mansion. It's the only place that's heavily guarded, much more than it was before. Though I have a plan for that too. I've already met some of the guards at a local bar not far from the estate. They go there after their shift and toss back a few beers. I've been in there. They haven't noticed any similarity between the person they are on the lookout for and the man I've become. Brown hair, a full mustache, and the start of a pretty good-sized beard have really helped. Add the contacts, and voila, I'm a new man. I've even donned some pretty stellar suits because a well-groomed man in a suit is not the guy they're looking for. No, they're looking for a blond, blue-eyed man who works out a lot and is an accountant in a small firm. Was an accountant, anyway.

I've always been good at numbers. Like the number one hundred and forty. The exact number of people between me and my girl.

Fourteen. That number signifies how many rows back I am from my princess.

Six. The amount of people I'm going to have to kill to have her in my life forever.

Chase will never stop. Neither will that pig Thomas Redding, especially if he keeps dating her best friend. Then of course there's still the cousin who looks like a fucking Ken Doll who's with one of her other friends. I can't imagine going through life looking like a little girl's toy. And of course yoga Barbie, though now I guess I'd say she's prego Barbie. Still looks hot. I'd definitely stick my dick in her. Never fucked a pregnant woman before. Might be worth a round or two, make Gillian watch so she can see how nothing and no one will ever stand in my way getting to her. And last but not least, Phillip and Maria. Now those two are a pair. I need to think up something definitely evil to take them out. They have both thwarted my attempts to cage Gillian too many times over the years aside from recent events. They were always hanging around, trying to take up my girl's time when Gillian and I were dating. Fucking annoying.

I stare at the six people, thinking about each one of them individually. Chase has all of them locked away, so I'm sticking with the theory that they are all at that mansion. Getting in there will be easy enough. Figure I'll be working as one of Chase's rent-a-cops in the next couple weeks. I'll just mention that I'm looking for work the next time I'm at the bar when he's there, give him one of my fake cards, and I'm in. Even if I have to take out one of the current guys to ensure an opening, that won't be too hard. I've already got one in my sights. He's a real piece of work. Fucks over his wife and kids, drinks his paycheck away at the bar. They'd be better off getting social security for his death than the mountain of debt I'm sure he's got going on.

My musings stop cold as I watch Chase go over to where Gillian is sitting with her friends. She stands, and he puts an arm around her and leads her to the front row. Dick.

"Let's all take a seat," says the priest at the front of the seating area where the casket is propped up like some kind of fucking altar.

The woman was a hideous bitch who yelled at my perfect girl and made her feel inadequate. No one is allowed to make my girl feel like that. And the woman wouldn't shut the fuck up. I warned her, but…she didn't listen. You can't blame a guy for taking her out. Anyone who has balls would do what I did. I put Gillian and the rest of the world out of their misery when I slit that old hag's throat. Man, and the waterfall of blood when I slid my blade clean through the pale skin of her turkey-like neck was quite a sight.

Standing over the bitch really gave me a good view of it, too. The blood poured out like a wave cresting on a sandy beach. It was magical. When I killed that tree-hugging yoga cunt, I was sitting behind her. Took away the cool visual. Though I'll never forget having my legs and arms wrapped around her body as she shook and took her last breath. Her body was still warm when I left her on that wooden platform, her blood coating the shiny surface. As I recall these recent memories, my dick becomes painfully hard. What would it be like to fuck a woman while slitting her throat?

I scan the crowd and see that pathetic assistant I was fucking. She was good as far as fucking whores goes. She would be a good candidate to test my throat slashing theory while taking her like an animal. I can just imagine the warm sticky blood flowing over her chest, sticking to mine as I slide along her body. Or maybe I'd slit her from pelvis to breast and let her insides coat me while I fucked her to death. Literally.

Damn, and I thought my dick was hard before. Not even close to what it is now after that little fantasy. Now I just need to make fantasy reality. Maybe the boring blond bitch will be my fun until I can get to my girl.

Speaking of my girl—she's ethereal today. So perfect in her black suit. Though it makes me sad that most of the marks I gave her have faded. Guess it just means she'll be a nice blank canvas when I get her back. Then again, I did notice she wobbled on her small heels when she came up the hill with the prick. Maybe the marks at her ankles are still there. That thought makes me extremely happy. Knowing that every day when she looks down at her ankles she'll be thinking of me. Of the time the two of us shared for four blissful days. And then she was taken. Stolen from me.

That will not happen again. Someone has to pay for that, and if it's not Chase, it's going to have to be her friends. I'm tired of these bitches. They're always there, hanging around, filling my Gillian's head full of stupid shit that doesn't matter.

And I was making such progress, too. I'd gotten her to eat a little, and she had put on the tank top I brought her. Those were steps in the right direction. A couple more weeks in her cell and she probably would have bent over backwards to get into the motor home. Now it's all gone. Seized by the fucking federal government as a crime scene.

I will not let that setback ruin me. As it is, I'm here, looking at my girl, though now she's twenty-two rows ahead of me, in the very front. Chase has his arm around her, his fingers rhythmically massaging her shoulder. I want to scream at him to get his hands off her, but I can't. I cannot let my emotions control me. I'm too good for that. No, I will have her back, but it will be in my time and when it best suits me. In the meantime, I think she needs to be reminded of what's at stake if she chooses to continue this farce of a relationship with the rich fucker. In the end, it's going to be me or the lives of the people she calls family. It's a pretty easy choice, but I know how stubborn my girl is. She may need some time to think about it. I'll give her that. And while she's thinking, I'll be taking action.

I look at the six heads of the people Gillian adores. Some more so than others. And then it becomes so clear. She works in a dark location that's not heavily guarded, easy enough to get to. Especially if I scope it out at night, set up some cameras, watch the place for a few days, get to know the routines of everyone there.

The San Francisco Theatre is an old building. Great architecture but easy enough to break into. All of those old buildings are. I watch my target as she pushes her long hair over her shoulder. It falls in a blanket of golden curls. Her brown eyes seem to have a story behind them. One most don't bother to ask. The quiet one. The one that no one suspects would be in danger, yet now, the perfect target to get my Gillian's attention.

I don't know why it never occurred to me before. Long hours at the theatre working on costumes. I'll bet there're very few people around her when she's doing her job, too. The cameras will tell me everything I need to know in a few days. Then I'll strike.

Kathleen Bennett, you've sewn your last masterpiece.

CHASE

CHAPTER SEVEN

It's unusual for her to wander off. Now that we're home—well, at the Davis mansion—I can usually find her in our room or with her friends. Never alone. Most of the time she's right on my heels. I find that disconcerting, but only because I know her mental health is suffering. Having her where I can see her at all times works for me. It speaks to the Neanderthal deep within my genome that wants his woman by his side, always within arm's reach. Except now. I left her on our bed resting peacefully for once, needing some time to think, to work through what I'm feeling about Mother's death, but she wandered off. I haven't come to any conclusions, other than a profound anger and hatred toward her murderer that resonates just under the surface of my skin since the attack and abduction of Gillian.

I walk slowly through the long hallways of my childhood home, passing the doors for each of my cousin's bedrooms. Memories of hide and go seek, games of tag, wrestling, and overall roughhousing with them flood my vision, making them so real it's as if I can reach in and touch them. Go back to that time when life was easy. Living with my Uncle Charles and his four children healed me from the experience with my father, bringing a frightened little boy back to life, giving me hope and dreams for the future. And I didn't waste a minute of it. I used every ounce of the second chance this family gave me and made something out of it. Now I'm as wealthy as the man who raised me from the age of seven years old. Richer actually. Though it wasn't a competition to my uncle. He only ever wanted the best for me and his children. Treated me like one of his very own from the start. I learned from him the power of working hard and going after what you want in life. Never stopping until what you seek is yours.

Like Gillian. The moment I saw her, I wanted her. Not just her body, though Gillian naked could bring any man to his knees. Pearlescent skin that shimmers when she's turned on. Her full breasts, nipped-in waist, and that tiny triangle of red hair that makes me salivate for a taste. All these things are physical reminders of her beauty, but it's her essence that drives me mad. Surrounding her form is something majestic that calls to a place deep inside me. Like now, I can feel her close as I make my way to the opposite end of the mansion. My mother's wing.

One of the double doors is open and I enter. The scent of lavender with a tiny hint of vanilla invades my nostrils as I make my way through the open living room area. Mother always smelled of lavender or flowers. The vanilla, that's *my woman*. I could pick her out of a lineup while blindfolded. I know her scent that well.

I can hear whispering as I get close to Mother's sleeping quarters. Again, the door is ajar, and I peek inside, keeping silent. My bare feet curl into the carpet as I stare at her. Gillian. She's kneeling at the side of Mother's bed as if in prayer. I wait, holding onto the door, digging into the wood with my fingers so that I don't instantly go to her. The fact that she left on her own is important. It's the first step toward healing, but why Mother's room? What called to her?

And then she speaks. "Ms. Davis…um, Colleen"—she dips her head down toward her hands that are in prayer and sets her lips on the tips of her fingers—"we laid you to rest today. I hope that means you're at peace."

From my position, I can see a tear trace down her pale cheek, and it almost catapults me to her. Seeing Gillian cry breaks me. Every tear seems like a failure on my part, proof that I've not done my job making her happy.

"Chase is okay. He's hurting, but I don't know what to do to help him." Her voice cracks on the last part, and she sniffs, wiping her nose and wet eyes on the sleeve of her robe.

I stifle a laugh. The women who came before her would never do such a human thing. No, they always had perfect manners and plastic bodies. Gillian is real, and seeing her now, on her knees, praying to my mother, fills me with a love so strong I've no doubt it will survive the test of time.

"I'm sorry that you're gone, for Chase and for me. I wanted the time to prove to you how much I love him, how I'd never forsake or take advantage of his love. And now you'll never know. Worse, it's my fault you're gone. How will he ever forgive me?" Her voice shakes, and a sob fills the room as her head falls onto the bed, her shoulders racked with the weight of her sorrow.

I can't handle it. I fall to my knees behind her, caging her body with my own, sheltering her, giving her the protection I wasn't able to give her two weeks ago. "There's nothing to forgive." I nuzzle the side of her hair near her ear. "Hear me. Really hear me. It's not your fault." She shakes her head and the sobs take over. I turn her around, and she scrambles into my lap, legs wrapped around my waist, head in my neck. Using the bed to help steady us, I stand, gripping her ass and her back.

While she cries, I walk us back to our room. We pass Phillip on the way, and he opens his mouth to speak, but I shoot him with a hard gaze and shake my head sternly. He closes his mouth and backs against the wall getting out of our way. Smart man. Right now, I'll take out anyone who tries to breach my woman. She's right where she needs to be, and I will be the one to comfort her, to bring her back to the happy, confident woman she is. Me. The man who's going to spend the rest of his life loving her.

We enter our bedroom, and she lifts her head with the click of the bolt going into place. Through her tears, her eyes are as green as shamrocks and just as wild. Her lips are moist, tears having coated them. I bring her to the bed and slowly lay her down. Then, I take her mouth in mine, tasting her sadness, her grief. It's beautiful and heartbreaking. She doesn't hesitate to open for me, and I dip in for a much more thorough sampling.

Christ, she's the sun, the moonlight, and the stars, positively shining under my touch. Methodically, I pull the tie at her waist and open her robe. She's wearing a pale yellow camisole with matching lace panties and nothing else. My cock hardens under my pajamas, and I push it into her leg. Her eyes widen, and she gasps.

"You still want me?" Her voice comes across sounding surprised, but for the life of me, I can't possibly imagine why.

I narrow my gaze at her, making sure she focuses on

me. "Gillian, I will always want you. You give me life, bring a purpose to my world that's much greater than the bitter existence I once lived. With you, I see possibilities. I have hope for more."

A tear tracks down the side of her face. I push up, pull off the T-shirt I donned, and push down the pajama pants.

"Commando?" She smiles and a little giggle follows it. Prettiest sound I've heard in a long time.

I grin. "I was worried."

Her eyes go soft, and she lifts her hands to my hair. Smooth fingers caress the side of my scalp until she lifts up to kiss me directly over my heart. "I want to be worthy of this," she says, placing a kiss there.

"There is no one more worthy," I say while pushing her robe off her shoulders.

She removes her arms and holds her hands up as I lift the hem of her camisole and pull it off. Her full breasts bounce free and catch my gaze like a hawk to its prey in the dead of night. In this position, me standing, her placing kisses all over my bare chest, I can only cup and lift her breasts, swiping my thumbs along the turgid peaks. She mewls but doesn't stop her ministrations. With my thumb and first finger I simultaneously pluck and pull at each tip, elongating the flesh, knowing how to best pleasure her. Pleasing this woman is ingrained into my soul. Soon she can't handle it, her eyes closing, hands gripping my hips as she feels every movement, every caress of my hands on her. I love how I can make her stop doing whatever she is doing just by touching her.

I kneel down alongside the bed just the way she was in mother's room before. With intent, I pull a nipple into the heat of my mouth. Her hands instantly fly to my hair, and she holds my head to her breast.

"I missed your love," she moans, letting her head tip back, her glorious curls falling down her back.

With the flat of my tongue, I lave around the areola before biting down softly on the tip. An unintelligible sound slips from her lips. Her usually pale pink nipples are now dark, wider, and pointing straight at my mouth in offering. They are mine, and even her body knows it instinctively.

Fire builds at the center of my groin and spreads out, my shaft filling with blood and aching with the need to plunge, to take, to own. I slip my fingers into the edges of her lace panties and pull them down as I lick a solid line from her breast, down her sternum, to the thatch of hair that drives me insane with desire. Her womanly scent is heady, and I inhale deeply, allowing the caveman within me to sense his mate intimately. With an urging press to her ribs, I guide her down to the mattress. Her hair fans out in a rush of color along the pink sheets. I watch her with her eyes closed as I trail my fingers from her shoulders, over each breast, where I stop to cup and fondle. Her back arches, pressing into my hands. I twist each tip enough to send jolts of pleasure straight to her center. Gillian fists the sheets on both sides of her, showing her restraint. She's letting me have my time with her. As much as she needs this, she knows I need to control this first time back with her body. Aside from the very fact that regardless of where she's been or what's gone on in the past…Gillian craves submission. Only that submission shouldn't come with a price other than extreme pleasure. With me, she'll never go without knowing the surrender of her control is a gift I cherish, one

I will keep safe and protect with every ounce of my being.

"I love your body. Love seeing my hands all over you." I paint a path all over her skin, caressing her everywhere. "Knowing I'm the only man that will ever get to see this, touch it..." I lean forward and nuzzle her center, inhaling full and deep the scent of her arousal. She gasps and twitches. Her legs tremble as I stroke her thighs and widen her legs for me. She's positively dripping with need, the lips of her sex coated in her essence. My cock hardens, becoming painful, weeping at the tip. "I am the only man who will ever see this pretty cunt open in invitation. Do you want that, baby? Me being the only man to taste your desire?"

Her eyes open, and the emerald orbs are sparkling, filled to the brim with lust. "Yes. Only you. Please," she begs.

I close my eyes, appreciating this moment for what it is—Gillian, bringing me back from the depths of hell, helping me find my way home. It's her. She is my home.

I open her thighs wide and lock my gaze with hers. Her mouth opens, and she's breathing heavily, possibly dying in anticipation of that first touch. And I give it to her with everything that I am. I lay the flat of my tongue on her pussy and slowly drag it along her weeping slit. Her arousal coats my tongue, my taste buds bursting with extreme flavor. Fucking sweet. My woman is so goddamned sweet my balls tighten, lifting up, reaching toward her. Closing my eyes, I suck her tiny clit into my mouth and reach my tongue way down to sop up some of her sugary nectar.

The plan was to go slow, ease her into one orgasm and then another before I took her, but I'm losing control. Every sweep of my tongue into her delicious pussy has every neuron and synapse firing. Electricity and energy sizzle around us as I drink from the woman I love. Before long, she squeezes her thighs and grips my head. Thank Christ! I suck, lick, and nip against her swollen center as she keens out to the room, her cries of pleasure music to my ears.

But I'm not done. I may never be done. Cupping her ass, I press her cunt hard against my face, smothering myself with her flesh. She cries out, but I don't stop. Can't. I need her too much. Inserting two fingers deep into her cleft causes her to buck wildly. Her head is moving back and forth against the mattress as if she's saying no, but her body, her cries of pleasure are saying, "Fuck, yes!"

I pull back from her, licking my chops, preparing for more but needing to see her—see on her face what my touch does to her. Keeping my hand busy, I stand up awkwardly and press a knee to the bed. Gillian must feel the shift in the mattress because her eyes fly open, and I watch her. Sitting on the side of the bed, I scan her body. Her pale skin now has a fine sheen of sweat and a rosy hue. She's panting and moving her hips along with the movement of my fingers deep inside her.

"Do you like my touch?" I ask her, quirking an eyebrow. Hooking my fingers, I tickle that spot inside her that makes her gush.

"So much," she gasps and closes her eyes.

"Give me your eyes. I want to watch you fall apart."

Her breath comes in short staccato pants as I fuck her with more force, the muscles of my forearm straining with the effort.

"Why?" she asks, her eyes rolling but coming back to me.

I lean forward to suck on her nipple, which gets me a

long drawn out moan, before I lean back up and watch her pretty face again.

"You want to know why I want to watch you fall apart?" She nods, but then cries out to God when I press a third finger into her wet cunt. "Because it's my job to put you back together again. Every time." I tickle along the wall of her pussy and her hips fly up. I push them back down, holding her pelvic bone with my thumb, my other three fingers hooked deep inside. It would be easy to lift her up just by her sex.

"I want to fall..." she whispers, and that request forces out the animal in me. "Catch me," she says while her body strains, becomes tight.

"I'll always catch you, bring you home. Now give your pleasure to me. Let yourself fall apart. I'll put you back together," I promise and pick up the pace. Fucking her with fast and rough fingers, just the way she likes it. It's as if my hand is working to physically pull the orgasm from her. Perhaps it is because her eyes go dark, her mouth opens in a silent scream, and her pussy clamps around my fingers so tight I clench my jaw. Her body arches up and down, thrusting in harmony with my own movements until she stops, her hips in midair, her shoulders still flat on the mattress. Slowly, her body loosens its hold, bringing her down one vertebra at a time. I wait until she's languid and smiling to ease my fingers from her.

I lie alongside her, my dick hard as stone against her hip, and kiss her. She kisses me back, and though I thought I tired her out, I couldn't have been more wrong. Instantly she turns the tables on me by throwing a knee over my hips, straddling me perfectly. Her wet cunt lands directly over my length, pressing down. I groan and thrust my hips on instinct.

A beautiful smirk adorns her face. "My turn to play, handsome."

"You have no idea what you do to me," he says while cupping my bum and crushing his erection between our bodies. Nothing but skin-on-skin contact. It's exactly what my ravaged heart and mind need. After going two full weeks without his touch, I feel like I'm starving, only it's not my belly that needs sustenance. I need him inside of me, so deep I forget what it's like to be me without being connected to him.

I lean down and suck at his lips. He tastes of man and me. A sexy mixture I haven't had in what feels like years but it's only been a couple weeks. One thing is for sure, Chase loves to go downtown. He almost always goes for the space between my thighs. To me, it's almost more intimate than the act of sex itself...except with Chase. Every act is intimate. He makes it so.

"I know exactly what I'm doing to you." His eyebrow quirks. "Really, I do." I smile and trace his lips with one finger.

"Enlighten me then, gorgeous." He grins, clasps his hands behind his head, and waggles his eyebrows. Smug bastard.

I sit up, giving him a great view of my naked body. He takes the bait, his eyes running the length of my torso and down where I slowly start to rub my slick center against his velvety cock. "You're turned on," I start.

"Given." He thrusts his hips, reminding me just how painfully erect he is.

I moan and then catch myself. "You're warm, everywhere." I lay my hands on his chest and smooth over the bumps and ridges of his abdominal muscles and square pecs. I'm one lucky woman, sitting here on top of a naked man who could double as a male model. His body is in such perfect shape. Only he's thinner, hasn't put back on the pounds he lost when I was abducted. I'm no better. I've only gained back five of the twenty-five I lost, although I know it's a process and I'm on the right track.

Chase gives me one of his heart-stopping smirks. "Very warm. I could be warmer if you'd sit more fully on my cock."

I shimmy my hips, stirring my ass in a circle. "Like this?"

"Mmm, yeah. And now maybe you could get up on your knees and open yourself to me. You know how I like it, baby. Let me see your pleasure."

"You're depraved, you know that?" I grin.

He clasps my left hand and brings it to his mouth. He sucks my first finger and middle finger into his mouth, swirling his tongue delectably around the fingers, and then pulls my ring finger in. It stops at my engagement ring. Thank the heavens my fingers were so swollen from the anesthesia that Daniel couldn't get my ring off. He tried. Lord knows he tried. Chase looks at the ring and frowns.

"This should be your wedding ring," he laments sadly.

I nod and bite my lip, not knowing what to say that could make it better for either of us. Finally I just tell the truth, trying to focus on the positive. "We're together, and that's all that matters. It will be…one day." I say it to him as if it's a promise.

"If I wanted to whisk you away and marry you along the side of a lake in a tiny church in the middle of nowhere, what would you say?" His eyes no longer hold mirth but focus intently on mine.

I look at the man lying naked below me. He's laying his heart out in the open for me to see. I place my hand over his heart and feel the steady, quickening pace of his heart rate as he waits patiently for my answer.

Tilting my head, I look at the man I love. Just look at him. Eyes dark with lust and love. Hair a stark brown against his lightly tanned skin. Lips so soft that I worry kissing him will bruise the perfect bow-shaped flesh. And his jaw, his beard now scratchy from a day of growth. Watching him, I can see not only how beautiful he is, but I can feel how much I mean to him. His hands come to my hips, and he methodically lifts me up. He centers the wide knobbed head of his cock at my sex and pushes inch by slow inch inside me. His manhood presses the walls of my pussy wide to allow for his thickness. My body clamps down around his length in greeting. Ribbons of heat and excitement spiral from between my legs up and out of my pelvis until finally, as if he had all day and night to make his entrance, he's seated to the brim. There is nowhere else left for his cock to go. I'm jam-packed with the heavy weight of his flesh and don't want to be anywhere else in the world.

"I need an answer," he says, grinding his pelvic bone into my clit from below.

I gasp and lean forward, shifting his cock and forcing

him into a new angle. An angle that penetrates to nth degree and then some. "Chase, baby…" I moan, swept away by our connection.

"Will you marry me?" he asks again.

I lift up and slam back home. That time, he growls and clenches my hips possessively.

"Of course I'll marry you. I already said yes. My answer didn't change in two weeks." I tip my head back and place my hands on his rock-hard thighs behind me. Without meaning to, I jut my breasts out and curve backward over the legs of my man. His thick rod pushes up into me with each thrust, hitting that effervescent place that only he ever reaches.

Chase groans and clenches his jaw when he responds. "I meant will you go away with me? Let me marry you far, far away, where it's only me and you and our commitment to be together, to have this…through infinity, baby," he roars, slamming me onto his cock. I scream out an orgasm, preparing to explode deep within my womb.

He lifts his legs up into ninety-degree angles, forcing his dick higher, if possible. Then he places his hands on my waist and lifts me up and down, rocking me back and forth on his cock. Tingles prickle along my body, firing off tiny bursts of pure bliss. Pleasure roars through me in a wave of uninhibited ecstasy. His thumb comes in contact with my clit and gives it a wild rubbing. That is the trigger.

"God, Chase," I scream as the orgasm shoots through me. My body puts down the vise lock on his erection, and he, too, cries out long and deep. Hot sprays of his seed bathe my insides with jet after jet of his essence.

I flop down onto his chest, incapable of movement. His

breath comes in heaving pants against the side of my hair, blowing a stubborn curl down the side of my cheek.

Chase's arms wrap around me, and I snuggle into his chest, my head on his heart, exactly where I'm meant to be. "We needed that." He states the obvious and I chuckle. The first true laugh I've had in two weeks.

While I lie there naked and perfectly content to doze on my man—he's now soft but still imbedded within me—I think about his request. Just get up and leave everything behind and escape... no, escape is the wrong term. Elope.

I lift up my head, clasp my hands over his chest, and rest my chin on them. "You want to elope?"

His eyes turn my favorite cerulean blue. "I do. I don't want to tell anyone, explain where we're going or how long we'll be gone. I just want to disappear with you. Then bind you to me, legally, physically, mentally, eternally."

I force myself not to shy away but to just follow my heart. "I want that too."

His eyes narrow. "You do?"

"Yes, I do."

He hugs me to him. "Does that mean we can leave tomorrow?" It reminds me of the first time he asked me to marry him back in our penthouse after that horrible evening with Megan.

"End of the week. Friday. Five days from now."

He nods, smiling wide. "I'll make the arrangements."

"Don't tell anyone. Make them yourself. Don't even tell Dana."

He scrunches up his brows. "Do you not trust her because of what McBride did?"

I shake my head. "No, that sick asshole played all of

us, me especially. I do not fault her for falling for him. He's very good at manipulation. She was just another pawn in his game. I just… This is about us. Me and you. We can make the plans together if you want."

This time he shakes his head and pulls me into a tight hug. "I'll take care of everything, but why the end of the week?"

"Well, we need to see Dr. Madison, and I need a day with the girls before we elope."

"You're going to tell them?" The tone in his voice holds a touch of accusation.

"No, I won't, but I haven't been a very good friend. These last two weeks I haven't been able to be away from you for more than ten minutes, and honestly, Chase, even that is excruciating. I was thinking maybe we could plan a girls' night in with some movies in the media room. You could work from home in your office…"

"You mean the office that's right next door to the movie room?" I purse my lips and look away. "Hey, hey, don't be embarrassed. I think it's a good idea and a good step forward. We'll have the chef make you some pizza, you and I can pick out some bottles of wine from the cellar…" he says, but I stop him.

"You have a wine cellar here? Like a dark dungeon-type one?" He chuckles and nods. "Is it big enough to have people eat down there?"

"Yes, I believe so. It's been a while since I've been down there, but we can fit a table in the center and work with the chef to serve a meal down there if you'd like. Do you want that?" His face contorts into one of surprise.

"Hell, yes! Only not now. Just the thought of being in a

cold, dark place messes with my head a little." He closes his eyes, and I kiss him until he opens them again. "Though it will be a good test down the road," I offer. He kisses me full, wet, and deep. Our chat time is almost up. I can already feel him getting harder within me.

"Again?" I ask.

He thrusts his hips, becoming fully erect. "With you lying naked on top of me? How can that surprise you?" He rolls us both over and sinks deep. I wrap my legs around him and let him slowly make love to me for a few moments.

"So we're going to leave on Friday?"

He thrusts hard. "And you're going to become my wife." His hands curl around my shoulders, and he hammers into me. I moan and arch into him.

"I cannot wait."

"Let's wait until I'm done fucking you." He laughs into my neck and sucks on the tendon there.

"Yeah, okay, let's definitely wait until after that." I scratch my nails down his long back.

He kisses his way up my chin and to my lips. "Then again, that might not work." Another powerful thrust, and I close my eyes, the heat building within.

"Why's that?"

He power drives his hips into mine over and over, crushing his pelvis against my clit in dizzying bursts of pressure. "Because…" He moves again, harder and harder. A hand comes to my ass and lifts me up as he presses down and up at the same time. "I'll. Never. Be. Done. Fucking. You."

He punctuates with each thrust until I'm gone, leaving the plane of existence and entering the space where only beautiful things exist, and all of them lead back to him and our connection. By this time next week, I'll be Mrs. Gillian Davis…if he ever stops fucking me.

DANIEL

CHAPTER EIGHT

"Welcome to the team, Elliott!" My new boss holds out a beefy hand. His hand grips tight but is no comparison to my strength. I could crush him with my pinky finger, but instead of doing that, I just smile.

"Thanks, Mr. Templeton. I'm happy to be here. I've worked some security jobs before but never for an estate like this," I say with fake enthusiasm. The guy nods, adjusts his belt as if he's important, and looks out the window over the vast landscape where a mansion sits at the top of a curved path. The guard's headquarters is a small building near the front of the Davis Estate.

"Yes, it's a beautiful home, and the owners are very kind, but security is tight. You'll have to be alert at all times." He walks over to a bulletin board, rips off a flyer with my picture on it, and holds it out.

I take it from him and look down at my smiling face. It's one of the headshots from the accounting firm I left when I saved my girl from making the biggest mistake of her life, marrying the fucker. And now I'm standing on the property where she's likely holed up. It's been a few days since the funeral, and I haven't caught sight of her anywhere. She has to be here. It's as if I can feel her presence.

"So this a bad guy or something?" I hold up the picture right to my face. "I mean, the guy looks pretty normal. He could even be my brother."

The fat man looks at the picture and then at me with narrowed eyes. Maybe I played it too close, got cocky with the disguise having worked so well. I place my hand into my pocket and feel for the small pocketknife I have there. With a flick of my wrist, I could have it out and into his jugular in a second flat. Sweat beads on my forehead as the man assess me.

"Nah, he's a pretty boy type. You look like you've got some balls." He grips his sac. I laugh out loud, mostly because of the absolute absurdity of this man running the security team at the rich bastard's mansion. It took almost no effort to get a job here.

"So what did this guy do anyway?" I hand him back the paper, and he tacks it back onto the bulletin board.

"Plenty. Killed a few people blowing up a gym."

I act surprised. "Really? He was the one who took out that gym downtown?"

Templeton nods, a grim line to his lips. Me, I have to clench mine to hold back a smile at the great work I did that day. I almost did mankind a huge favor, taking out that prick Phillip. Another time, I promise myself.

"Yep. Also slit a woman's throat at a yoga place." Totally deserved, I think to myself. The world is better without that tree-hugging hippie in it. Templeton continues, "Apparently, he meant to kill one of the chicks that's staying here. Beautiful woman, big and pregnant, though, with one of the other fellas that survived the blast at the gym."

Bingo. So Yoga Barbie and her bastard child along with

Gillian's first fuck are staying here. That has to mean my girl is here.

Templeton rests a pudgy thigh on the wooden desk. It groans and creaks under his considerable weight. "The reason we're here though, and that there are armed ex-military walking the premises, is because he kidnapped the boss's fiancée. Well, technically the man who owns the place is Charles Davis. And Ms. Gillian, she's the fiancée to his nephew, Chase Davis. You'll see them come and go when you're on point at the guard shack, accepting visitors in and out. To start though, we'll have you walking the grounds with another guard until you get up to speed on procedure."

I nod. "So this woman, the one who got kidnapped..."

"Wait until you see her. She's somethin' else. Beautiful. Sexy in a way that has a man hard in seconds."

I bite down and clench my teeth together. It takes every ounce of strength I have to not pummel the fucker into the ground for speaking about my woman that way.

Templeton looks off at the house again. "She's up there now." Those four words enter my chest, wrap around my heart, and send anticipation skittering through my veins.

She's here.

"Tonight, she and her friends are staying in, so we just need to make sure the grounds stay quiet and no one gets in or out. You got that? No one enters on my watch," he says while lifting his belt once more over his beer belly in a portrayal of self-proclaimed importance.

Smiling wide, I say, "No one gets in or out. Got it, sir."

"All right then, let's introduce you to the men. Get you suited up in uniform along with a Taser. All of us carry them, but the veterans have loaded weapons. The rest of us have the communication lines here." He points to his earpiece and a receiver. "We check in with our group on the regular and report back. If we see something, we call for reinforcements. Come on." He waves a hand. "We'll talk and walk."

We go outside and start walking up the path to the house. As we walk, he's rattling on and on about the job. I half pay attention. I'm far more focused on how many windows there are, what the access entries could be, how many men are patrolling and where. And then I see her. Sitting outside in a patio chair, soaking up the sun.

Templeton points to my girl. We're a few hundred feet from where she's reading. The sun is shining off her bright red hair like a homing beacon calling to that place deep within me that knows its mate. She's ethereal in a pair of jeans and a tank. A pair of sunglasses perched on her perfect button nose. I want to go to her, step up and take her.

"That's the one I was talking about. Name's Gillian Callahan, but she's the soon-to-be Mrs. Davis." He points her out, but I know where she is. I felt her the second we walked up. "Oh, and that's Mr. Davis." I watch with barely controlled hate as the bane of my existence exits the French doors and hands my girl a drink. Then he leans down and kisses her. She accepts his kiss, looking to be really into kissing him back. The rage swirling just below the surface turns white-hot and spreads like the plague over my senses. I thought she understood her place. Her lips should not be on another man's…ever. I'm going to have to punish her severely for that transgression.

Without realizing it, I start walking toward the couple my hand in my pocket, ready to pull out my knife. A firm grip pulls me back. "Elliott, man, you can't approach them. This is their home. We're supposed to be on the periphery so they know we're here, but we never ever intrude on their lives."

I suck in a slow breath. "Sorry, I was just thinking I should introduce myself."

Templeton shakes his head. "Nope, we're invisible to them unless shit goes down. Other than that, we do not make eye contact. Stay close but not so close that they feel your eyes on them, but that they know you're there and feel safe. That's our job. We protect and serve," he says with a heaping dose of pride as if he were a fucking officer of the law. He didn't go through the years of training to become a civil servant to "protect and serve" like he boasts. He's a goddamned rent-a-cop with a fat gut and a false sense of importance.

Without voicing my real opinions, I look at him and nod vigorously as if he's really gotten to the heart of me. "I completely understand, sir. Do not approach. Stay close but not enough to warrant concern. Got it."

He claps a hand on my shoulder. "Good man, now let's go meet some of your team and saddle you up with a trainer."

Templeton leads me along the path, and I keep my eyes glued to Gillian and that motherfucker. He's sitting on her lounge chair with her feet in his lap. She laughs at something, and he brings her foot up to his mouth and kisses her ankle. She rewards him with peals of laughter. I miss her laugh. When Gillian found something funny, she'd laugh with her entire being. It's been a long time since I've heard it. Soon.

I look over at her one more time before we go around

the building and she's out of sight.

Soon, my love. I'll have you back.

Closing the door to the home office most of the way, I sit down with Thomas Redding, Agent Brennen, and Jack on the U-shaped leather couches. I left the door slightly open so I could keep an ear on Gillian. If she happens to look out the door, I want her to know I'm close. Being away from me has been extremely difficult for her, and I can't complain. Having her wanting me close at all times right now works for me. Yes, it makes me a sick fuck that I, too, am having trouble having her out of my sights, but we've been dealing with a traumatic situation, and I have no desire to have her anywhere but near me. It will be so much easier to work through when we find McBride.

"So what do you have?" I ask the three men.

Agent Brennen speaks first. "Not much. We expected him to go to the funeral, but our snipers didn't pick up any suspicious activity. No one approached her who wasn't part of her normal crowd, and the ride to and from didn't have any unmarked vehicles to trace."

Thomas takes the pause in Brennen's reiteration of the obvious to make his own opinions known. "We think he might have gone underground or left town to stay off the radar for a while."

I grind my teeth, and my jaw aches with the amount of times I've done that very thing over the past three weeks.

"Jack"—I look at my most trusted confidant, the one

man I trust beyond all others—"do you think he's gone underground or left town?"

His steely eyes focus on mine. The slicked back hair and his sheer width make him a very menacing individual. He shakes his head in a tight movement. "No, I don't. If anything, he's closer than he's ever been." My stomach drops. "McBride has anticipated almost every move we've made. Now that we know who he is, he'll be doing more to disguise himself, but he's confident. Overly so. He didn't think we'd figure out who he was, or that we'd find out where he was hiding her. He won't make that mistake again."

"So what are you saying?" I push my hands through my hair and grip the roots.

Jack leans against the side of the desk. "She goes nowhere without the best protection."

"We have bodyguards on her 24-7. What more can we do?" My tone is harsh, but Jack knows it's not him, that it's directed at the severity of the situation.

"Sir, she needs the best. I'm the best. She goes nowhere without me until he's found. Including you, sir."

I open my eyes wide and look at him. "What does that mean? Are you insinuating I can't protect the woman I love? I'd kill any man who comes close to her." I mean it with every fiber of my being, and Jack just crosses his arms and tilts his head.

"That's exactly why you are not going to be able to protect her. She needs someone on her at all times who has an eye on everything around her, not her as a person. I will be watching every move that's made near her, the people she comes into contact with, and anticipating everything. You will be focused on her emotional needs and your connection with her. I don't have those feelings about her. For me, she's a job, and my job is to make sure that she stays alive and within our circle of protection."

I sit down next to Thomas and put my head in my hands. "Fine, whatever. I just want this madman found. Now. What do we need to do?"

"We need to find a way to get him to come into the light," Thomas says.

"Are you suggesting we use Gillian as bait?"

Thomas scowls. "Not exactly, but in a way, yes. What if we planned something that would ensure there was no way he could get to her, but once he got close, he'd be on lock-down?"

"Such as what?"

Agent Brennen leans forward. "We don't have all the details. I've got a team of people coming up with a scenario. Once we have the plans drawn, the location chosen, we'll discuss it with you."

"When?" I ask, entirely done with this conversation. I need to check on Gillian. My need to be close to her is starting to suffocate me.

Agent Brennen looks at me with kind eyes, ones that have been through far more experiences than I could ever grasp. His mustache seems to ripple when air passes his lips and he speaks. "We should have everything lined up within the next ten days or so."

I stand up. "Fine. I will tell you that Gillian and I are leaving in two days. The destination will not be provided to anyone. Jack, pick your best two men and plan to leave town. I'm not going to allow Gillian to be a sitting duck."

"Sir, McBride could figure out where you're going.

Flight plans can be hacked."

"That's why every single plane in my fleet will have the five of us—you, me, Gillian, and your two men—listed as passengers. Only one of them will actually fly to the destination I've chosen. I do not believe McBride will be able to determine which location we actually end up in, nor can he afford to visit all those locations."

Thomas lets out a long breath. "Damn, that's going to cost a pretty penny."

I look at Thomas with hard eyes. "I can afford it." Without further ado, I offer my hand to Agent Brennen. He stands and shakes it. "Get on top of that plan. Call Jack on the new burner phone he'll give you tonight. We'll return when the plan is in place and not before."

"What about the girls? Maria is going to be pissed," Thomas starts to say, but I cut him off.

"Ms. De La Torre is your woman and your problem. From what I understand about those women, they will forgive one another for anything. Gillian can handle her relationships. I will handle Gillian. Have I made myself perfectly clear?"

"Crystal," Thomas says and stands. He holds out a hand, and I shake it before turning and exiting the room.

Across the hallway, I can hear the sound of laughter. I push open the door and find four women draped over different pieces of furniture in the ugliest polka dot pajamas I've ever seen, and three out of four of them are drunk as skunks.

"Baby!" Gillian squeals, runs across the room, and catapults into my arms. I catch her in a tangle of limbs, my body flying back a few steps. When I've caught my balance,

I barely take a breath before her lips are all over me. My neck, my face, my lips all kissed in an array of wet presses of her mouth. "You are so fucking hot!" She turns her head around, addressing the girls while clutching my neck, her legs firmly wrapped around my waist. "Isn't he hot?"

"So hot!" says Kathleen.

"Sexy as hell," Bree says while rubbing her massive belly. She's popped out considerably over the last week.

"*Muy caliente*," Maria says, her Spanish side coming out in full force.

Gillian kisses me, and I allow it, needing to connect with her physically after the meeting I just had. She tastes of rich red wine, and if she weren't having a great time with her friends, I'd whisk her to our room and take her in a completely visceral way. Gripping her head and tilting it to the side, I take long, slow sips of her sweet mouth. She moans full and deep, and the sound ricochets through my body and settles heavily in my groin, my dick taking notice.

"Hey, get a room. Wait a minute, no, we're having a chick date. No boys allowed!" Bree harrumphs and sits down in a chair, pouting.

"Yeah, no fair. Carson is up in our room watching the game. Go hang out with him!" Kathleen admonishes.

I chuckle against Gillian's neck. She, on the other hand, does not in fact care what her friends think. Her lips are planted on my neck, and she's licking and nibbling to her heart's content.

"Just a moment, ladies," I say and walk out of the room with her clinging to me like a baby koala bear. Once I get her into the hallway, I press her into the nearest wall and show her exactly what she does to me. Her answering moan and tightening of her thighs does not help me in my desire to be the good guy here.

"Baby, if you continue to attack me with your lips and tongue, I'm going to set you down, pull down your pants, and go to town on your pussy right here, against this wall."

Her eyes go wide, and she nods. "Yes please. Do that." She accentuates her need with a thrust of her hips against mine. The move sends jolts of pleasure splintering from my cock and over the rest of me.

I shake my head and cup her neck, holding her chin up with my thumbs. "We're going to have all the alone time we want in a couple days, remember?"

Her entire face lights up with a smile. "Yes, I remember," she says loudly as if she's gotten the question right to a game we're playing. "We're going to get marr—" I cover her mouth with my hand.

"Shhh, it's a secret." Her eyes go wide, and then she licks my hand. I pull it away as if it was burned.

"You're a bad girl. Do you have any idea what I'm going to do to you tonight when I get you alone?" Her eyes burn with intent and lust.

"Spank me?" Her response blows me away. That is not at all what I'd expect coming from her mouth after her history.

"Would you like me to spank you? Make the cheeks of your heart-shaped ass light up?" She moans and then squeezes her thighs again. "I'll make them nice and pink, just warm enough that when I fuck your tight little ass, I'll feel the warmth from your spanking against my skin."

She groans and closes her eyes. "Would you like that, baby? Me fucking your perfect little hole, after I spank you into a blinding orgasm, and then follow it up by stuffing you full of my cock until you come again? Is that what you want?"

Her entire body is squirming against me. With a quick glance in both directions and my ear to the door where her friends are, I make a decision. I need her, now. Loosening my pants and zipper, I pull out my cock. It's as hard as a hammer and just as ready to pound. I push down Gillian's pants enough that I can wedge my dick straight into her wet cunt. Her head flies back and smacks against the wall. Shit, I couldn't hold her and protect her head. She's going to feel that tomorrow.

"Baby, are you okay?"

"No, fuck me," she says far too loudly.

"Shhh, they'll hear you."

I pull back my hips and slam home, pressing her harshly into the wall. Her pants are pulled tight above my cock and rub against the skin at every pass into her wet sheath. She starts moaning loud. I cover her mouth with mine and kiss the daylights out of her, stealing her sounds. They're all for me anyway. It doesn't take long for me to pound an orgasm out of her. The liquor mixed with her desire made her hair-triggered.

Listening close, I can hear the women on the other side of the door only a few feet away. They are talking about the movie they have playing and seem to be pretty involved with it. Once Gillian comes down from her orgasm, I pull out. She whimpers until I set her feet down on the ground, push her pajamas and underwear completely down, and cover her pussy with my mouth, shoving my tongue way up inside. She clasps onto my hair and looks wildly around the hallway. At any moment, anyone could walk down this hallway, and yes, it would be embarrassing, but I don't give a fuck. I've got my woman's sweet pussy all over my face and her sugary nectar from coming around my dick all over my tongue. There is absolutely nothing like her taste, and the desire I experience from touching her, tasting her, being with her.

After soaking up her cream, I stand, turn her around, and push her feet wide.

"Chase…" she warns. "Someone could come."

"Someone is going to come," I growl into her ear before I hammer into her from behind in one long stroke. "Me!" I promise, and she moans and then bites her lip, bruising the sweet flesh.

This position doesn't allow me to go as deep as I'd like, but being able to see her pert ass and play with her little hole is enough to have me almost ready to shoot my load deep within her. I fuck her hard for a series of strokes, making sure she's close, and then I lick my thumb, twist it around her tiny rosette, and on a particularly strong thrust, plow my thumb straight into her warm ass. She cries out, not being able to stop herself. At this point, I'm too far gone to care. My balls are aching with the need to come, my dick so hard and fat inside her I'm losing my mind, taken to a place of sheer ecstasy with every penetrating thrust. Gillian mewls softly as I fuck both her entrances, wanting her to feel me for the rest of the evening, knowing that I took her good and will continue to take her whenever and wherever the fuck I want. There is nothing she can do about it either. She is as powerless to the lust raging between us as I am.

"Get there," I tell her. "Put your hand between your

legs and twist that little clit the way I would. Don't be shy. I want to see you touch yourself. Makes me so hard, baby."

She does what I ask, bringing one of her hands between her legs, the other holding her up against the wall. When she hits the spot, her hips buck wildly. "That's it, stroke yourself for me. Show me how much you like me fucking you right here, where anyone can come down the hallway can see your naked ass and pussy being taken." She drops her head and pushes back into my strokes. That makes me insanely hot.

I watch her hand move in a blur between her legs, her chest heaving with the movements of her pussy and ass taking me in over and over. Then her body tightens, the telltale sign that she's about to have one mother of an orgasm. I fuck her faster, pounding into her flesh until she places both hands against the wall, only able to take the pounding movements. Her pussy is stretching wide over the fat head of my cock as I plow in and out. With a twist of my pelvis, I hold her hips and slam home. And that's when we both lose it, shaking with the effort of our combined release. Her pussy milks my cock with tight compression and releasing motions until I'm essentially milked dry.

She leans her head against the wall, and I kiss her neck, push away her sweaty hair, and lick up the white column. Her body responds with another strong clamp and release before I pull out, tucking my softening cock back into my pants, and button up. As I lean down to pick up her panties and pajamas, I can see my cum sliding down her leg. The sight sends a flicker of lust back into my dick. I love seeing my mark on her, knowing that a piece of me is inside of her for days. Makes me want to fuck her all over again and fill her full to the brim so she'll never be without me.

Pushing my piggish ways aside, I sop up between her legs with the handkerchief I have in my pocket and then help her back into her clothes. Once I turn her around, she has that beautiful, fully satisfied look that I strive to put on her face every day.

"I love fucking you," she says drunkenly.

I rub my nose alongside hers and get close. "I believe it was me who was fucking you." I grin and snatch up a kiss of her sweet mouth. "But I agree. I love fucking you, too."

This time she kisses me softly but then stops abruptly. A whimsical lilting voice singing comes from the doorway. "She's singing. I have to hear it!" Gillian pushes at my chest and runs into the room where her friends are.

I peak in, and Bree is singing an incredibly beautiful rendition of "Wild Horses" a cappella. Kathleen and Maria lock waists with my girl and start to sway along with the song.

Gillian has so quickly become my world. But her friends are a package deal. I look at each woman, seeing the undying love for one another. It's a true sisterhood. The same way I feel about my cousins Carson, Craig, and Chloe. Cooper, on the other hand, can go to hell.

These women, though, are true friends who love my woman. With time, I'll get used to sharing her with them. Today will be the first step. I turn away and head back to my office across the way, but this time I leave the door completely open. If she needs me, I'll be here, but I think she's fine with her girls.

Time to finish the plans for "operation make Gillian my wife and fool a madman."

GILLIAN

CHAPTER NINE

"Gillian, dear heart, please, come in. I can't express how disturbed I was to hear of your abduction. I'm relieved to see that you're okay." Dr. Madison pulls me into his warm embrace. Chase clears his throat behind me and I smile. Possessive doesn't even begin to describe my man. Dr. Madison pulls back, holding me at arm's length. "I see we still have the strapping young lad to ensure your honor." He looks over my shoulder. "Welcome, Mr. Davis. Do come in."

"I was planning on it," he growls, before curving me into his side and leading me to the long couch. I look longingly over at my favorite fluffy individual chair, but don't say anything.

Chase has an issue with how good-looking Dr. McHottie is as well as how much this man knows about me. More than any man, but in a very different way from Chase. I do find it mildly entertaining that Chase is jealous over my shrink. My doctor has never been anything but perfectly professional over the past few years. Never once has he tried to hit on me or make any overtures other than concern for my well-being. It has taken us years to get to a greeting hug. That was actually part of my therapy. Touch. Letting a man touch me, even platonically, used to set my panic-o-meter flaring, but I worked through it with Dr. Madison. To this day, I have him to thank for the fact that I'm even able to have any form of romantic relationship.

Dr. Madison sits in a chair across from the couch. I suspect he does couples' therapy in this part of his office.

"I imagine you want to talk about what happened to you in the past three weeks. Being kidnapped on your wedding day, Chase's mother being murdered in front of you, and then being held against your will in captivity is a lot for anyone to take on," he starts and I nod. Chase tightens his hold around my arm, his fingers digging into my shoulder. The doctor notices it. "And for you, Chase, this has to be equally hard, losing your mother in that way, your fiancée taken from you. Not knowing where she was for all those days."

Chase grunts an affirmative sound and looks away, neither of us wanting to bring light to everything that has happened.

The doctor waits patiently for one of us to speak, moving his eyes to Chase and then to me and back. The room seems to fill with a cloying humidity, making the space around my body feel clammy and uncomfortable. Chase's lips turn into a flat line, and that grip he has on my shoulder seems impossibly tight.

Instead of mentioning anything about the abduction or losing Chase's mother, I blurt out, "Chase and I are eloping tomorrow!"

The doctor's eyes widen, and Chase chuckles and shakes his head. "Baby…" he says on an exasperated sigh.

I turn and look at him. "Well, we are!"

Chase lets out a breath. "Yes, we are doing that, but not

only did we agree this was a secret, I also doubt the good doctor is interested in this particular line of conversation."

That's when Dr. Madison perks up. "On the contrary. I'm very interested in why the two of you think it's appropriate to elope after you've experienced so much in the past three weeks. One would gather that it is a veiled attempt at controlling your life."

Chase's eyes go from warm to icy in a second. "I am very much in control." His tone is scathing.

"As you are used to feeling, I assume. But nothing you've experienced in the last three weeks has been in your control. That must make you feel agitated." Dr. Madison's eyes narrow, and his head quirks to the side.

I can feel Chase's body tense. His hands turn into white-knuckled fists on the top of his thighs. That's when I slowly scooch back. He doesn't notice. The doctor, however, does. I close my eyes. I know for a fact that Chase would never hurt me that way, but when a man has gone through what we've gone through, you never know what type of things come out, and my natural self-preservation technique is to remove myself from the situation as quietly as possible.

Chase stands up abruptly. "You don't know how I feel!" His words are angry and sharp as nails, directed at the good doctor.

Dr. Madison leans back against the leather chair and looks up at Chase, who stands off to the side of the room looking out the French doors. "You're right, Mr. Davis. I don't. Why don't you tell me how you feel?"

Chase looks over his shoulder, scowls at him, and runs a hand through the layers of his dark hair. I hold my breath, desperately wanting to know how Chase feels about everything. He hasn't said a word. He's spent the last two weeks taking care of me, making sure I want for nothing. "Inadequate," he says on a loaded sigh. It's as if the entire weight of the universe is on his broad shoulders.

My own eyebrows rise along with Dr. Madison's. "How so?" the doctor asks.

I know this game. I've played the therapy game for years, and this is how it starts. Dr. Madison provokes you into telling him what's plaguing you. It's genius, really. I'm just glad it's happening to Chase and not me. Finally, I get to find out how he's feeling instead of constantly crying into his chest. Maybe if we both get it out, we'll be able to move forward, let go.

Chase turns around, hands on his hips, his jacket flaring out. He holds a hand out to me. "My future wife was attacked and abducted on our wedding day from one of *my* resorts guarded by *my* men." He points to his chest, wearing a disgusted expression. "My wheelchair-bound mother's throat was slit in front of Gillian before she was taken against her will and held in a fucking ten-by-ten cell with only a goddamned pot to piss in!" he roars, his voice reaching maximum strength. His face is red, the tendons in his neck are bulging, and he continues undeterred. "She was still in her fucking wedding dress almost five days later, her face and chest beaten black-and-blue, her ankles and wrists cut deep because of rusty shackles that were attached to a pulley system above her head. Those same shackles gave her a massive infection. One that could have very well killed her! How the fuck do you think I feel, *Doc*?" Chase's jaw is locked down so hard I'm worried he'll break teeth if he keeps going the way he is.

"Jesus Christ," Dr. Madison whispers, his eyes on me. Because I know him so well, I see the concern in his gaze. To anyone else, he would appear calm and in control. "Gillian"—he presses his hand to his mouth, swallows, and clears his throat—"we're going to work through all of this. Thank you, Chase. Thank you for being so candid."

Chase harrumphs and starts to pace. "Now, tell him what's fucking with you." His eyes are fierce, leaving no room for pussyfooting around.

"Um, well…" I take in a tortured breath. "I seem to have a bit of an attachment issue."

"A bit?" Chase growls.

I nod noncommittally.

"Doctor Madison, if I left the room right now…" He starts to walk toward the door.

Instantly, the hairs on my neck and arms stand at attention. My heart pounds in my chest so loudly I can hear it like a drum next to my ear. I turn around and sit up on my knees while gripping the back of the couch.

"No," I whisper just as Chase's hand touches the handle. "Don't leave!" I beg, tears rolling down my cheeks. He turns around, closes his eyes, and leans against the door.

"See what I mean?" He lifts a hand, and I glance at Dr. Madison.

Dr. Madison brings his hand to his mouth and leans back in his chair. He pulls off his spectacles and looks at me in wonder. "How long has this been going on?"

I don't answer, just sit back down, and look down at my lap, not wanting the eye contact. I'm tired of being the one always under a microscope. I just want to go back to a normal life. One where I can work and visit my friends when I want to without the fear that someone is going to attack me or kill the people I love.

"The first time I noticed this particular fear was when she woke up in the hospital two days after being found," Chase says, coming back from the door to sit next to me. I curl into his side, feeling instant relief.

The doctor nods and writes a few things down. "Gillian, what happens to you when you think Chase is going to leave? Meaning physically?"

I lick my lips and focus on my fingers, twisting them together. Chase puts an arm around my shoulder, and I can breathe again. "Um, my heart pounds. I get a little nauseated, shaky, my hearing becomes very acute, or I lose it completely. Much like my panic attacks."

"And does that happen when you're in a room with other people?"

"Depends on if I know where he is." Dr. Madison's eyebrows rise into points at his hairline. "Like last night, the girls and I had a movie night at the Davis Estate. As long as I could see Chase's office and I knew he was there, I was fine. I could enjoy the time with my friends." Dr. Madison nods, writes a few things down. "What's wrong with me?" Chase hears the fear in my voice and instantly works to calm me. Taking my hand, holding me closer, kissing my temple.

The doctor shakes his head. "Nothing. What you're experiencing is an acute panic disorder that manifests in panic attacks after dealing with a traumatic event." Both Chase and I look at him with matching expressions of confusion. "Essentially, you're having a fear that Chase will abandon you, which in response brings on the attacks," Dr. Madison clarifies.

"I'll never abandon you, baby," Chase promises immediately. He turns my face to his and cups my cheek. I lean into it, appreciating his warmth. "We're going to get past this together. But I can't say that I'm un-fond of you needing me close." His grin is sexy but honest.

"That"—the doctor's voice inflection rises to one of concern—"on the other hand, we need to get to the bottom of, Mr. Davis." Dr. Madison uses his stern no-nonsense tone.

Chase's own voice changes, sounding gruffer. "Excuse me?"

"You have an excessive need for control, are habitually possessive and demanding by nature. It's not all together a healthy way to deal with a woman who's been victimized in the past. Though, I know it's those ways of yours that attract our dear Gillian."

He is not wrong. Not by a long shot. I've always sought out men who are confident, strong, self-assured. It's just a lot of times that comes with the downside of those traits that are controlling and demonstrative and the worst of all... abusive. Chase is a lot of things but never abusive.

"He'd never lay a hand on me, Dr. Madison. Of that I am certain. His mother was a victim of domestic violence, and Chase abhors a man taking a hand to a woman." Chase nods at my response.

"I'm sorry to hear that," the doctor says to Chase.

"Thank you. It was a long time ago. I've moved on. Right now, my focus is on Gillian and her well-being, mentally and physically. We're leaving tomorrow. I plan to spend the next couple weeks or so allowing us to be free. To have her feel safe in her own skin, as well as make her my wife." Chase adjusts his jacket and leans forward.

"Is there a reason you're in a rush to get married, Mr. Davis?"

Chase and I both shake our heads. "No," he says with conviction. "It just feels like it's something that keeps getting *taken* from us. To tell you the truth, Doc, I wanted to marry her the day after I proposed." He turns to me. "I'm regretting letting you talk me out of that." He grins, and his eyes twinkle when he smirks at me. "But then we ended up waiting for her wedding dress to be designed, and then it was Phillip and the explosion, and then we finally get to the day and she's abducted. I've wanted nothing more than to claim her as my wife since shortly after we met. I'm tired of waiting to make her mine."

"Do you feel like she'll be more yours if you are married?" Dr. Madison asks.

"Yes, I do. Legally, she'll be connected to me, she'll wear my ring on her finger for the world to see, have access to my fortune, never want for anything, and I'll have my own family. With her," he says matter-of-factly—no mincing words for my guy.

"I see. And you agree with this plan, Gillian?" The doctor looks to me.

I'm still stuck on Chase wanting to be a *family* with me. Ever since my mother's death, my friends have been the only family I have. When I marry Chase, he'll be my family. Officially, legally, mentally, and physically. "I can't imagine anything better than Chase and me becoming our own family."

Chase's smile is so bright it removes all the dark from the conversation and only lets in light. It warms my heart and my soul.

"Then I agree. You should have what you desire, because it comes from your love for one another, not from the desire to control a situation in your life. So for that, I issue my congratulations."

"I can't believe we sneaked out in the middle of the day and no one is the wiser." Gillian laughs, clipping her seatbelt in place. The flight attendant hands me, and then Gillian, a glass of sparkling pink champagne. "Ooh, it's pink!" She shimmies in her seat happily. I knew my girl would appreciate the feminine aspect of this champagne.

Holding her hand in my left, I hold up my glass. She does the same. "To our future, baby," I say, and she leans close.

"To becoming a family," she says breathily, while clinking our glasses together. We take a sip, and then I lean forward and capture her lips in mine. She tastes of champagne and strawberries, both of which I had ready to go when we arrived at the airport in Sacramento.

I made sure that several of my planes left from San Francisco International, Oakland International, San Jose International, and Sacramento International all with our names and the names of the three men accompanying us. When we left the Davis Mansion, Jack had ten blacked-out Escalades at the ready. Two were set to drive to each airport and two just driving around. If McBride was watching the estate, he'd have no idea which one we entered since we loaded up in the underground garage. Not even security knew what the plan was. Only Jack and his two most trusted men. The two men had been flown in from other jobs. One was on leave from his assignment on the presidential detail with the Secret Service and one who was in the SAS in the UK. Jack had served with both men and gave his word they'd protect us with their lives. We met them on the plane. Both of them were very large, fully equipped with weapons, and had an air of authority about them. Instantly, I approved of his choices. Right now, they were discussing our plans in the small office on the plane, giving Gillian and me our privacy.

"So are you going to tell me where we're going?" she asks, all smiles.

I look at my woman and am so taken with her. She has her legs up and under her ass. The blouse she's wearing is giving me a lovely eyeful of her creamy, white breasts, and her hair... Christ, her hair drives me wild. It's down, curly, like a fiery halo surrounding her. I lift my arm and tunnel my hand through her silken locks. She mewls prettily.

"Do you have any idea how you make me feel?" I ask her. Her green eyes open, and I swear I could lose myself in them.

"Probably similar to how you make me feel." Her voice is a whisper.

"And how is that?" I turn it around on her.

She smiles shyly, still rubbing into my hand. "Safe. Protected. Cherished. Loved." So softly, she kisses the inside of my wrist. I can barely feel the wet imprint of her succulent mouth on my skin, but it's there, burned into my memory forever.

I suck in a breath and press back the desire to unclip her

safety belt, pull her into my lap, and show her exactly how I feel. Instead I hold her gaze. "You make me feel whole. It's as if I've been searching for my other half and I no longer have to. I found myself, in you."

Her eyes fill with unshed tears. "Chase…" She leans forward and kisses me. Her lips are moist and full as I allow her to lead the kiss. When her tongue enters my mouth, I groan, pulling her in deeper, taking over. She doesn't protest. I sip from her mouth, sliding my tongue in and out in a slow dance that's making us both needy for one another. Kissing Gillian is a new experience, yet somehow beautifully familiar. Like déjà vu. I've been there before, but something makes it slightly different.

I pull away, slowly nibbling on her bottom lip, and then her top. "I could so easily get carried away."

"Why don't you?" she challenges in that voice that makes my dick hard. Then again, everything about this woman makes my dick hard.

Smiling, I take a sip of my champagne. It's magnificent but tastes better secondhand from her mouth. She brings up her glass and drinks. "Anticipation, my sweet. I want you so gone for me that we barely make it to our destination before you beg me to take you."

"And that destination would be?" she asks again.

I've made a point to avoid telling her. Not because I don't trust her, but I don't want her to be disappointed, once again, if our attempt at eloping is thwarted. Now, sitting on my plane, I'm confident that, in the next couple days, she will be my wife and we'll have the honeymoon we deserve.

"Ireland."

Her pretty mouth opens and her eyes turn a breathtaking

shade of bright green. "Our honeymoon," she gasps.

I nod. "That's the one place you said you wanted to go in all the world. It's my job to give that to you."

Within seconds, she sets down her glass, unclasps her restraint, and straddles my lap, her lips on mine. Warm hands hold onto my cheeks as she kisses me long, full, and deep. I grip her ass and press into her, taking her mouth and pressing her into me wholly.

"I love you"—*kiss*—"I love you"—*kiss*—"I love you." She peppers kisses all over my face until she tugs my bottom lip into her mouth with her teeth, and at the same time, grinds her pussy into my erection.

I groan and hold her close, keeping our mouths connected until we've both lost our breath. We move away panting, breathing in one another's air. Little puffs blow against my heated skin, but it doesn't cool me. Quite the opposite. I want her.

"Chase, we're going to get married in Ireland," she says in a tone I've not heard in a while. Awe. It's devastatingly beautiful. Right then, I promise to put that look on her face as many times as possible throughout our shared lifetime.

"We are, baby, and it's going to be perfect."

She kisses me slowly and nuzzles her nose against my own. "It is, because it will be just the two of us. I thought I wanted the big to-do, to have everyone there to witness our love, but it doesn't matter. Yes, I'll miss the girls and Phillip, but I'm tired of waiting. I want to be your wife. I want to be connected to you for eternity."

I grin and look at her neck. "Infinity, baby." Bringing my hands to her neck, I circle the column and drag my knuckles between her breasts. She sucks in a breath, and her eyes water. Something's missing. As I stare at her bare neck, it dawns on me. "Where…"

Gillian cuts me off. "He took it." Her teeth dig into the flesh of her lip. "I don't know what he did with it, but he saw it and ripped it off my neck. It's gone." One tear slides down her face.

That fucker took the infinity necklace I had made for her. The one she was wearing on our wedding day. Not only was that important to me, it was yet another fucking thing he stole from us. "Doesn't matter. I've got you. And I can get you another necklace." I clasp her left hand and place kisses all around her engagement ring. "He didn't get this, and soon I'll be adding to it."

She smiles wide, the moment of anguish leaving her. Then, her pretty lips turn into a frown. "But what about the ring I got you? Maria had it that day." Our wedding day. "I didn't think to get it from her."

"Gillian." I cup both her cheeks. "Honey, you know I take care of you. Right? I asked Thomas to find the ring and give it to me. Said I'd hold onto it until the time was right. He didn't think anything of it."

"Did you look at it?" Her eyebrows narrow, and I shake my head.

"No, baby, I didn't. I did ask Thomas to open it and make sure it was there, but that's it. I did not want to see what you purchased as a token of your love until our wedding day, when you slide it on my finger."

Her smile at my words is splendid.

"Good. Because it's personal." She flattens her forehead against mine, getting impossibly close. "And private. I want it to be for that day and every day after."

"I will wear whatever symbol you have given me with pride, baby. I want the world to know you own me."

She rubs her lips along mine, not really kissing, just letting her lips graze along mine. "I give you me. Everything that I am, Chase…is yours."

The words hit deep, curl around my heart, leaving a delightful impression. "I'll want for nothing more in this lifetime."

X

DANIEL

CHAPTER TEN

It's been two fucking days, and no sign of her or the rich fucker. No one seems to have any idea where they are. The Italian bitch has come and gone with her bodyguard, so has pregnant Barbie, her first fuck, and his bastard daughter. Also that dressmaking, hippie-looking chick and the cousin have been back to the mansion, but not my princess or the prick with a little dick.

I groan and pace the security office. Anger swells deep inside, making sweat rise to the surface of my skin, prickling and tingling. Something's not right. Maybe they went back to the penthouse? The penthouse is tricky. It's guarded, but the biggest problem is needing a fingerprint to access their home. Then again, the blond bitch I was fucking, Dana, could get me in. If she won't do it willingly, I'll cut her hand off, let her bleed out. Problem solved. She's no longer of this Earth, and I've got my fingerprint scan. Of course I'll have to find a way to disable the security camera with no one being the wiser.

Again, I pace back and forth until my boss arrives, breaking my concentration. "Elliott! Buddy, you about to start your rounds?" the fat fucker asks, using my fake name.

It was pretty easy to get. I just pilfered it from my adopted stepbrother. The one I'm staying with while I figure out how to get Gillian back and take her away. My stepbrother is one of the only people who's ever been consistently nice to me. Probably because he's just as big of a bastard as I am, only he doesn't hide it very well. And he likes money, which I have a lot of. It was nothing to give him ten grand to let me hide out with him, no one being the wiser. So far, it's worked like a charm.

"Yes, sir. Just checking out the cameras. Making sure everyone is accounted for. You know what I found strange?" I lean forward and pretend to look at the wall of cameras.

"What's that?" He looks over my shoulder.

I point to one camera. "There's Mr. Parks and Ms. Simmons and the little girl. And there, that's De La Torre with Ms. Bennett and Carson Davis. What's weird is that I haven't seen Chase Davis or our top protection priority, Ms. Callahan."

"Not strange at all." He shakes his head and walks away.

"Yeah? How so?"

"Because they're not supposed to be here."

I narrow my gaze at him. "Do they have another home?"

"Well, yeah, Mr. Davis is extremely rich. Like more money than you and I would ever see in a lifetime, and he makes that in a day."

That just irks me. He makes it sound like the fucker being rich means something. It doesn't. I can take him out just as easy as I could a poor man. We all bleed fucking red.

I pretend to act relieved. "So good. They're at one of his other homes."

He shakes his head. "Nah, they left on an airplane. No one knows where."

"What?"

Templeton's eyebrows rise.

"I mean, we're security. We need to be aware of these things, told where they're going and when they're coming back, right? So we can make sure they're safe?"

"Mr. Davis planned something big. A bunch of Escalades went to four different airports. Not sure which one they were in or where they went. I was told by Mr. Jack Porter, his personal guard, that they'd be gone for an indeterminate amount of time and to focus our protection on the charges you see on the screen." He points a fat finger at Gillian's bitches.

"Seriously? No one knows where they went?" I'm certain my entire body is about to light up in flames. Anger burns like acid in my gut, and I'm ready to strike, charge out of here, and kill one of her stupid bitches in retaliation.

"Yeah. It's a good idea if you ask me. Scoop that pretty little thing up and get her out of the country. Makes sense, right? He's rich enough, and that guy did a number on her. Poor thing is completely scared all the time. Haven't seen her once without Mr. Davis locked to her side. Word is she freaks out when he's out of the room. Probably took her away to make her feel safe."

I suck in a harsh breath, grind my teeth, and stare at the monitors. He clasps a hand on to my shoulder and squeezes it. "Like that you're paying such close attention though, Elliott. You're a great man to have on the job."

He praises me, but it doesn't sink in. Nothing does. All I can think about is that he has her somewhere far away. Fuck, I should have stayed on yesterday after my shift, found a place to hide out. Had I not gone home to get a bit of shut-eye, I'd know where they are. And now, they could be anywhere in the world. With his money, fuck, he could have her on a tiny island off of Asia or Australia. Halfway around the world. That's how far I plan on taking her. Though I think the tip of Canada to start with, until we get settled as a couple.

"Elliott, I'm going to make my rounds, feel free to stay here, watch our charges."

I nod and wait until I hear the door close to grip the chair in front of the wall of monitors and squeeze with all my might. *Fuck…think Daniel, think.* How the fuck am I going to get her home? I look at the blond-haired little girl being lifted and then dunked into the indoor pool. The pregnant one in a bikini. Gotta admit, her body, even with that giant fucking bump with Philip's bastard child in it, looks mighty fine. I'd fuck her for sure. My dick hardens. It would be best to fuck her while Phillip was tied up, bleeding from multiple stab wounds. I'd protect the girl though. She deserves fucking better than him.

Next, I see the Italian cunt and her hippie bitch sitting in one of the lounges. One is talking adamantly to the other, swinging her hands around. They both have a glass of wine in their hands and are smiling at one another. How I'd like to rip those smug smiles off their pretty fucking faces…with my knife. I could scratch all kinds of words into their skin, watch blood spill out and smear over their features. Again, my dick gets painfully hard. It's time to release this pent up need inside, and it's not one that will be taken away by sticking my cock in a whore. No, it's been too long since I've seen blood flowing from a warm body. Then, it comes to me like a winning million-dollar lottery ticket.

The bitches. Easiest way to get my princess back on terra firma is to take out her bitches. The stupid cunts she calls her soul sisters. Whatever the fuck that means. No guy knows. It's made up shit women come up with to give certain women higher status than the others in their lives. At this point though, it works in my favor.

I touch the screen that feeds the live images of Kat and Maria. It's going to be too easy. They both work at the same place. A very old building. One I've already scoped out. The time is now. The next day they are both together, it's going down…and the place is going up in flames.

When I wake up, I'm surrounded by warmth. Every inch of my body is pressed up against Chase's. He's holding me close, even deep in sleep. We arrived last night. The countryside was pitch black, and the limo had darkened windows making it impossible to see anything, so I didn't bother. Instead, I fell asleep with my head in Chase's lap while he stroked my hair. It was lovely. At some point, we arrived at our destination, and I awoke in Chase's arms as he carried me up a flight of stairs before laying me down on the softest bed. Reminded me of our bed at the penthouse back home. Our real home. Not the Davis Estate.

Slipping from Chase's, arms I sit up. The room is vast and charming, cottage-like, with a cathedral ceiling, exposed wooden beams, and plush furniture. Large wooden dressers line the walls with high back chairs facing a fireplace. Even though it looks a bit rustic, I can definitely see the hints of luxury. I expect nothing less from my over-spender. Moving out of the bed, I see the bathroom. It's smaller than what we have back home, but so is the bedroom. However, it does have a wonderfully large claw-foot tub that definitely can fit two. It's the biggest bathtub I've ever seen. I can't wait to enjoy it with my man. The shower looks like it was right out of nature. It's one hundred percent made of rocks, giant boulder-looking things that give off the scent of the Earth. I find the toilet and take care of business, wash my hands, and exit on bare feet. I'm in Chase's T-shirt, and it smells deliciously like him and me.

On quiet feet, I pad over to the French doors and open them wide. That's when my breath leaves my body in a whoosh. "Oh my God," I whisper, still clutching the handles of the door. A warmth hits my back and two arms wrap around my body. Chase presses the length of himself against me and kisses my neck.

"Beautiful, isn't it?"

I look in wonder, in complete and utter awe of the luscious rolling green hills that drop off to a cliff where the ocean sits beyond. "Beautiful doesn't even begin to cover it."

"I'm glad you like your present."

"What do you mean my present?" I press into him, wanting to look into his eyes but not capable of letting go of this view just yet. It's too much, too incredible to not give the entirety of my attention to it.

I can feel Chase grin against my neck as he holds me. "I bought you this house. All that land you see, all the way to those cliffs is ours. Once your name is Mrs. Davis, you will get a copy of the deed."

"Chase," I gasp. He has given me a home and land as a

present. "It's too much. Jesus, look at it. No one should own this. It's God's country. It's God's gift to the world."

He shakes his head against my neck. "Nope, it's my gift to you. And you will gift it to our children one day. Then maybe, our daughter or son will come here for their honeymoon and look out at this and dream of the children they're going to leave it to. Then the Davis name—our legacy, my love—will carry on through them. To infinity," he says while rubbing that very symbol into the soft fabric of his shirt at my rib, just under the fullness of my breast, below my heart. Figure eights, over and over again. He paints such a beautiful image I want to have it with me always, and I get an idea. One I cannot tell him about. For it will be my gift to him on our wedding night. The wheels are turning in my mind as I stare out on the most stunning view I've ever seen.

"I love how you see our future," I say while bringing his hand up to my lips and kissing it slowly.

"What do you want to do today, baby?" he asks, clasping his hands around my hips and lifting the shirt up incrementally.

"You mean after you make me scream your name over and over again?" I grin, turn in his arms, and plant my lips on his. He slides his hands under my shirt, planting them firmly on my ass, and lifts me up. I wrap my legs around his waist as he takes me back to our bed in our new countryside home in Ireland.

★ ★ ★ ★

Hand in hand, we walk along the sidewalk up to a sign that says "Welcome to Bantry Beanntrai, National Tidy Towns Gold Medal Winners" and stop. There are boats dotting the surface of the water, giving the small town a coastal feel that reminds me of home. On the right side of the street are lines of multicolored buildings only three to four stories high. Each building is attached to the next but painted a different bright color. Chase and I both silently take in the beauty of the small town we are now a part of. It feels like our first real connection to our new life together.

"I love this place," I say into the open crisp air, swinging Chase's arm.

He pulls me close and lays a kiss on my temple but doesn't stop walking. We come up to a square of sorts where a giant anchor sits on the concrete. It looks like it came from a huge ship. I pull out my phone and push Chase in front of it. "Baby, I want to take your picture."

He chuckles and stands in front of it, posing like Superman. He is my Superman, and seeing him being silly lifts a huge weight off my chest. I snap a couple photos of him and then go over to the sign. "Says it's an anchor from the French Armada force in 1796. It was discovered off the northeast point of Whiddy Island in Bantry Bay back in 1980 by a Dutch salvage company. Trippy."

Chase looks up at the huge anchor in the middle of the town and then slowly brings his stunning gaze to me. "I like the symbolism. An anchor. We should get one for our home here."

I smile wide, run over, and jump up into his arms, legs back around his waist, and kiss him. He swings me around, and I tip my head back, allowing my hair to flow in the breeze. He lifts me up, kisses me, and sets me on my feet. "What was that for?"

Shrugging, I take in a breath. "I'm just so happy."

"I'm glad, baby, because from here on out, it's me and you, kid." He holds my hand, and we start walking once more. One guard is walking behind us, but I haven't really seen him, just catch glimpses of him now and again. Jack is across the street. He's much easier to spot because I know him better, can anticipate his bulk. The other guys, I have no idea. Chase said they're somewhere in front of us, making sure to keep an appropriate distance so we don't feel they are invading, but he knows we're safe. For me, I feel completely free of the burden we had back home.

"Coming here, leaving San Francisco was the best decision we've made. I feel free here, Chase."

He nods. "Me too. The moment we got off the plane and then made it to the new house, there was something different in the air. It just felt right." I smile and sidle into his side, looping my thumb into one of his belt loops. "You hungry?"

After we woke, we made love, showered, and then hopped into the little sports car Chase had in the garage. How it got there will always be a mystery, but I've come to understand that Chase just has things. He doesn't worry about getting rentals or planning travel. It just comes easy for him. Then again, when you have that kind of money at your disposal, I'd imagine getting a car parked in the garage of your new home wouldn't be that hard.

"Famished," I say while people-watching.

Chase leads me to a place uniquely named Box of Frogs. It is a coffee house and bakery right under a bright sunflower-orange building. The rich smells of cinnamon, sugar, and coffee make me salivate. We enter the warm space, and I instantly brighten at the wide variety of perfectly dressed cupcakes. "Chase, we have to get some of these for the house!" I waggle my eyebrows. "You know, dessert for later."

He grins one of those panty-melting grins. "Absolutely, my sweet."

I roll my eyes. My sweet is the newest endearment he's been trying on for size. I don't mind. When he said it, his intent was clear…to remind me of exactly how sweet he thinks I taste. So that makes it worth it.

"Babe, they also have a ton of cookies! You love cookies." I point to the glass in front.

He hugs me around the waist. "I do, indeed. We'll need to get a few dozen."

"A few?"

He shrugs, and I shake my head. We are greeted by a woman in a red apron and a hat that I usually attribute to old men who golf. I glance at the few men and women hustling around the bakery. They all seem to be wearing them. "I like your hat," I say.

"Oh, it's day-cent," the woman says. "You look like one of us, but you're American." She smiles, her Irish accent very thick.

"We're here for our wedding and our honeymoon. We actually bought a home up the way."

"Ah, big, faces the ocean?"

I nod happily. "That's the one."

She whistles, and Chase puts an arm around my chest from behind and nuzzles my neck.

"Making friends with the locals, baby?" He kisses my neck.

"I am."

"What can I get ya two lovebirds?" she asks. I find that I want to find ways to make her speak. Her accent is adorable.

"I'll have one of those scones." I point to the item.

"It comes with jam and whipped cream." She hits a few buttons on the register.

"Um, why?"

Her eyebrows scrunch together, and Chase laughs. "Baby, that's how the Irish eat a scone."

"Really?"

"When in Rome." I giggle. "I mean, when in Ireland." The attendant waits patiently, likely having dealt with Americans before. "Okay, and my guy here with a sweet tooth would like to have a variety of your cookies."

"Biscuits."

This time I'm confused. "No"—I point to the case of cookies—"cookies. Say three dozen?"

"Make it four, baby. You know how much I like them."

"You mean biscuits," the overly perky, now annoying Irish woman says.

Just when I'm about to correct her again, Chase puts a hand on my shoulder. "Honey, biscuits are cookies to them."

"Then what do they call a biscuit?"

"A scone."

I snap my head back. "But that's absurd."

This time he shrugs. "Were not in Kansas anymore, Dorothy."

"Obviously not. I hope I can get the hang of this." I cringe.

He places our coffee order and leads me to a small table.

The first bite into my scone makes it very clear why it needs the jam and whipped cream. It has absolutely no sugar in it. But with the jam and whipped cream, it's heavenly. My vanilla latte, on the other hand, comes with a perfect amount of tasty white foam that was made into a lovely leaf. I sip the liquid and moan around the cup. "I'm going to need another one of these." I suck back some more of God's sweet nectar.

Chase laughs, leans back, and slips on his shades. He has a blue polo on, a sweater over his shoulders, and a pair of aviator sunglasses. Me, I'm wearing a long army-green skirt, knee-high brown leather boots, and a cream cable-knit sweater, compliments of my new wardrobe. Chase didn't pack any clothing. He called Chloe, who was already in Europe, and had her stylist buy and ship over clothing. The house assistant removed tags and placed everything in the closest and dressers. So technically, she knows where we are, but since she's in Europe and hasn't been part of everything that's happened, she has no reason to share. And Chase assures me she's not going to interfere.

"You look handsome," I say, pulling out my phone again. "Smile for me. I need a new background on my phone, and I want to remember you, right now." He appeases me and then decides he wants one of his own.

One of the café busboys walks up to us. "Would you like a photo together?"

I smile at him and move my chair closer to Chase's. He pushes his glasses onto his head and gets closer to me. We lean toward one another, and the boy takes a photo and hands me back my phone. I look at the picture and notice how happy and relaxed we both are. I show him the photo. "That's a keeper," he shares.

"It is," I agree. Once we finish breakfast, we continue

our journey through the town of Bantry. Chase sees a camera shop at the same time that I see an antique shop. "I want to go in there." I point over to the quaint-looking store and start to pull away.

"You sure?" Chase's eyes hold concern and maybe something else.

I caress his brow, pushing aside the uncertainty that's showing there. "You get us a camera so we can capture all this." I point to the beautiful streets and vistas. "And I'll check out the antique store. Perhaps I'll see something we can add to our new home away from home?"

Chase cups my cheek. "I really like the sound of that." Chase looks up and gestures with a hand. Out of nowhere, Jack is by our side.

"Sir?"

He looks at me and tilts his head. "Gillian wants to go to that antique store while I get us a camera. Can you escort her please?"

"Of course." He mumbles into his wrist, and then again, like a magic trick, the two men, who were apparently closer than I thought they were, appear by our side. He directs one to stay on the street, and the other to go with Chase.

"Shouldn't take long. I'll meet you over there in fifteen or twenty minutes. Okay?" He leans in and kisses me softly.

"'Kay." I look at him, the most handsome man I've ever known, and I'm going to marry him this week. In a few days, really.

Without any concern or worry, I cross the street, and Jack is quick on my heels as I enter the little shop. The smell of dust and flowers permeates the air. An old woman with white hair piled up on her head in a bun is sitting in a rocking chair knitting a sweater, one much like the one I'm wearing now.

"Go on ahead and look around, dearie. Maybe you'll find something from the past that will enrich your future."

I like that thought but don't tell her that. As I scope out the furniture and knickknacks, I find a tapestry hidden half behind a large scrollwork mirror. "Jack, can you help me pull this mirror back?" I ask. He lifts the mirror with little problem and shifts it aside. Staring me in the face is a seven-by-ten foot tapestry of the Celtic trinity knot. It's blue and green, just like my tattoo. "Oh my!" I whisper, and the woman looks up.

"Yep, will look really lovely in the master bedroom of that house you just bought."

I turn around. "How do you know that we just bought a place here?"

The old woman looks up at me over her glasses. "Honey, there isn't much in Bantry that I don't know about. 'Sides, the home was expensive, knew a classy woman and man probably bought it since no one around here could afford it. It's been empty for a couple years now. And the population is only thirty-two hundred. I've been in Bantry all my life and will die here. I know everyone."

I smile and nod. "Well, I definitely agree. How much?"

"Two thousand," she says, and I suck in a breath. Jack looks at me with hard eyes.

"You can put the mirror back."

"Not before you get that tapestry," he rumbles.

I shake my head. "No, it's okay. It's really beautiful though," I say, loud enough for the woman to hear.

"Excuse me, Ms. Callahan, but you're about to become

Mrs. Davis. He will be very pleased if you purchase something to add to your new home." Jack's dark gaze holds mine. For the first time, I can see real unguarded sincerity there.

"It's expensive."

"It isn't. He will think that is a pittance. She'll take the tapestry, and I'll purchase it on behalf of her fiancé," Jack tells the old woman.

"I have money." I narrow my eyes at him and place my hands on my hips.

Jack scowls. "Yes, of course, but if someone is tracking your credit card and bank account, there will be problems. We will use the card I have."

"Good point." I breathe in slowly.

The old woman stands. "I believe I have something else that might be of interest to you, my dear." I turn around and follow her. Jack stays close, which is annoying and comforting at the same time.

She leads me to a tall armoire. "Oh, I'm sorry. The furniture we have is all new and looks great."

"It's not the furniture you'll be interested in, precious." She opens the armoire doors, and hanging within is a gown. A lace wedding gown.

The woman smiles as I hold my hand over my mouth and my eyes tear up. "I married my Henry in this gown sixty years ago. It was made by my mother's own hand. I've held onto this as Henry and I were not blessed with children. He passed almost ten years ago now, and there isn't a day that goes by that I don't miss him."

"And you're willing to sell it to me?" A tear slips down my cheek as I look at the most perfect dress in the world. Absolutely ideal for a tiny wedding in a small church in

Ireland.

The dress has a lace cap sleeve, a sweetheart neckline, and fits close to the body until you hit the knee where the lace flares out enough to give it some body. There's a nude-colored underlay because the lace is a wide pattern. The shape reminds me of fans that flare out meeting with a flower shape in the center of each fan. It's incredibly intricate. The back has a one-inch wide scalloped lace piece to hold up the top, and then is cut out and open to the lower back. Showing just enough of my bare back that Chase will lose his mind.

"No, precious," the woman says, and my heart sinks. I know—I just know this is the dress I must marry the man of my dreams in. And then she blows me away with her next words. "I'm going to give it to you."

CHASE

CHAPTER ELEVEN

"Hey, baby." I pull my woman back against my body as a little old woman in front of her zips up a garment bag. "Buy something?"

Jack hands the woman a credit card, and she looks up to me. "So this your young man?" She looks at me over her glasses. Gillian snuggles back into me and puts an arm around my middle.

"It is."

"Strapping young fella. Big." Her eyes widen as she takes in my appearance.

"Making new friends again?" She shakes her head. "What did you get?" I point at the garment bag.

Gillian sighs and looks up at me. "Only the best things ever."

I tip her chin back and look into her face. Her pale skin is pink at the cheeks and her eyes a forest green. I'll never tire of looking at her face. "Which is what?"

"A tapestry for one. It's the trinity! Can you believe it?" She points a finger behind us, and I see the symbol. The design is beautiful and the craftsmanship perfection.

"It's lovely. I'm sure it will go great in our home, and I know how much you love the trinity."

She nods happily and pulls out her phone and takes a picture of it. "I can't wait to show the girls. They are going to die!" Then her face scrunches up into a frown, as if she just grasped what she said. I pull her back into my arms and tip her chin up.

"Hey, it's okay. I know what you meant." I slide my thumb across her cheek and pet her plump lower lip. She kisses my thumb.

"Here you go, sweetheart. I'll have one of the young fellas I have working for me deliver the tapestry to your place tomorrow. They can hang it for you too."

Gillian claps her hands together. "Fantastic!"

"What's in the bag?" The woman hands the garment bag to Jack. He treats it as if it's precious cargo.

Gillian shakes her head. "It's my wedding gown." I open my eyes wide, and she nods. "You'll never believe this, but Mrs. McMann here gave me her wedding dress. The one she wore to her wedding when she married her husband over sixty years ago, and, Chase…it's just, well"—she looks down and then back up to me, moisture in her eyes—"it's perfect."

I turn my head to the old woman. "Mrs. McMann, thank you. Thank you for putting this smile on my bride's face. You can't know this, but we've had a very rough year, and what you're doing for her—this means a lot. If ever you need anything, anything at all, consider it done." I pull out one of my business cards and lay it on the antique table she uses.

"Chase Davis." The old woman studies the card. "Well, I've got no use for business-related things, but sometimes I don't mind eating a meal out with some new friends."

"Absolutely. Gillian and I have just bought a home

here. After our wedding, we'll be visiting as often as possible. We'll make time to spend with you on our next visit."

"Much obliged," she says and turns to Gillian. "Now come on over and give your new granny a hug, precious."

Gillian wraps her arms around the old woman. She's the happiest I've seen in her in months. I'd go a long way to keep that smile on her face, and if this little woman and her shop can give her that, well, I'll make certain we give some time to her.

"We'll be back. And thank you for taking such good care of my girl here."

"You make her happy now, young lad."

"With everything I am." I wink at her and she winks back.

I lead Gillian out of the store, and she's practically skipping with excitement. "Can you believe I walked into that store, found an amazing tapestry, and met a lovely woman who gave me one of the most special gifts of my life?"

"Knowing you, how big your heart is, yes, yes, I can."

★ ★ ★ ★

Today's the day. Gillian is arriving an hour after me in a separate limo to the Gougane Barra Church in the city of Macroom. It's about a thirty-minute drive from our home in Bantry. The church is remote and sits alongside a lake. The chapel is small, planted out in the open greenery with the backdrop of a pristine sky and lovely lake. Swans swim in the waters peacefully and the trees sway in the breeze. The church is made up of multicolored grayish blocks that prove its age around the 1700s. The entire building goes up and into a point, making it seem very much like a triangle. Two large red doors sit at the mouth of the building. A priest exits down the small stairs and holds out a hand.

"You must be Mr. Davis."

"I am."

"I wanted to thank you myself for the considerable donation we received. The town will do much good work with such a sizable contribution."

I smile at the older gentleman. "I'm pleased that I could help. Obviously, it wasn't entirely selfless, as you are presiding over my wedding today."

"Indeed. And how many should we expect in attendance? I have several parishioners and townsfolk at the touch of a button to assist in the activities."

Putting my hands in the pocket of my tux, I look out over the lake, thinking how picturesque this will be, wishing I could see Gillian's face when she sees the location. "It will just be me, my bride, and our three bodyguards. Two of them can serve as our witnesses. One will walk the premises."

The man of God looks nonplussed. "I assure you, Mr. Davis, the town of Macroom and our church are very safe. You won't need guards."

"I'm sure you're correct, Father. However, I've learned recently one can never be too careful. You see, my bride was kidnapped at our wedding almost four weeks ago. Today is our second chance, which is why there will be no friends or family attending the nuptials. Just she and I. Though, I would appreciate your assistance with one thing, if possible."

The father places a hand on my shoulder. "Anything, my son."

"If you happen to know a photographer who could come out, I'd be happy to pay him or her handsomely to capture our ceremony and take some photos of us by the church and this stunning lake. I believe my bride and our future children would love a memento of this day."

The priest puffs out his chest. "My brother is such a man. He will take fine images of this day. I shall call him now."

"Thank you." I nod to him as he turns and enters the church. Mentally, I go over the vows I want to say to her when I take her forever. In my pocket, I rub my thumb over the velvet box and then take it out. I open the small square, and within lies a diamond band. The sun glints off the many diamonds that make an entire circle. It's just how I see Gillian…simple and elegant.

The wind blows my hair as Jack helps me out of the limo. The view is unlike anything I expected. Chase has outdone himself. He's giving me a dream church wedding, the kind you see in fairy tales, and he's the handsome prince who will be waiting at the end of the aisle to take my hand. Clouds slowly creep by as I take in the lake with its charming ducks and swans swimming dreamily along the surface. The trees surrounding the lake, hills, and this quaint church give off a storybook quality. The church is pointed, and old, very much so. It has two red doors with those big black brackets running at the top and bottom to hold their heavy weight.

Jack crooks his arm, and I slide my hand onto his. "Shall

we get you married?" He smiles. Jack Porter, Mr. Linebacker, Mr. Grumpy, Mr. I-Don't-Like-You-Gillian gave me a smile. A real one, too.

"That smile looks good on you, Jack."

He purses his lips, holding back a grin. A grin! "I'll have to remember that." Before we get to the step, Jack turns to me, stopping our progress up the stairs. "Look, Gillian, I've only ever wanted what's best for Chase. He's more than my charge. He's like a son to me."

I place an arm on Jack's forearm. "I'm not ever going to hurt him. I promise you that. I love him."

Jack tightens his jaw. "I know that, now." His dark gaze holds mine for a second more, and then he puts out his arm again. "I think someone is very ready to make you his wife."

We take the few steps and enter the church. One of our bodyguards is standing to the side of the entrance. The church's ceiling is a peachy hue with wide sweeping white columns curved into a half-moon shape. Several empty rows of wooden pews sit in lines, ready for guests who aren't going to be in attendance. For a moment it saddens me that the girls aren't here, and Chase's family, but all of that disappears the moment I look up.

Chase.

He's there at the end of the aisle, hands clasped in front of him, waiting for me to walk to him. Jack lets me go, walks up the aisle, and stands at Chase's side. What I didn't see before is the little old woman who stands at the very front. It's Mrs. McMann, the woman I met two days ago, the woman whose dress fits like it was tailored for me. Having someone standing on my side, even someone I don't know very well brings tears to my eyes. Her wrinkled hands come up to her face. A handkerchief is clenched tight in one gnarled fist.

I hold tight to the bushel of daisies I wrapped in a single white ribbon. I'm wearing the dress and a blue sapphire ring that belonged to Chase's mother on my right hand. It's something old, something borrowed, and something blue all in one, he reminded me early this morning. I think it's perfect.

Taking a deep breath, I look into Chase's eyes and hold them as I walk slowly down the aisle. There isn't any music, but I don't need anything. The music is our love, and it's leading the way.

When I get to him, he takes my hand and kisses it. "You have never looked more beautiful than you do in this moment. I'll remember it always."

The priest says a few words, skipping over some of the parts that would matter to a church full of people, or to a Catholic couple, but neither of those things matter, not to the two of us.

"Chase, Gillian, I believe you have your own vows."

I turn and hand Mrs. McMann my flowers. "Would you?"

"Of course I'll hold them, dearie. It will be an honor," the old woman says, and I smile.

Chase clasps both my hands and brings them up to his mouth where he places a kiss on the knuckles of each hand.

"Gillian Grace Callahan, I promise to love, cherish, and worship the ground you walk on every day of my life. I'll strive every day to be the man who's good enough for a woman like you." Tears fill my eyes and slip down my cheeks. He cups both of them, and I rest my hands on his hips. "When you cry"—he moves forward and kisses each cheek—"I'll kiss away your tears. When you love"—I look deep into his blue eyes and see they're a startling shade of aqua—"I'll love you in return. I will never forsake you, and will always make you priority number one. Today is the first day of the rest of our lives as one whole. I feel as though I've spent the last decade trying to find my other half, and I've found you. You're it for me, baby. Through infinity."

He once again kisses the tears off my cheeks and then my lips. "I love the taste of your joy."

And more tears.

Finally, I get it together, taking a long slow breath. "Chase William Davis, I promise to love, cherish, and allow you to worship the ground I walk on." He chuckles. I hold onto his hands and kiss his knuckles the same way he did mine. "I'll never put another man higher than I hold you and your love. I want to be the woman you believe in, the one you come home to at night, the woman who bears your children. Today we become a family. A real family. There is nothing more important to me than the sanctity of that binding. Every day, I will do my best to make you proud you chose to spend the rest of your life with me. Today I give you me. My body, my mind, and my soul. Please take care of it," I whisper as the tears fall again. This time as I look into Chase's eyes I see they, too, are wet.

One tear falls down his cheek. "I will, Gillian, I promise I will," Chase says.

"I believe you both have your rings." Jack hands Chase's ring to me and mine to him.

The priest speaks, "Bless, O Lord, these rings that he who gives it and she who wears it may abide in thy peace and continue in thy favor, unto their life's end, through Jesus Christ our Lord. Amen."

Both Chase and I respond with, "Amen."

The priest continues with the ceremony. We exchange rings, repeat after him, and wait while he says the Lord's Prayer. Finally, he finishes with, "Amen."

"You may now kiss your bride," he announces.

Chase cups both my cheeks and brings me in. His mouth covers mine, and the entire church, the priest, Mrs. McMann, Jack, and the world disappear. It is just the two of us. His kiss is slow, thorough, and filled with enough happiness and energy to light up a small town. I kiss him back with everything that I am, wrapping my arms around his neck and holding on for dear life. Because that's what being married to Chase is going to be like, me holding on for dear life. And no matter what I know, he'll always keep me close. Cherished. Loved.

Finally we pull back, and both Jack and Ms. McMann clap and offer their congratulations.

Chase tunnels his hands into my loose locks of hair. I left it down because I know he prefers it that way. "You're my wife," he whispers, his forehead planted along mine.

"You're my husband," I whisper back.

"I've never been happier than this moment. You give me that, baby. Life. A life worth living."

"I love you." I caress his cheeks and kiss him softly.

The priest clears his throat, and Chase smiles against my lips. "I think that's our cue."

"It is indeed."

When we turn, I notice the flashes. Someone taking our pictures. "Has he been taking them the entire time?" I ask while Chase leads me down the aisle toward the light showing through the church doors.

"Yep. And now he's going to take some of us by the lake. Would you like that?"

I smile huge and squeeze his fingers. "More than anything."

"Well come on, wife, up you go!" He hooks an arm around my hips and lifts me into his arms in a princess hold. I tip my head back and laugh as he carries me out of the church and down the steps to the lake. The camera is clicking like mad and I don't care.

Once we're outside, I scream out, "I'm Mrs. Davis!"

"Damn right you are!" Chase bellows.

He sets me down when we reach the edge of the lake. There he holds me by the hips. In return, I place my hands on his shoulders. It looks almost like we're dancing. The camera clicks away, but I don't care. There won't be any boring placements, no stand here or there—just Chase and me.

"Was it enough today? Would you like another ceremony when we get home, one where we can invite the world and your friends?"

I shake my head. "No. This, us being here, is more than enough. You, Chase, you will always be everything I need."

He looks down at his ring and lifts it. The infinity symbols are a delicate yellow gold and intermingled with the platinum of the ring. "Infinity?"

I nod. "Look inside."

"Body. Mind. Soul," he reads. "Look at yours."

I lift up my ring, pull it off, and then read the inscription. "All that I am is yours." I smile wide, put my ring back on, and jump into his arms. He kisses me, spins me around, and dips me down, where he kisses me again.

When we come up for air this time, Chase tugs on my hand. "Let's take a couple photos in front of the church and then head home. I have a dinner for two overlooking the ocean, music, and champagne prepared."

"That sounds heavenly."

We take a few more photos, thank the priest, and thank Mrs. McMann for the dress, and Chase pays the photographer. He hands the man a rather large handful of bills. "I'd like to buy the camera along with the photos. We'll have them developed in the States. Will ten thousand euros do it?"

The priest's eyes widen and so do the photographer's. The man nods, unable to speak. In a tiny town like Macroom, ten thousand euros for a camera is a lot of money.

Chase hands the camera to Jack, who places it the front of the limo before opening our door.

"Over spender," I chastise and shake my head while entering the limo.

Chase slides in next to me. "No, wife, I'm just making sure that these pictures don't end up in the hands of the paparazzi. Here in Ireland they don't know who I am, but all they have to do is look up my name and we've got company. Plus, these pictures would be worth a lot of money, and they are not for anyone's eyes but our own. We'll share them with the people we care about, not the paparazzo."

I tap on his temple. "Always thinking."

He grins and lifts me onto his lap. "I'm thinking about how insanely beautiful my wife is right now. I'm thinking about how I'd like to slowly remove this dress and get to her body underneath. I'm thinking about how many times I'm going to make her come."

"Really? Sounds delightful," I say, nuzzling his neck and biting down on the tendon there. He growls and squeezes my breast through the lace of my gown. Wetness pools between my thighs. "How many times?" I ask.

"So many, baby. I'm going to make you come so hard and so long you're going to beg for me to stop. But I won't. Because it's now my job to know what you need. To make my wife sing with pleasure. I plan to fuck you until you pass out."

"How romantic." I snicker against his jaw, dragging my mouth along the smooth surface.

"You bring out the romantic in me," he jokes, and I pull back laughing. "No really, though, I just want to make love to my wife all night long."

"Well, your wife thinks that's an excellent plan."

X

DANIEL

CHAPTER TWELVE

The building is dark as I enter through a small window connected to the janitor's closet. The window creaks and groans as I slither through. I can hear music and the sound of bare feet hitting the wooden floor when I open the door to the inside of the building. The stage. Even though it's midnight, there's still a crew here. Just as I suspected. Good news—I know for a fact that the dancer bitch is on that stage right now.

Weaving through the dark corners I scan the stage from my hidden location. I chose to wear all black. Even my face is hidden behind a ski mask, aiding me in the goal of being invisible. I could be wearing bright pink and the ten or so people on the stage wouldn't notice. They are so stuck on themselves, and they're dancing around like little fucking fairies. Watching their muscles move and flex is exhilarating, but only because I can see the exhaustion there. They've been here since early morning. I've been watching Gillian's old roommate Maria since she arrived. She hasn't left this theatre. I'm unsure if the director asshole even brought food in. It makes me happy to think she's been here all day, not a bit of food in her. Her suffering makes me happy.

My eyes zero in on the tall raven-haired beauty. She is

beautiful. Anyone can see that. Her body is made for sin, and she flaunts it like the two-bit whore she is. Always wearing tight leggings and tank tops that her giant tits almost fall out of, or worse, the booty shorts she walks around Gillian's apartment in, even when I was there. It was like she was showcasing her body to me in invitation. Stupid slut. Like I'd ever go for a dancer. A dancer is just a fancy name for a stripper. If that man clapping and pointing, the director or choreographer or whatever his stupid fucking title is, told her to take off her clothes and jump around in front of all these people, she'd do it. Just like a fucking stripper. She's no better.

Sneaking behind the stage door, I walk along the long hallway unspotted. When I reach the end, there's a door leading down into the belly of the old San Francisco Theatre. It should be a basement, a place they store things, but it's not. It's been turned into a workspace, and Gillian's seamstress hippie friend works down here. She also arrived earlier today, but much later than dancer bitch. Around noon. Must be nice to work when you feel like it. I'll give her credit. She has been here twelve hours. Though what she's doing is completely idiotic. Making costumes. It's a glorified way of saying she plays dress up or Barbie dolls but with real living people as her toys. And they eat this shit up. Pay her to make clothes. They could just as easily buy the shit on the Internet. Whatever.

Slowly, I make my way down the stairs and into a flurry of lights. Thank God I scoped this place out earlier. Within minutes, I'm behind one of the dressing screens. I move one of the slats barely open. There she is, hunched over a garment, her back to me. The soft glow of the light above her head makes her blond hair shine. Classical music pumps through the room—some piano concerto I've heard before and actually quite like. Her music tastes aside, I look around the room. There is one small window at ground level with the theatre.

This is going to be too easy. For on the other side of that window, I've nailed in a wooden two-by-four on the top of the window and the bottom. They wedge perfectly to shorten the width. Making it too small for even a thin woman like her to get through.

With one last look, I sneak back to the door at the bottom of the stairs. She's so focused on her work she doesn't see or hear me shut the door. At the top of the stairs, I tip over the gasoline I brought and squirt the accelerant down the stairs like I'm getting ready to light up a charcoal barbecue. This is going to be one helluva cookout. Charred human flesh. I can already smell it. Reminds me of home, when I burned the bodies of my parents.

Once I've doused the space, I grab the other can I've hidden and walk along the hallway, leaving a trail of gas as I go. I'd be whistling right now at how happy this makes me. I can already feel my temperature heating up, preparing for the fire. My veins are pounding with adrenaline, and I can't wait to see this building go up in flames.

With ease, I make it back stage where the dancers are still going at it. Some are sitting on the sides of the stage. Maria, however, is on her hands, legs up to the sky and in a wide V-shape. Two men lift her up by the thighs. It's an erotic move and just proves how skanky she is. Letting two men hold her up like that. Their hands are so close to her snatch, their heads along her leg. They can probably smell that dirty cunt. I pity the men who have to get close to that whore.

Oh, well, not for long. With as much control as I can muster, I spill out the rest of the gasoline, open a fresh bottle of accelerant, and stick a tissue in the top. A flick of my wrist and my Zippo lights. Same Zippo I used to light up my family and watch those fuckers burn. Now I'm going to do the same to Gillian's bitch friends.

Over in the distance, I can see Maria's hired rent-a-cop and Kathleen's walking along the back of the theater. Shit, he better not make it to her location before the fire does. With no time to waste, I light up a hard piece of cardboard and toss it to the floor.

Instantly it turns a bright orange. Then I see it take flight, zipping and lighting along the line I walked down the back of the stage, straight to the costume bitch's closet...or should I say grave.

I make my way easily to the janitor's closet again, wedge the door shut with a broomstick, and drag myself back through the window. On quick feet, I jog to the building next door, climb up the fire escape and to my perch where I've left my binoculars. They are centered on the front of the building with a clear line to the window, where I can still see Kathleen hard at work. Not for long.

Alarms instantly start blaring. Kathleen's head comes up, and she pushes on a remote control. Probably turning her music off. She stands and goes to the door. It must be hot to the touch because she pulls her hand back as if burned. Then she runs to the window and opens it. Smoke has already seeped into her space. Sweat beads on the surface of my skin. My dick hardens painfully as I see her open the window and scream for help. No one comes. They can't hear her over the alarms.

Fuck. This is too good.

Right about now, I can see the dozen dancers rushing out the front of the old building and flying down the steps. Maria is there, and she's screaming and pointing at her bodyguard. The other bodyguard is rushing back into the building. Too late fucker. She's going to be swathed in fire soon. You'll never get to her. I laugh and watch as Maria tries to run back into the building. The guard holds her back. She kicks him and punches him the face. He gets her in some type of body lock, and I feel giddy for the first time in years. I wish I were closer and could hear what they're saying, but at least I've got eyes on the show.

I swing my binoculars back to Kathleen. She's moving away from the window. I feel as though I could jizz in my pants right now. She has an arm over her mouth. The smoke is getting really thick. She grabs some type of garment and goes back to the door. I can almost feel the intense heat along my own skin as the stupid fucking cunt does exactly what I hoped for!

Waiting with baited breath, I watch as she holds the handle with the garment, turns, and pulls it open. A wall of fire slams into the side of her, knocking her back and to the ground. I jump up and fist pump the air. Finally, I've taken one out! Once my girl gets word that her bitch is dead, she'll come running back to town.

Just as I watch the smoke fill the room to the point where I can't see Kathleen lying prone on the floor anymore, something blocks my vision. Backing up, I see that it's Maria. She's screaming into the window. She tries to push the front of her body in but can't fit. I laugh and watch. Maria turns on her ass and kicks at the two-by-fours with her bare feet. Seriously, bitch, that takes some balls. Then her fucking bodyguard pulls her away and kicks at the first and then the second. The open window breaks, widening the space, and he removes one and then the other two-by-four. Only the big asshole is too big to fit in there.

The smoke pouring out the window is black and angry, fitting my soul as I watch. Maria and the guy fight again. She pushes him away, gets on her belly, and presses into the hole. She screams out, the bottom of the window cutting the bare skin of her stomach up good, but she doesn't stop. Soon she disappears into the hole. This could work out in my favor. Two for the price of one. She's exhausted, having worked the last sixteen hours. I can't imagine she'll be strong enough to get her friend out.

I am wrong. After a few minutes, I see the bodyguard take off his jacket, place it over the window seal, and lean his arms into the hole. To my extreme displeasure, he sits on the ground, wedges his feet on the sides of the window, and lifts a limp body through it. Kathleen is pulled out and laid on the ground. Then I see Maria's arms, which he gets a firm grip around, only she's no longer moving. The bodyguard jerks and roars as he now hefts her body out of the window.

Some of the dancers have taken notice and are pointing and running down the back of the building. A couple firemen follow. One lifts up Kathleen's limp body. I see that one of her arms is seared black all the way up to her neck and down her ribcage. Hopefully she's dead from the burn or the smoke inhalation. She was in there a long fucking time. Though Maria still isn't moving, and the front of her belly is covered in blood. They are two dead weights in the firemen's arms. Can it be too much to ask that my plan took out both of them? I'll settle for one. As long as my princess hears about this, regardless of whether they are dead or alive, she'll come running home. That is my ultimate reward.

When the limo arrives at our new home in Bantry, Chase leads me by the hand along the walkway around our home. It's lit up with swinging lanterns to guide us. When we hit the soft grass behind our home, I see that a path has been made all the way to the edge of our property near the sea. The path is lit with more lanterns and littered with white, pink, and red flower petals all the way to a small white tent.

"Wow," I say, as he leads me down the long flowered path to the tent. When we enter, it's much larger than I expected. At least a fifty-foot perfect square. On one side is a table for two set with flickering candles in glass holders, flowers, and two metal circular trays covering the plates. On the other side of the tent is a bed. An enormous cloud of pillows in rich burgundy, gold, and white. Flower petals are floating along the coverlet. That's not the most stunning part. No, that's the open view of the ocean. The tent is closed on the three sides, but the flaps of the fourth are pulled back to give an exotic 180-degree view of the ocean midafternoon.

"Chase," I gasp, and he pulls me into his arms.

One hand holds me around the waist, and the other cups my cheek. "Do you like it, Mrs. Davis?" I can already tell he's going to call me Mrs. Davis every chance he gets.

"I do, Mr. Davis. I can't believe you planned all this. It's... It's incredible."

Chase gives me one of his best smiles. The sweet, lovable only-for-me kind. I pet his lips, lean forward, and kiss them briefly.

"Anything for my *wife*."

"I like the sound of that, *husband*." I grin, and he uncharacteristically swings me around like he did at the church.

"As do I. Are you hungry?" He sets me back on my feet.

"Famished."

Chase leads me to the lovely table. There's a bucket of champagne in a standing unit. Two bottles are nestled there. He opens one and the cork goes flying out of the tent. We both laugh as he pours the sparkling pink champagne. I hope it's the same kind from the plane. That one was a burst of dry berry notes on the tongue. We hold up our glasses, and Chase looks deep into my eyes.

"To our forever," he says.

"To our forever." I clink his glass. We both take a sip, and I moan in delight at the crisp, wonderful taste.

Chase stands and walks over to a small table where a stereo has been set up. He presses a button, and the tent fills with the sound of a lilting woman's voice. It's an opera singer I've heard before. Just as Chase makes his way back to the table, a man in a suit with a white towel over his arm comes in. "Sir, I do believe you said to enter once the music plays."

"Yes, thank you, Colin. I'd like to introduce you to the lady of the manor, my wife, Gillian."

"Good to meet you, Mrs. Davis."

I smile at the red-haired older gentleman who's probably in his late forties if not early fifties. "You can call me Gillian."

"Yes, ma'am," he says before approaching our table.

"Gillian, Colin is our house handler. He will be taking care of everything that is the Bantry home. He lives with his wife in the guest house off the side of the property, down the path."

Colin smiles and removes the two metal covers over our plates. "Sir, ma'am, for this evening we have a special filet mignon with a garlic buttered potato, fresh vegetables from your garden in a special sauce me better half prepares on special occasions."

"Your wife cooked this meal?"

The man beams with pride, his chest puffing out. "Yes, ma'am. My Rebecca is a master chef. She will make all your meals while you're in Bantry. She looks forward to meeting you."

"As I do her. Thank you, Colin. Please give her my compliments."

He nods and leans back. "Will there be anything else, sir?" he asks Chase.

"You've set the dessert and utensils over there." Chase points to a side of the tent I haven't seen.

Colin nods. "Yes, sir. And I hope you don't mind, my wife found a lovely topper. Please consider it as our gift to you. We look forward to getting to know your family through many years to come."

Chase stands and shakes Colin's hand. Then he claps Colin on the shoulder and squeezes. "Thank you, my good man. That will be all until tomorrow's breakfast. Please have Rebecca prepare it in the sun-room but not too early." He grins and smiles wide. I blush.

So does Colin before he clears his throat and holds back a smirk.

He bows toward me. "I hope your first night as man and wife is everything you hope. We shall see you in the morning. I will take my leave."

"Thank you, Colin. Everything is perfect. Please share my thanks with the missus."

He nods and walks out.

Instead of eating, I hop up and rush over to the table with a cake on it. Chase laughs at my enthusiasm but comes up to hold me from behind. A small two-tiered cake sits on the table. It's white with intricate swirls and Celtic symbols weaving through it. At the very top sits a ceramic heart with two hands holding it with a crown on top.

"It's a claddagh." I touch the cool ceramic.

Chase holds me close. "What does it mean?"

I grip his arms around my waist, pressing into his front. "It's a traditional Irish symbol. It represents love, loyalty, and friendship. The hands are meant to represent our friendship, the heart our love, and the crown represents our unending loyalty to one another.

"Then it's perfect."

I turn in his arms and hug him close. "It is. Everything about today is perfect. Thank you for giving me my dream wedding. And all of this, I couldn't imagine better."

He kisses my forehead and then my lips softly. "Me either. Now let's eat. You're going to need your strength."

I grin, and he leads me back to the table. The steak is

mouthwatering tender, the potatoes seasoned to perfection, and the veggies crisp and delicious dipped into the special glaze Colin's wife made. "This is the best meal I've ever had."

Chase chews and nods. He takes a long swallow of his champagne. "It is. Maybe we can get Colin and Rebecca to come back to San Francisco with us."

My eyes widen and my mouth drops open. "You'd get rid of Bentley?"

Chase laughs and sits back in his chair. "No, but I'd love to challenge him."

I shake my head, and we spend our dinner chitchatting about our wedding, the church, the town, and how beautiful it is here.

Every so often I see Chase spinning the ring around his finger with his thumb.

"Does it make you uncomfortable to wear a ring?" I ask, sipping the yummiest bubbly in the world. As a matter of fact, it's making me a wee bit tipsy.

"Not even a little. Surprisingly, I like its weight there. Knowing I'm married to you—it's very grounding."

Not being able to be away from him anymore, I stand and make my way to his side of the table and plop into his lap.

"Was that seat no longer working for you?" He leans forward and starts to lay kisses all over my neck.

"This one is far more comfortable." I press my fingers into the layers of his hair at the back of his head. His mouth trails down my neck to where my breasts are pushing up at the sweetheart neckline of my gown.

Chase groans against my breasts. "You know, Gillian,

when you entered that chapel, I about swallowed my tongue. Seeing you in this dress, willingly walking toward me, choosing me as your husband..." He shakes his head and bites down on my breast. In response, a moan slips from my lips. "I'll never know anything more enchanting than you. Baby, you have the power to destroy me."

With those words, I slant my mouth over his and take him in a deep kiss. Our tongues slip and slide against one another until Chase stands. He turns me around, sweeps aside my long hair, and unbuttons the two buttons holding the lace together at the top of my neck. The dress delicately sweeps down my curves into a puddle on the floor. I step out of it. Chase instantly picks it up and lays it over the chair I sat in while we ate.

I turn around and stand there, clad only in a pair of lace panties that curve around the edge of my hips and cut in deep along my ass. His eyes blaze with heat and hunger. My nipples become ridged and erect as the cool breeze of the ocean air tickles my bare skin.

Chase's nostrils flare, and he sucks in a harsh breath. In what seems like the speed of light, he removes his tux jacket and bowtie. His belt is the next to go. I just stand watching him disrobe. It's the most fascinating and thrilling experience to be standing almost completely naked while the man of every single one of my deepest fantasies removes his clothes. His pants open, and I can see his cock stretching the fabric. Then he moves to the top of his dress shirt and undoes each button. I watch, rapt with attention to this normally mundane task that has turned into one of the most lust-inducing performances I have ever seen.

When his shirt is completely undone, he opens it,

revealing the hard slabs of thick muscle. His abdomen flexes and moves, making me want to lick every inch of his exposed skin, and I plan to. He's my husband now, and I can do whatever I want.

"I like the sound of that, baby," he growls, and it dawns on me that I said that last part out loud. "Like hearing you call me your husband."

I grin and slip my fingers into the sides of my flimsy panties, about to push them down, when he stops me.

"Don't. I want to remove my wife's panties." His eyes burn with a desire so bright he could blind me.

His pants and boxer briefs drop to the floor in a heap. He kicks them to the side, not taking the care he took with my dress. We stand looking at one another—just looking, appreciating the raw desire filling the space around us.

"I'll never know beauty like you," he whispers, and it sounds like a prayer.

"Yes, you will. You see it when you look in the mirror every day," I quip, wanting him to know that I find him just as breathtaking.

As if he's moving in slow motion, he approaches me. When he gets close, one hand grasps the nape of my neck and the other my hip, and that's when he slams our bodies together. He takes my mouth in a savage kiss—all lips, teeth, and tongue. He sucks my lips and tongue into his mouth over and over, driving me insane with his carnal need to claim me.

"Need to love you hard this first time. Want you lost in me...in us."

I groan pulling my lips from his. "Yes. I want you, everything you have to give. It's mine now."

He growls and leads me to the bed where I fly into a cloud of soft pillows. He lifts my legs, opens them wide, and then his mouth is over the skimpy fabric of my panties. Licking me over the fabric, rubbing the texture against my clit. "Gonna soak these panties in us, and then I'm going to take them off you and keep them with me. So that anytime I want, I can smell your sweet pussy from our wedding night."

"Jesus, Chase, the things you say…" I gasp when he bites down on my clit through the fabric, and I'm so wound up that's all it takes. I grip his hair in my hands and ride his face through my first orgasm. He doesn't stop, biting and licking, destroying me with every pass at my sex until my orgasm settles. Like he promised moments ago, he pulls off the panties and sets them on the table near the bed.

"Saving those," he says before he places his mouth over my sex again and spears his tongue deep into my cleft. I jerk my hips up, but he holds them down. "Fuck! Your cream is so fucking good. Delicious. And. All. Fucking. Mine." He holds my legs wide, using his thumbs to splay the petals of my center wider to accommodate him. I look down just as he presses his tongue deep and starts up this flicking motion inside me. It sends shivers of ecstasy rippling along the surface of my skin to the point that I'm panting.

The pleasure is coming to the surface again. "Chase, baby, need you inside. I'm gonna come again."

CHASE

CHAPTER THIRTEEN

"Chase, baby, need you inside. I'm gonna come again."

Her voice sounds almost pained. I like that more than I'll ever admit. Knowing my woman needs my cock in her—there's something that digs deep into the roots of my manhood. Like a calling that only I can fill.

I push her up the bed and bring her knees up high and wide. "Does my wife need my cock?"

She moans and her head flies from side to side. "Chase…" she pleads, and it's the prettiest sound in the world.

"Say it. Say you need your husband's cock. Tell me how hard you want me to take you," I growl and press just the tip of my dick to her clit, rolling my hips to give it a nice twirl.

She gasps and lifts her hips for more. "I want…" She loses momentum, focusing on my dick pressing against her clit.

"Oh, no, you don't," I chastise and place just the crown of my cock into the tight heat of her pussy. "Tell me what you want. I need to hear it."

"I-I want my husband to make love to me."

Those words, though they aren't what I asked her to say, are far more honest than I could have hoped for. I push her legs back farther, into her chest toward her underarms, holding her behind the knees, center my cock, and enter her very slowly. The walls of her pussy cling to my dick as I glide in. When I'm balls deep, I stir my hips, and her eyes fly open, meeting mine. They are greener than the rolling hills of our Bantry estate.

Pulling back, I come almost all the way out of her. She closes her eyes in bliss and opens them again. Her mouth opens on a gasp when I slam home. This—making love to my wife—this is our home. When we're joined, it doesn't matter where we are because as long as it's the two of us, we'll always be in the right place.

"I love you, Gillian Davis," I say, closing my eyes and hammering into her over and over. She takes it. Hard. Soft. She always allows me to set the pace and take love from her body any way I need it.

I grip her legs, pull them around my waist, and lift her up. She hooks her feet behind my back, and I hold her around the back of her neck, cupping her head so I can kiss and plunge my tongue deep into her mouth. She moans, probably tasting herself. That always drives her lust to another height. Removing my hand from her head, I grip her waist. I curl the other arm up her back and cup her shoulder, clamping her to me in an upright seated position. She's hung up on my cock, and when I heft her up and slam her back down, she cries out, her pussy clamping around my cock like a vise.

"Fuck," she swears, and that riles me up even more. My wife rarely swears, and hearing it come out of her mouth means she's losing control. She's becoming lost in us. Exactly what I want.

I slide her up my cock and then lift my hips at the same time I haul her down on me.

"So hard," she gasps. "So full...I can't." She clings to my shoulders, and I lean her back a bit, clamping my mouth around her turgid nipple and biting down. Her pussy becomes impossibly wetter, gushing as I suck long and hard from her sweet tip. "Chase," she warns with a little mewl, her body shaking with the effort to find release.

I lean her back down on the bed and cover her body with mine, intertwining our fingers together next to her head as I thrust deep with my cock and my tongue.

When I pull back, her eyes are open, glazed, and teary. "My Chase, my love, my husband." A tear slips down her cheek, and I kiss it away, loving the taste of her happiness.

"My Gillian, my love, my wife," I repeat her words, only geared toward her, clench her fingers tight, and with everything I have, I take my woman and myself over the edge in slow even thrusts. It isn't hard and fast, like I thought we needed. No, it is slow and beautiful. Making love to my wife on our wedding night is the single best sexual experience of my life. And I tell her so.

★ ★ ★ ★

Once I clean her up, I hand her a silk cream-colored nightgown that comes to the middle of her thighs and a robe I have hanging on a rack in the corner of the tent. I slide on a pair of matching pajama pants.

"Matching?" she says with a hint of a smug smile. She's figured out that I like us looking united in all things, even if it's bed clothing.

"Got a problem with that?" I quirk my eyebrows up into a point. The one that dares her to say anything more about it.

She shakes her head. "Nope, I like it." She pulls on the nightie and robe and then comes over and gives me a hug. "You realize you just rocked my world, right?"

I lick my lips, still tasting her on my tongue. "Plan to for the rest of your life, baby."

She graces me with her sweet smile and then walks over to the cake. "Want to cut the cake and have more champagne in bed?" Her eyes light up as if she's just seen the eighth wonder of the world.

"Absolutely."

Sitting next to the stereo, I spy the camera. I grab it up and take a picture of our wedding cake, knowing this is something she'll want to capture. Then I turn it on her and take a bunch of pictures.

"Chase!" she scolds and stomps her little foot. "I've got sex hair!"

I look around the camera. "I know." I grin and hold it back up to her stunningly gorgeous face. She's backlit by the ocean behind her. That red hair of hers is indeed looking very mussed and extremely sexy. Finally, she lets out a breath, looks at me, and smirks. That's the picture I'll be printing and putting on my desk back at Davis Industries. I want to see that look on her face every day.

"Okay, so traditionally, we cut the cake together and then serve it to one another."

I grab the knife and hand it to her. She holds it, I cover her hand, and together we cut our wedding cake. She cuts a giant piece, one I know she couldn't possibly eat herself, but

I don't say anything. I'll finish whatever she doesn't.

Once she's got the cake on a plate, she cuts two small squares and picks one up. "Now you grab yours. And don't smash my face with it."

I think about it for a minute and then decide against rubbing it all over her face, mostly because I've got a better idea.

We take a bite from each other's fingers, and the burst of lemon and vanilla is scrumptious against the palate. "That's really good," she mumbles around another bite. I still have the sticky confection on my fingers. With my other hand, I pull her close, undo her robe, and let it fall to the floor. "I just got that on," she pouts.

With one finger, I press down the shoulder strap of one side. Her large breast comes into view, and I wipe the remaining frosting from my fingers to her breast. She gasps when I lean forward and lick the sugary taste off her voluptuous tip. It tightens and elongates under the force of my suction.

I pull back and lick my lips, slip her strap back up, and look into her lusty gaze. "It's better on you."

Her head tilts to the side. "Really?" she says and sticks her finger in the frosting, pulls back a dollop, and smears it onto my nipple. Then she comes forward, brings her pink tongue over my flesh, and goes to town. She sucks hard, making sure she licks all around the flat disk. I groan, holding her to me. She moves back, dunks her finger in the frosting again, and spreads it on my other nipple, repeating the action. Within seconds, my dick is hard, pressing into the satiny fabric between us.

Again, she gets a large amount of frosting, but this time

she doesn't put it on my chest. No, she drops to her knees, tugs down my pants, and smears the white frosting all over the top of my dick. Before I can respond, her mouth is surrounding me and my hands are in her hair. She takes her time, licking off the frosting, swirling her tongue around the tip before taking me deep. Rivers of pleasure rip through my shaft, up my pelvis, spreading low in my back. It curls there, the desire, the need to fuck her.

I place my hands in her hair and grip tight at the base, pulling against the roots. She's sucking so hard I have no choice but to thrust down her constrictive throat. Somehow she tips her head a certain way, relaxes her jaw, and then I'm there, all the way down her throat. Quickly, I pull back, and she protests with a whimper. I shove my dick back down her throat, and she swallows. That muscle squeezes the crown of my sensitive dick so hard I can feel my balls getting hard and high, ready to shoot my release. "Baby, I'm going to come down your pretty throat. You suck me too good, make me weak."

Gillian moans around my cock and pulls against my hips. That's her sign that she wants me to fuck her face. Gripping her head with both hands I begin a steady rhythm, of pressing deep into her throat, pulling back, letting her get used to it. She swallows every time I get to the end, and I'm losing it, her mouth is too soft, too hot, too exceptionally tight for words.

"Fuck." I thrust deep. "Woman"—thrust—"you"— thrust—"own"—thrust—"me." I hold my cock deep into her throat as my cum spills into her mouth. I pump in large spurts over and over until I'm shuddering with the effort to remain standing. Gillian swallows all of me, pulls back, and licks my softening dick clean.

"You're right. The cake does taste even better paired with you." Her innocent eyes are sparkling as I haul her back up into my arms and take her mouth.

Finally, I pull back, needing to catch my breath. "Christ, woman, you'll be the end of me."

"I hope not for another seventy years. Now can we cuddle in bed with our wedding cake?" She licks her lips, and it makes my dick twitch. I lean down, pull up my pants, and hand her the giant piece.

"That for us both?"

She looks down at the large piece, her eyebrows coming together. "Does it have to be?"

Her sweet grin is my undoing. I tip my head back, laugh, and cut myself a large hunk of cake, refill our champagne glasses, and get back into bed with my wife.

We spend an hour talking about nothing and everything at the same time, eating cake, kissing, touching, enjoying one another.

When night falls, I make love to her to the sound of the ocean waves crashing against the cliffs. Then, I wrap her body and take her to our official bedroom within the house, as it will get far too cold to sleep out here even wrapped around one another. She doesn't move as I walk the lit path.

Colin is waiting at the door, holding it open.

"Everything okay, sir?"

I look down at the most precious gift I've ever known. "Everything's perfect, Colin. Thank you. I'm taking my wife to bed. We'll be down late morning."

He closes the door, and I carry my cargo to our room and place her in the center of our bed. I unwrap her naked body like a present. I can see the imprints of my teeth along the plush surface of her breasts, the red rubbing along her thighs where my stubble grazed along her creamy flesh. She has told me before how she loves to see the marks from our lovemaking on her, and in this moment, I can't agree more. They are only on the surface and given with extreme pleasure and adoration. Just like the streaks from her nails I feel marring my back and the hickey she sucked into the indent at my hip. Her favorite spot.

Slowly, I get her under the blankets. She sighs dreamily and whispers "Love Chase," in her sleep. I curve my naked body around hers from behind, push one of her legs forward so I can wedge my own between it, and curl my arm through hers and encase one of her large breasts. I squeeze, and she moans. Even in sleep she wants me. Boggles the mind.

"Today was the best day of my life," I whisper into her ear.

She hums and says, "Love Chase."

I chuckle into her hair and close my eyes. With my wife locked into the safety of my arms, I can finally rest.

"Where are we going?" Chase asks while holding my hand in the back of the limo.

I smile and lean into his side. "You'll see. I told you, it's a surprise."

He brings my hand to his lips, presses a kiss against the top, and sets it down on his thigh. It takes about thirty minutes to get to our destination, and when we get out of the car, Chase looks at the sign and then back at me. Above a bright yellow Cash Express is a building marked Raven Tattoo Studio right in the heart of Cork, Ireland.

"Am I missing something? You want to send money to someone?" His dark hair blows in the breeze, making my fingers itch to run through the strands. He lifts up his aviators. The blue of his eyes startles me, and I momentarily lose my train of thought.

"Um, no, actually, see the sign above, on the second floor?" I point at the white, red, and black logo in swirling letters.

Chase takes a breath. "You've got to be kidding me."

I grin wide and tug on his hand. "Nope. Not at all."

"Baby, you don't need to mark this pearly skin. I love it just the way it is." He rubs his thumb over my bare shoulder. I wore a tank top so it would be easy for what I have planned.

Without responding, I grip his hand, open the door, and walk up the stairs. A petite woman with purple spiked hair and more rings in her face than I thought would be possible greets us. If she didn't have that jewelry hiding her features, she'd be a really beautiful woman. As it stands, she's still pretty and probably a knockout to a man who likes that type of flair.

"I have an appointment with Raven. My name is Gillian Davis," I say matter-of-factly, and Chase grips me from behind nuzzling into my neck.

"Love hearing your new name, baby. Makes me hard all over again." He presses the sizable proof of his statement into the crack of my ass. I can feel the heat of his meaty length through my jeans, and it makes me wet. I press back quickly, giving him a shove back so he'll get the hint. He totally doesn't get it.

"Not now," I warn, and he chuckles as I scan the space to see if anyone can see what he's doing. Jack has followed us into the tattoo parlor but has not said a word. He looks out the window, scans the area, basically presenting a menacing front to anyone who dares look his way.

A large hunk of a man enters from a back room. His hair is dark as night and curly, reminding me of Maria's ebony waves. He's tall, taller even than Chase, and that's flippin' tall. Guy's at least six foot four or five. His eyes are as black as his hair and shoot right through me. I shudder at the intense gaze. Within less than a second, Chase is sliding an arm around my waist and claiming his woman in front of this godlike man. There's muscle upon muscle visible through the thin cotton of his white T-shirt that would make any woman openly drool.

"You Gillian?" the man asks with a grumble that reaches through my chest and spirals right down to curl my toes. Damn, this guy is crazy hot. Not as hot as my husband, but he's a fine second.

Chase steps forward. "This is Mrs. Davis." He holds out a hand. "I'm her husband."

"Raven." He holds out a strong hand. A hand that is surprisingly free of any ink. Makes me wonder where all his tattoos are.

"Well, apparently my wife made an appointment with you. Though I'm not sure why."

"What we talked about on the phone?" His eyes sparkle when he addresses me, and I nod.

Raven's gaze goes to Chase's, which is icy steel as he clutches my hip possessively. Raven grins. "I see. Hey, man, if I had a wife who looked like her, I wouldn't have been married and divorced twice already."

That bit of unwarranted personal information, however, does not make Chase loosen his grip. "Are you certain you want to go through with this?" Chase asks me.

I nod quickly. "Can't wait." I bounce on my wedges and give him a luxurious kiss. He takes the opportunity to palm my ass, grinding his now softening erection into my pelvis. I push away. "Okay, I'll be back."

"Should only take twenty minutes. Come on, beautiful." He gestures to me, and Chase positively growls.

"I'm going with you." His jaw is locked tight, and the muscle I love so much is ticking away like a time bomb.

I stop mid-stride and turn around on a toe, my hair flying behind me. "No! It's my gift to you. I want to surprise you with it." I catch his gaze with my pleading one.

He speaks through clenched teeth, "Tell me you're not taking off your pants or even unbuttoning a single button."

I cross my heart for his benefit. "I swear."

"And you're keeping your shirt on." His tone is a low warning.

"Um, completely on, yes." I smile and he groans.

"Gillian, I will not have another man's eyes or hands on my wife." He grips my hips, fingers digging in. Usually this move excites me. Now, it's positively annoying.

Taking both his cheeks in my hands, I lean very close. "Trust me."

He closes his eyes and takes a breath. "Jack," he says on a growl, "go with her."

I cringe and open my mouth to dispute it. He places two fingers over my mouth. "It's my only compromise.

Anything else, nonnegotiable."

Grinding down on the back of my teeth, I look into his blue eyes and see that they are pure white-hot fire. He's not happy about this idea. I can only hope he's happy with the end product. "Okay, deal."

He doesn't even smile, just dips his chin tightly.

"Come on, sweet cheeks, I've not got all day."

"Dude, do you have a death wish?" I ask, turning around and looking at him but find that Jack has the man up against the wall his hand locked around Raven's throat.

"Jesus Christ, let him go, Jack!" I scream.

Jack speaks directly into the man's face, only a scant couple inches away. His voice is low and his tone deadly as his words lay out a true warning. "You do not speak of Mrs. Davis in that manner. You will respect her and give her the tattoo she wants as quickly as possible so we may take our leave. You will be paid four times the price to keep your eyes on the design and not on her body. Got me?"

Raven nods with the little space Jack allows between the vise grip he has on the man's neck.

"I'm glad we understand each other." Jack lets Raven go, and he slumps back against the wall. Jack readjusts his jacket, clearly making the gun holster he wears visible to the artist. As suspected, Raven's eyes widen, he adjusts himself to full height, and gestures to the back.

"Come on, Mrs. Davis."

I walk back to the room and look over my shoulder. Chase is already pacing the floor, clearly mumbling to himself.

"Go on and lie down on the table and show me where you want it. I've got everything ready," Raven says.

I lie down and pull up my tank top, folding the fabric over my breasts. You can probably see the bottom of my lace bra and that's it. Jack looks at me and scowls. I point to my ribs just under my breast on the same side as my heart. "Right here."

Raven places a piece of paper over that spot, presses down, and then methodically removes it. He hands me a mirror. I hold it up and look down to see the transfer of the ink on my skin. "It's perfect. Let's do it."

He grabs a seat and his tattoo needle and gets to work. The minute the needle touches down on my sensitive skin I brace, grit my teeth, and wait for the moment the slight pinch of pain turns into euphoria. It doesn't take long. I felt the same thing when I got my Trinity tattoo on my wrist with the girls. They all thought I'd be the wimp, but it turns out, I barely flinched. The color actually hurt worse than the black outline but for this one, it's all black.

The buzzing lulls me into a hyperalert state. Raven is actually really professional. He's focused one hundred percent on the design and not on my bare midriff or the lace and satin of my undergarment. At one point, his black gaze lifts and he catches mine. "You good?"

I nod. Jack hovers at the end of the bed, watching every move Raven makes as if he's my overbearing father instead of a hired bodyguard. I can only imagine how Chase is doing out in the waiting area. The thought makes me chuckle, and Raven's eyes widen and his brows rise. "Something funny?"

"I'm just thinking about how much my husband is freaking out right now." I glance at Jack, and he's still wearing a frown, only the corners tip up a bit like he's forcing himself not to smile.

Raven laughs. "Yeah, I've seen protective men, but he takes the cake. Hiring you a bodyguard." He gestures over to Jack. "You two got married yesterday?" he asks while digging deep into the portion that cuts across my rib. I wince momentarily and take a breath. "Okay?"

"Yeah, thanks. We were supposed to get married a month ago, but some unfortunate things got in the way. We eloped and got married at Gougane Barra Church, the little one by the lake. It was magical." I think back to Chase spinning me around, my dress flowing in the breeze after we pledged our love to one another.

"Gougane Barra Church?" He whistles. "That must have set him back quiet a penny. It's a historical site now. I'm pretty sure they don't usually allow people to marry in it."

I smile and flinch again at a particularly painful spot. "My husband is comfortable monetarily."

He glances at the bodyguard and then back and me with a grin. "I kind of gathered that. You two heading back to the States soon?"

"I hope not. We bought a home in Bantry and plan to spend our honeymoon here for a while. Then we'll head back to San Francisco."

"Never been." Raven shrugs.

"To San Francisco?"

He shakes his head. "Nah, to the States, though one day I hope to get around to it."

"You should. We have a lot of beauty in our lands too."

Raven wipes my skin with a cool cloth. It grates along the freshly tattooed area. He hands me the mirror again. I look down at my skin and see it's exactly what I wanted. I just know Chase is going to love it, seeing his mark on me, knowing it's for him. I can't wait to show him! "I love it!"

The artist wipes some type of gel on the wound and gives me the rundown for keeping it clean and dry. I've heard it before.

When we're done, Chase jumps up from his seat and looks me all over. "Well? Where is it?"

I turn my back from the men as Jack sidles up to the cash register to pay Raven. I watch Chase's eyes as I lift my shirt, peel back the bandage, and watch his eyes change color.

He drops to his knees in front of me, his eyes glued to the tattoo. "That's the most perfect wedding present you could have ever given me."

I smile wide and watch as he looks at the symbol I've permanently placed on my body for him.

He traces the design over the clear plastic bandage with one finger, and I close my eyes.

CHASE

CHAPTER FOURTEEN

When Gillian lifted up her shirt earlier today and showed me the infinity symbol with the word love intertwined, I about took her on the floor of that tattoo parlor. Knowing that she put that on her body permanently for *me*, giving me a gift that will last through the end of time… It makes me want to worship the ground she walks on. Good God, my wife makes me insane in all the right ways, not excluding mentally, physically, and emotionally.

After her kidnapping and my mother's murder, I thought nothing could heal that wound, but having her near, officially with me as my *wife,* is stitching the very heart of me back together. Making me something that I wasn't before, but somehow better. Gillian makes me want to be a better man—a good man, one she can be proud to call her husband.

Husband.

I'm someone's husband. I shake my head and chuckle as we enter the Bantry home. Gillian turns, looking over her shoulder, her hair a wild mess of red curls down her back, the smile she's wearing so pretty it could light up a dark day.

"What?" Her eyes are an intense green and swimming with curiosity.

I shake my head and press her into the room with a light touch to her lower back. Colin approaches, a grim set to his features. "Colin, something the matter?" I ask.

"I'm afraid there is, sir. Have you checked your cell phones?"

I tap my pockets and shrug. "On my honeymoon, my good man, the phone is off." I grin and pull Gillian into my arms, snuggling her from behind.

Colin frowns. "I suggest you turn them on. There has been news from the States that I'm certain you'll want to hear."

Jack enters with our bags from our shopping excursion after the tattoo parlor. Gillian and I wanted to add things to the Bantry home to make it our own. We found several knick-knacks and pieces of art to add to the already beautiful décor. It was important to her to choose these items together. She says they give the place a more lived in and loved feel to us each time we visit.

"Colin, what is it?"

He glances around the room. "Shall we go into a more private location?" he asks, waiting for me to decide if I want him to speak in front of Gillian and Jack.

"No need. Answer my question." My tone is bordering on annoyed, which does not bode well for the evening I had planned with my lovely new wife.

The frown he's sporting deepens. "An Agent Brennen called from the Federal Bureau of Investigation. Unfortunately, I have to be the bearer of some very unfortunate news. It seems two members of Mrs. Davis's family have been harmed in a fire." Colin holds his hands in front of him and bows his head respectfully.

Gillian's hand comes to her mouth. "What? Oh my God, who?" Her eyes instantly fill with terror.

"The gentleman didn't say—he just left the note to call." Colin looks to Gillian. "I'm sorry, ma'am.

As Gillian's hands start to shake, I can already hear Jack on the phone. "Brennen, Porter here. What's happened?"

Gillian sits on the couch and holds her hands near her face, her fingers clasped. She sits with her eyes closed and moves her lips. I sit next to her and hold her close as we wait to hear what Jack learns. "It's going to be okay, baby. We'll handle this together." She starts rocking, and her fingers whiten from the strain of holding them in such a firm grip.

"We'll be on the next plane out," Jack growls into the phone. "You should have called me, Brennan. I understand. We're on our way."

Jack comes over to the two of us sitting on the couch and sits down on the table directly in front of us. Gillian's eyes are wide, filled with fear as she looks up to hear the news.

He clears his throat before speaking. "Gillian, your two friends, Maria and Kathleen—"

Gillian instantly lets out a sob at hearing their names. I pull her closer.

"They were in a fire. The two of them were working late at the San Francisco Theatre when the blaze happened. Maria is being treated for wounds around her midsection and smoke inhalation. She's going to be just fine. Absolutely okay."

The way he stresses how Maria is going to be okay and not Kathleen sends an icy river of fear down my spine. Gillian holds my hands tight.

"And Kat?" Her voice shakes as the tears over take her.

Jack sucks in a breath and does something I'd never expect him to do in a million years. He reaches out a hand and clasps her knee. Her face crumbles, and a sob escapes at the comforting gesture. "Kathleen is in serious condition. She sustained considerable burns over fifteen percent of her body as well as extreme exposure to smoke. That's all we know at this time.

"What happened?" I ask while attempting to comfort my wife.

"It looks like arson. Someone set it up so Kathleen would die in the fire."

Gillian whimpers and I cut my eyes at Jack. His eyes narrow in response, but he continues undeterred.

"The only reason she didn't is because Maria was ruthless. Once she got out of the front of the building she went around to the back and kicked at the small window near Kat's office. The guard I had on her helped, and she entered the small space, pulled Kat out. But not without getting harmed herself. Her injuries, however, are superficial, whereas Kathleen..." He shakes his head. "I'm sure you want to get home right away. I'll call for one of the planes."

Gillian stands. "Let's just go. Take whatever flights out are next."

I look at my wife's tortured face, and the anger within simmers deep, curling and curving around my ribs up my chest to awaken a monster I haven't met yet. That motherfucker did this to get to my wife. He will pay for every inch of pain he has caused Gillian and her friends. I'll see to it or die trying.

We find out that the private jet we took here can be

ready within the hour. Gillian and I go to our room. When we get there, she gasps. Hanging directly over our bed is the trinity tapestry she purchased from the little old lady she met and who incidentally attended our wedding unannounced.

My wife walks over to the large tapestry and fingers the fabric. "It's perfect."

"It is, and we'll come back and enjoy it very soon. I promise you. This is our home away from home. We can bring all your friends here to vacation together. Just as soon as this is over. And it will be over soon." I place my hand on her shoulder as she stares at the intricate design. On a sob, she twirls around and cowers into my chest, her shoulders heaving with her grief.

"I wasn't there. If I had been there, maybe he would have gone for me and not them." She cries out as if she is in physical pain. Sometimes the emotional strain is far more painful than the physical. I know that all too well after spending years seeing my mother beaten to a bloody pulp until my father took his hand to me.

I shake my head and pet her hair. "Baby, no. This man is sick. It doesn't matter. He's going to strike wherever he wants to strike. There is no possible way to know what he's going to do next, but we're working with the FBI and the San Francisco PD. I'm certain when they go through this fire investigation, they'll come up with something. A lead. In the meantime, we're working on a plan. Okay? Let's just focus on getting home and checking on the girls."

Gillian nods, sniffing loudly, her tears running so quickly down her cheeks it's as if they were two identical waterfalls. I hand her the handkerchief in my pocket and she wipes her nose noisily against it. Then she sucks in a long, slow breath, bringing her body back in control and pushing her emotions to the wayside. It's amazing to watch how she slowly puts herself back together. With effort, she straightens her spine, breathes deep, clears her throat, and tilts her head. "Okay, let's go."

We gather up a change of clothes, our phones, which had been off and left on the nightstand, and are now are flaring with a large numbers of notifications. It's as if each ding is another spike into Gillian's bleeding heart. It's going to take mammoth effort to keep her together.

Soon we've said our good-byes to Colin and Rebecca with our apologies and promise to return soon.

★ ★ ★ ★

The plane touches down at SFO International after an eleven-hour flight. That did not include the drive to the airport, getting through the airport, and the taxiing time. Overall, the trip has been a good sixteen hours, and I for one am drained. Gillian finally fell asleep after taking a couple sleeping pills. I stayed up most of the flight, working with Jack and the additional guards on a plan. We'll need to talk to Agent Brennen and Thomas Redding, but we think it's a good one. None of us can continue to live like this—always on edge, waiting for the next person to get hurt. McBride is too intelligent. He seems to be a step ahead of the team. Our plan, however, is designed to draw him out of the shadows. The three of us agree that it's foolproof. It has to work. No more waiting. This time next week, McBride will be ours.

Jack drops us in front of San Francisco General Hospital,

a building I now know all too well. It's sickening that I've been to this hospital more in the past year than I've been to a grocery store or a library. I know too many of the hospital staff by first name, and it fills me with a sour seed that's setting roots in my gut.

Gillian rushes to Intensive care, not even needing to look at the directory or the signs. She also knows this place well.

When the elevator doors open, we can see a crowd of people at the end of the hall, the easiest to recognize is the six-month pregnant woman who's pacing the floor, hand to her lower back. Carson, Phillip, and Thomas are sitting in a line of chairs opposite her, pacing. It's as if time stops when she looks up. Her pretty face with the big blue eyes and soft features seems to disintegrate into a massive ball of devastation. Gillian runs to her, pulls her into her arms, and holds her close.

"I'm sorry I wasn't here," she cries into Bree's neck.

Bree's long blond waves cover them like a shroud. She speaks softly to my wife, their foreheads pressed together. Both of them cry, hug, and hold one another.

"When can I see them?"

Bree shakes her head. "They haven't let any of us see either of them, but supposedly they'll let us see Maria very soon."

"Excuse me?" I ask, my voice a heavy timbre in the otherwise quiet space.

Bree sniffs and pushes her hair back. "They aren't telling us anything about Kat, but I guilted one of the nurses who's a client of mine. They said we couldn't see her because of something about her being too serious and the potential for contamination. All we know is that she's stable, for now, but she's undergoing serious burn treatment." The tears rush down Bree's face, and she hiccups. "They said…they said…she was going to need a lot of surgeries to repair the damage to her arm and that she may not…" She chokes, and Phillip stands next to her, holding her in his arms, running a soothing hand up and down her back. He calms her down enough that she can finish. Gillian locks her arms around me. "They said she may not ever be able to use that arm again. She's going to have severe nerve damage, and the scarring…" She shakes her head. "Please, God, let her be okay." Bree crumbles into a fit of sobs as Phillip holds her, leads her to a chair, and scoops her into his lap.

With as much patience as I can, I take hold of my girl and maneuver Gillian into a seat, lock my arm around her shoulder, and keep her pressed into my side where she belongs. She leans heavily against me and silently lets the tears fall.

Across from Gillian, I lock eyes with Carson. He looks shattered, half-dead, and from what I gather, hasn't been able to see his woman. The turmoil pumping off him is thick and ripe with fury. I nod in his direction, and he shakes his head. His position and those blue eyes devoid of anything speak for him. He might as well have a sign around his neck that says "Back off." I won't approach, not right now. Now we wait.

After an hour of sitting, Dr. Dutera enters the waiting room. Man, this guy has had far too much time with our group of friends. His eyes widen when he sees Gillian and me.

"Thought this group was familiar," the doctor grumbles.

"Need an update. How are Maria De La Torre and Kathleen Bennett?" I ask.

The doctor frowns. "Mr. Davis, you are not direct kin of either of these women."

"No, but I'm listed as the direct medical contact for both of them, as Kathleen's parents are separated and live in other states, which obviously"—Gillian makes a point to look around the room with her hands out wide before continuing—"they haven't been contacted. Maria doesn't have any family but me," she continues.

The doctor's eyes assess the validity of her statement, and he must believe it because he finally gives us the rundown.

"Ms. De La Torre has been moved to a regular room. She was treated for slight carbon monoxide poisoning and several surface wounds on her abdomen and feet."

"Her feet?" I ask.

"Apparently she kicked at some wooden beams and glass with bare feet to get your friend out," the doctor confirms.

Now that, I believe. That Italian Spanish fireball would do anything to save her friends.

Then Dr. Dutera's look turns somber, and I know he's about to give us bad news. "Ms. Bennett didn't fare as well. She's being treated for severe smoke inhalation, a collapsed lung, and third-degree burns over her left arm, side of her neck, and down her left side ribcage. All layers of the skin in those areas have been destroyed. The damage extends into the subcutaneous tissues, and she'll need grafting in order to heal. Right now we've managed the lung, gotten her stable, and are dealing with the poisoning. She is on one hundred percent oxygen, is heavily sedated, and will undergo many rounds of hyperbaric oxygen therapy until her levels have come back to something resembling normal. She is not out of the woods. We will take her prognosis one day at a time."

"Can we see her?" Gillian looks at Carson and waves him over. She clasps his hand. "This is her boyfriend, and we're her best friends." She loops her arm around Bree's waist. "We have to see her with our own eyes. Make sure she's okay."

Dr. Dutera lets out a pained noise and a loud breath. "We'll take each of you one at a time."

As much as I can tell Gillian wants to go first, she allows Carson the honor.

I pull her into my side. "That took a lot for you to let Carson go first, baby. I'm sure he appreciates it."

She nods into my side and holds on. The tears are over, but they are close enough to the surface that anything, even the wind blowing the wrong way, could bring them on again.

X

Not dead. Of course those stupid little bitches would survive. Luck is a cold-hearted bitch, and I've fucked her too many times to catch a break. Doesn't matter though. The dancer and the hippie being unconscious up in the hospital brings the one thing I need back into my sights.

Gillian.

I watch with extreme pleasure as she enters the hospital. Felt like for-fucking-ever. She must have been really far away to take most of a full day to arrive. I wonder where the bastard took her. As far as I could tell from the security logs, they were only gone three days.

Using the same path I took the last time I was here, I weave through the hospital staff, my scrubs in place, a cap, a pair of fake glasses, and a stethoscope I got at a pawnshop around my neck. This getup works so well I could just as easily be invisible.

Making my way to the Intensive Care Unit, I take precautions to move at a smooth interval until I can see the group. One bright star of shiny red hair is present amongst them. Fuck, she's beautiful. My body gravitates toward her. I need to be closer.

I've investigated every inch of this floor, and I know that near where they are is a supply closet. I head straight there, open the door, and enter without anyone really noticing. Keeping the room dark, I prop open the door just a half-inch so that I can hear what they're saying, but mostly so I can see her. If I could only take hold of her arm, feel her smooth skin along the palm of my hand, the rage within would simmer to a more bearable level. Right now, I can hardly control the intensity, the need to get to her, take her, claim her for my own.

As I watch, I bite down on my lip, disgusted by how he's holding my girl close, rubbing her shoulder. It should be me comforting her. Only me. Forever me.

That pregnant cunt sits near my girl, and Gillian lays a hand on her belly. Her engagement ring to the fucker is still there, sparkling so bright I swear the thing is burning a fucking hole into my retina. Piece of shit. Had to buy her a showy-ass diamond ring, one that when she swelled up from the heat, I couldn't rip it off her finger. I got his necklace though. I took that symbol, ran a chain around it, and put it around my own neck. His failure, my gain. With my thumb and forefinger, I bring it out and rub it between the pads of my fingertips. It was on *her,* so I feel close to her when wearing it, but I know he gave it to her. Just the look in her eyes was enough when I touched it that first day she woke up in the storm cellar.

Gillian makes a surprised face and squeals in delight. "Baby, feel this." She grabs Chase's left hand and places it on the fat cunt's stomach. He moves his hand into the right spot, and that's when I notice it.

The room I'm in seems to get darker, my vision zeroing in on a small point on Chase's hand. Sweat trickles around the hair at my nape and slides down the center of my back. As I look, it becomes clearer.

No! Fucking no! I want to scream. I want to take out a gun and shoot every last one of them. I grit my teeth together and pull my fists into my sides.

Feel it, Daniel. Let this feeling consume you, because when you have her back, she is going to pay dearly. She made the ultimate betrayal.

I can't stop staring. As Chase moves his hand, the tiny diamonds sparkle against the light like little ice picks being driven into my eyes.

Gillian's hand comes up to Chase's face and she leans in, pressing her nose against his, and kisses him. Holds her mouth to his, her hand splayed along his cheek, proving my worst nightmare in living color. A wedding band has been added to her engagement ring. Sitting on Chase's finger is his own wedding band. The need to vomit is extreme, but I push it down, way down to where that rage is being contained...barely.

She married him.

Left me here in San Francisco to rot, went away, and married that rich fucker. How could she do that? I wanted to give her everything. Every. Fucking. Thing.

He had to have made her do it. Had to. Drugged her, used her, promised her money and fame. With every ounce of control, I stand and watch them. Even during this horrible time, they still find ways to touch one another, smile, kiss. Disgusting pig.

It's not possible that she's happy with him. He's got her brainwashed. Made her believe that he was the one she was supposed to be with when all along it was me. Me that perfect girl was supposed to marry. Me who she was supposed to be with until the end of time, not some Matt Bomer look-alike suit-wearing snob who uses money and power to emasculate people and manipulate them into believing they are important. That's what he's doing to my princess. He's manipulated her into believing he's the one.

Fuck! She's so far gone she's now willingly drinking the Kool-Aid. It's going to take years to get her through this bastard's twisted influence. But I'll do it. No matter how long it takes to bring her mind back to who she truly loves. The one who will always be there for her.

I love her. She loves me. End of story.

Now I just have to find a way to make her mine.

GILLIAN

CHAPTER FIFTEEN

Something ruffles the hair alongside my temple. A scratchy material presses into the sensitive skin of my cheek as I blink open my eyes, staring into the sky, a clouded gray-blue expanse that I know well.

"*Cara bonita*, what will Chase think when he finds out we've slept together?" she asks, her voice a hoarse, gravelly sound, one that reminds me of the times we've woken after a night screaming and cheering for a band we saw the night before.

I blink carefully and look at her. Just *look* at her. Even having undergone a traumatic experience, two full nights in a hospital, and carbon monoxide poisoning, she's still incredibly beautiful, her face the picture of serenity.

Her fingers smooth through the hair at my scalp, the same way she's done a million times before, soothing me even though she's the one lying in the hospital bed. I smile, remembering her quip, and as the tears fall, I lift up from where I was hunched over her bed asleep and curve my head toward the man sleeping curled up in a chair, one far too small for his large frame, and respond, "He'll say it was an exceptional experience sleeping with two women."

Maria laughs, but the jovial full sounds are not there,

instead replaced with a wheezing, painful cough. She sits up and groans, clutching at her abdomen. I try to help settle her in a seated position, fluffing her pillows, tucking the blanket into her sides.

Once she seems comfortable, she holds my hand and tugs me to sit on the side of the bed next to her hip. "I tried, Gigi. I tried to get to her faster." Tears fill her icy gaze, making her eyes a darker blue. "Tell me, did she make it?"

I swallow and bring her hand to my face, nodding. "She did, but she's hurt bad. We won't know her true condition for another few days, the doctor said."

Maria's jaw tightens, and her features turn hard. She's turning on the façade. I've seen it before, and I hate it. Hate that she feels she has to guard her emotions, her heart.

"Not with me." I cup her cheek and slide my thumb over her brow. "No hiding from me." The mask drops, her lips tremble, and the tears finally fall.

"I should have tried harder. Should have thought to go to her room sooner. Then there were these boards nailed into the window pane, and I kicked and kicked." Her raspy voice gets worse, so I place my fingers over her lips.

Shaking my head, I stop her from hurting herself. "No, you saved her, Maria. You. She would have died had it not been for you!" I say the words with as much sincerity and force as I can muster in this small room, trying to be quiet, trying to keep our conversation private.

Maria brings her hand up to mine, the one cupping her cheek, and rubs into it like a cat would. "We're going to take care of her. Whatever happens…we take care of *nuestra familia*." Our family. Her eyes close, and soon she falls back asleep, the drugs pumping steadily through her.

I stand at the side of her bed, lean both arms on the edge, and that's when it happens. My shoulders shake, my spine curving down, and I fall to my knees. It's too much. Every pore in me seems to feel pain—bone-crushing, gut-wrenching, soul-aching pain. And it doesn't stop. I clutch at my knees and let the tears overwhelm me. The room goes black and I go back to that place.

I'm curled into a fetal position as he stands over me. He kicks at my ribs again. The pain ricochets from my ribs, through my chest, and out each nerve ending. I scream in pain, clutching at my abdomen, trying to protect our child.

"You missed your fucking period? You say you're pregnant?" He kicks at me again. "With whose baby, you good for nothing whore!"

"Justin…" I beg. "It's your baby. Ours…" I try again as he kicks me viciously. The crack of one, possibly two ribs, sounds unbearably loud. I clutch at the floor with my fingernails, trying to move, to crawl away, but he doesn't stop.

"We used protection. Every fucking time. That means you were fucking that study buddy. I knew this whole time. You said you loved me. And now, look at you!" he roars. "Knocked up from a tiny pencil-dicked geek." He pulls me out of my position, forces my arms wide where he holds them down with the weight of his knees. I try to kick and turn, but the pain is so intense I'm losing my vision.

"You know I'm going to kill him with my bare hands. Strangle him until he's lost all breath, and then I'm going to cut off his balls and feed them to him one at a time for touching my property!" He spits in my face and starts back up with the punching. At some point I lose consciousness, praying that my baby will survive the

blows and in equal hope praying that it doesn't because this is no life for an innocent child.

Cold. So cold. My teeth are chattering as a warm hand slides up and down my back in smooth even movements. "Come back to me, baby. Come home."

I hear the one voice that instantly brings me relief. Chase. He's here, not Justin. Small kisses line my temple and my forehead. When my body comes back online, I clutch at him, his strong shoulders, legs wrapping around his tight waist. I feel weightless; he's standing, and I feel only him. Then I'm back down. He's sitting, holding me close. Slowly opening my eyes, I can see I'm still in the hospital. The room has a soft, muted glow. I see Maria, asleep in her bed. I'm still here.

"That's it, honey. You're okay. I'm right here. I'll always be right here, bringing you back to me," Chase coos into my ear.

I grip onto his shoulders and lean back. I press my forehead against his and close my eyes. "I'm sorry," I whisper, not knowing what else to say.

Chase holds me low at the back and shakes his head. "Nothing to be sorry for. You had a moment, baby."

I nod and breathe in his comforting sandalwood and citrus scent. It fills the air around me, and I nuzzle into his neck, portions of the flashback still clawing at my psyche.

I'd missed my period. Told Justin I was pregnant, and he beat the living shit out of me. Every time I recall that night, I wonder what I could have done differently, how I could have turned things around. Perhaps killed him before he killed my baby.

Then it hits me. "How long has it been since our wedding?" I ask on a rushed breath.

"Four days," Chase says instantly.

I chuckle and rub into his chest, laying my hand over his heart, feeling its steady, strong beat. "No, since Mexico."

He groans but responds, "About five weeks." Then he curls a hand around my neck and tips my head up. "Why?" When I look into his eyes, they are filled with love and concern, for me. Nothing but me. I know Chase, the man who loves me, my husband, would go to the ends of the earth for me.

"Five weeks!" I let out in a breath, the two words sending a nervousness so acute it rattles my teeth.

Chase nods, his eyes narrowing. He positions me so I'm straddling him, and he tunnels one of his strong hands into my hair, holding me at the nape. He maneuvers my head so I'm looking into his gaze. "What's wrong?"

The last time I told a man this exact thing he beat the shit out of me. Instantly, I feel the tremors of panic starting to build.

Chase can sense it because he tightens his hold, bringing me even closer, and shakes his head. "Nuh-uh, no way, breathe, baby, breathe. You're safe. You're here with me, your husband. Nothing can happen to you here in my arms. I'll protect you."

His words are exactly what I need to hear, the reassurance necessary to continue.

"You promise?" I choke out, shivers racking my frame as I fear telling him what I need to say.

"Never gonna hurt you, baby. I promise. You're safe."

"Chase," I whisper and look into his eyes—still love

and concern there but now hints of fear. He's afraid. I lick my dry lips and swallow.

"Tell me." He lays his head against my forehead. The connection is all I need. His warmth, holding me close, his hands soothing me in long unhurried caresses.

"I missed my period," I say so softly I'm not sure he heard it. His body tenses, and then mine does in response.

He pulls back and looks into my eyes. "What? When?"

"Um, I should have gotten it the week after our wedding." His eyes go wide, but not in the scary way Justin's did. More like a surprised holy shit way.

Chase licks his lips and cups my face. "I'm no expert, but doesn't that mean you should have had it again, meaning you missed it twice?"

I nod. "Okay," he says softly. "Have you been taking your pills?"

This time my eyes get big. Huge. Probably the size of half-dollars if I had to guess. "I-I...uh...no," I finally admit.

Chase smiles softly, his blue gaze turning an honest-to-God aquamarine so blue it steals my breath with its beauty. "When was the last time you remember taking them?" There is not even a hint of anger in his tone, just the simple question.

I think back, the reel of memories of the past few weeks sweeping through my mind in a giant rush.

Getting the tattoo, the incredible feeling when Chase went down to his knees to inspect it.

Making love for the first time as a married couple in the tent with our ocean view.

Saying our vows in a tiny church in Ireland.

Finding the wedding gown and the tapestry.
Our emotional visit with Dr. Madison.
The hospital stay.
Being locked away in that disgusting storm shelter.
The look of hatred in Danny's eyes as he tore the front of my wedding dress and fondled me.
Chase's mother's throat being cut, the blood pouring out over her chest.

I close my eyes tight, the memories flooding by so fast my temperature rises, but Chase is there. Laying a calm hand to my cheek.

The yacht where he gave me the infinity necklace.

The yacht. "It was on the yacht. My pills. That's the last time I remember taking them. Then there was the wedding, your mom, being taken, the hospital stay…"

He presses his lips to mine, cutting off my excuses. His mouth is soft over mine, his kiss worshipping in its sweetness. He pulls away and cups both my cheeks.

"It's okay. We'll get through this together. It might be nothing. It could be the strain of everything that's happened right?"

I nod and wait for him to finish his thoughts. "So we're not going to worry. We'll handle this together. Husband and wife. Right?" I nod again, tears pricking at my eyes. "No crying. Me and you."

Holy shit. Holy. Fucking. Shit. This is not at all something I planned for. Not something *we* planned for. I'm holding her hand and leading her out of Maria's room. We're on a mission. Well, I am. Get as many fucking pregnancy tests as possible and confirm the results. Fuck!

"Where are we going?" she says, her voice so small it stops me in my tracks. I turn in the hall, the bright lights of the hospital bearing down on my wife's tortured face. The pit in my stomach that formed when she said the words "missed my period" deepens further.

I cup her cheek. "Hey, none of that. We're just going to get the tests and confirm what we suspect one way or another. Okay?"

"You're not mad?" Her voice trembles, and that sound sends knives into my chest. I want to kill, torture, and maim every man who ever made her afraid to be honest with me.

I pull her close into my arms. "God, no. Gillian, we have been through so much over the past few months. If anything, this could be one of the good things."

She backs away from my hold. "Really?" Her breath catches, and her eyes search mine. I smile, even though my insides are screaming to run to the nearest pharmacy and find out if my wife is carrying my child. Our baby. I need to stay strong. Not show how much this news is affecting me. I'm not sure how to feel. All I know is that the desire to find out for sure is leading all actions from here on out.

Jack walks up to us. He was waiting outside Maria's room. I've got guards once more on both Maria and Kathleen, though Kathleen is still in ICU.

"Sir? Davis estate?" Jack asks in his usual no-nonsense timber.

I shake my head. "We're stopping at a drug store and then going to the penthouse."

Jack's jaw tightens, and I cut my gaze at him so sharply he doesn't respond, just nods. Thank Christ. The last thing I need right now is insubordination. Not that I treat him like any of my other employees, but right now, I'm sure he can feel the tension filling the space around me. I clutch Gillian to my side, holding her close. Fuck. I can't get her close enough. If she'd let me carry her through the hospital, I would. She could be growing my baby within her right this very minute. That thought speaks deeply to the caveman within me. As we walk by, I want to growl and bark at any person who so much as bumps into her.

I clench my teeth, and we walk briskly out of the hospital. Jack ushers us into the blacked-out SUV, and we're off.

I have Gillian wait in the car while I go into Walgreen's alone, to Jack's extreme discomfort. At this point, I don't fucking care. It's none of his business what I'm doing, and I don't want her worrying about anything. She's been through too fucking much already. When I find the right aisle, I'm shocked by how many options there are. Shouldn't it just be one? Take this test and find out pregnant or not. Instead of dealing with reading them, I grab one of each and head up to the register.

"Whoa, dude. Sorry, man." The young man looks at me knowingly while ringing up each test. "Had a few scares myself," he offers, and I want to punch his backwards hat–wearing pimply face in the teeth, just so he'll shut the fuck up. I narrow my gaze at him and hand him two hundred-dollar bills when the total comes out to one hundred and eighty something. I snatch up the bags and leave without getting a receipt or the change.

"Dude, your change," the kid yells.

"Keep it," I growl over my shoulder. Jack has parked directly in front of the store, blocking the entrance. He's already opening my door when I come out. He glances down at the tests clearly visible through the mostly translucent bags. Fucking cheap bags. His eyes widen and a small smirk appears.

"Not a fucking word." The words come out as if dipped in acid.

Jack doesn't care about my overbearing, demonstrative ways. He's known me far too long to give a shit about ruffling my feathers. "Never, sir," he says anyway, a small smile on his lips. Again, the need to punch someone in the face roars through me.

We make it across town to the penthouse. I'm gripping Gillian's hand so tight she's caressing the top of my hand, trying to soothe me. When the hell did the tables turn around so that she was comforting me? She hasn't said anything since the hospital. I'm worried about her—the flashback, the stress of seeing Maria and Kathleen in the hospital, and now this.

It's not as though I don't want to have children. I do. Ever since she put the idea in my head all those months ago, I've wanted to see her bloom with my child growing inside her, but I'd rather have it be during a time where we can both focus on growing our family and nothing else. A time like this should be about us and our desire to have a child. Not about the psychotic madman who's after her and the people she loves while dealing with a prospective progeny.

When we arrive at the top floor of Davis Industries, Jack does a cursory sweep, and then we enter. I walk her straight back to our master bathroom and dump out the contents of the two bags.

"Okay. I got one of everything."

"Chase, seriously? One would do."

I shake my head. "False positives. We need to be sure."

She blinks up at me and then nods. I can't place where her emotions are right now. She's definitely solemn yet not giving anything to let me know how she feels otherwise. This has to be a hit to her psyche. I wonder if I should call Dr. Madison. Have him come here, talk with us once we know. Either way, she's going to need to work through this. I just hope she can do most of that with me. I want to be the one who can soothe her, bring her back to the happy, beautiful self I know that's hiding under all that pain. The woman who was carefree in Ireland. Right then, I promise to take her back there, to put that smile on her face once more.

I pull out the first three tests in the bag, rip open each package, and dump them on the counter. "You need some water?"

She nods, so I fill the glass by her vanity and hand it to her. Like the appeasing woman she can easily turn into, she downs it all. I hand her three sticks. "Think you can urinate on all of them at once?"

That question gets me a grin. A full-fledged knock-down drag-out beautiful one. "Do you like sex?"

"What kind of question is that? Of course I do." I stumble over the answer, and this time she smiles wide, all hints of fear and nervousness leave her.

"Then don't ask me stupid questions, and I won't ask you stupid questions."

I chuckle. "She jokes." I grip her outstretched arm, pull her close, and kiss her with everything I have in me. The fear, the anticipation, and all the love I have for her. I pour it into that one kiss so she knows, can *feel* what I am incapable of telling her. That no matter what happens, we're together, and we can take anything on. That I love her and will love our child if that's what's meant to be for us.

She pulls back and her eyes are glazed, brimming with love and lust even now during this tense time. "Christ, I love you," I growl against her succulent mouth and then take her lips again.

Breathless, she pulls back. "It's a good thing, because I love you right back," she says with a wink and then takes the three tests and enters the little cove.

While she's in there, I grab a shoebox from our closet and dump out the new Louis Vuittons Dana must have purchased for Gillian. My girl rarely shops, and when she does, it's always bargain basement. That little reminder of what we used to be puts a smile on my face as I bring the empty box to her. She opens the door with the three tests in her hand.

"Put them in the box." She does, and I set it on the counter, grab her hand, and then bring her to our bed. As she stands there, I unbutton her shirt and push it off her shoulders.

One of her eyebrows rises into an arch toward her hairline. "What are you doing?" she asks.

"Need to feel your skin," I say, and she nods, standing there in pants and a camisole. With one hand, I pull my shirt over my head. Then I remove her pants, leaving her in her tiny shirt and panties, and then remove my own so I'm in only boxers. Grabbing her hand in one of mine and pulling back the comforter with the other, I lead her into our bed.

We face each other, our bodies touching everywhere… and we wait.

"Are you scared?" Her voice shakes a bit, but she lets it out with a slow breath.

"Yes," I answer instantly. "But not for the reasons you think."

She licks her lips and pushes a lock of my hair off my forehead. She's done it a million times before, but somehow, now, it means more. I close my eyes and just feel her touch. It's like a balm over the jagged edges of my psyche. "Tell me," she pushes.

"I'm scared that he'll get to you and possibly our baby." I admit the fear needling against my chest, making my heart pound. I put a hand over her stomach. "If my baby is in there, it's my job to protect it and its mother. I haven't done a very good job of protecting you, and the thought of not being able to protect our child guts me."

Tears fill her eyes and she kisses me. "Chase," she whispers against my lips. "You're the only one who can protect me. Keep our baby safe. Don't you know that?"

I groan, roll on top of her, and settle between her thighs. She holds me close, arms wrapped around my back. We hug for a couple minutes until my phone alarm goes off in the bathroom. "That's the buzzer for the tests." She gasps and cuddles me close. For a moment, we just hold one another while the annoying beep goes on and on. "Okay, I'm going to get it." She nods.

Entering the bathroom feels like I'm walking into a flame. This moment could change our lives forever. I grab the box and the paperwork that came with the tests without looking down. I want us to do this together. Everything together.

I settle the box directly between us as we both sit Indian style on our bed. "Okay, you want to look first or together?" Her eyes are so green and filled with so much fear.

I lean forward and kiss her. She holds my jaw and kisses me back with a fierce possession I haven't felt since our wedding night in Ireland.

Finally, she pulls back. "You read them to me." She sits back and clasps her hands in her lap.

I nod and then look down into the box at the first one. "Two lines?" I look up at her, and her eyebrows come together in confusion, and she grabs at the papers. "What the fuck does that mean? Two lines for yes, two lines for no." She shakes her head and moves to grab for the papers.

"Read another one," she says.

"One side is a line, the other a plus symbol. What the fuck?" I look up, hoping she'll know what that means, and she shakes her head, skimming the materials. "Christ!" How can this be so goddamned difficult?

"What's the last one say?" She blows out a breath, her red hair moving with the effort as she pores over the three different papers.

I look down and stop cold. The last one is digital and definitive. There is absolutely no guesswork needed, no searching through the paperwork to understand the symbolism of one line, versus two, a minus or a plus symbol. "Um, Gillian, baby." I hold up the test.

Her eyes zero in on the words that I'm staring at. Her hands come to her mouth on a gasp.

The little test has a gray screen with bold black writing. The text is clear as day as the indicator clearly says the exact word we needed to see to be certain.

PREGNANT

GILLIAN

CHAPTER SIXTEEN

It's as if the little screen starts flashing. *Pregnant! Pregnant! Pregnant!*

I open my mouth to say something, but words fail me. Chase gets up and starts pacing the room. His hands tunnel into those dark locks and yank on the roots. He really needs to stop doing that. He's going to end up bald if he doesn't. For now, though, the situation warrants an extreme response, and while I can't come up with a thing to say, I'll allow him his own freak-out. I watch as he walks from one side of the room to the other, back and forth. On the tenth cut across the plush carpet, he stops and looks up to the sky on a sigh.

I can't help but enjoy the view. My husband's body is magnificent—golden skin, tapered waist, muscles everywhere they're supposed to be on a twenty-nine-year-old man. A man who's about to become a father.

A mother. I'm going to be someone's mother. I lay a hand over my stomach protectively while looking down. I caress the skin that's there, hoping that my baby feels the unconditional love I'm sending.

As I'm bonding with the idea that I have a baby growing inside of me, I feel the bed dip. Chase crawls over to me and lies on his stomach. His head is uber close to my stomach when he looks up. "Can you feel it? I mean, our baby?" The question is so innocent, so unlike the demanding business tycoon I met almost a year ago. Chase is so different now than he was then. All that's happened to us—the stalker, the abduction, his mother's death, our eloping, and now this—and he's still here, worrying about me.

"No." I smile softly and lick my lips. "But I imagine him there, growing, a testament to our love. That's what he is."

"He?" Chase's eyes turn up to mine, his question laced with hope.

I shrug noncommittally. In my mind, Chase is so powerful, his swimmers must be, too. So yes, I think our baby is a he. Another perfect specimen of mankind made to drive women of the world absolutely insane.

"Chase…" I swallow, not knowing how to ask this question, not wanting to but knowing I need to know where he's at with this. I can't go one more minute knowing I'm going to be a mother with the thought that I'll have to do it alone. Abortion is not an option, never would have been when Justin took motherhood away from me all those years ago either.

My husband pulls my hand away from my stomach. He grips my hips and pushes my legs out so they are caging his body. I allow the movement, not knowing what he's doing but appreciating him close anyway. Once he gets my legs spread and his body lying on top of me, he scoots my body down, my head falling to the pillow. He has his face hovering over my stomach, so close I can feel the warmth of his breath. He leans forward, pushes up my camisole, and kisses every inch of my belly. Every single last inch he presses his lips to and holds for long seconds. It's as if he's making sure that with every press he's giving his love.

"Mine," he growls while covering my entire stomach and pelvis with his two large hands.

Tears fall before I ever realize I'm crying. I don't have to ask him how he feels. Of course, I know instinctively his reaction. It's Chase. When it comes to me, our future, our child, he's going to be possessive. Dangerously so. He looks up at me, his eyes a steel blue—the kind that would normally issue fear in the person they are directed at. But not me. I know him too well. He's just feeling too much too quickly, and when he does, especially when it involves me, he loses his shit.

I stay quiet while he connects with this idea of being a father, and I let him finish whatever he needs to say or do to make this reality sink in. Chase leans his head down to my stomach and listens. To what, I don't know. The fetus couldn't be more than the size of a lima bean. I can feel his body tense all around me, his hands cupping where the baby is nestled safely within my womb.

"This is *my* child. No man, no woman, no one, will *ever* lay a harsh finger to our baby. I will protect you and our child with my life. Know that, Gillian."

"Chase, baby, I do know that. I know you will never hurt me or our child. Daddy," I say to lighten the thick pressure of the mood he's in. His lips turn up and he grins.

"Holy fuck. I'm going to be someone's daddy. And you're going to be a mommy!" he tosses back, and I giggle and nod.

"Looks like it."

"We're going to need to get you into the doctor right

away. I'll call Dana after."

I narrow my brows and purse my lips. "After what?"

"After I fuck my pregnant wife," he says deadpan.

"Is that right?" I say with as much sex appeal as I can muster.

"Oh, I'm going to show you what's right. And that's me, balls deep inside that perfect pussy," he growls.

Jesus. There are so many layers to this man I can hardly keep track. One moment he sounds angry, the next possessive, and now, horny. And his words, they seem to smooth along my skin like silk and wrap around my libido, making me insanely needy for him.

"Does the idea of taking a pregnant lady turn you on?" I say, stretching out my limbs above my head, pointing my toes and moaning at the way the muscles bend and stretch, relieving two days' worth of tension.

I'm so happy to be back in our bed after all the travel, the nightmare of dealing with two more of my friends hurt, falling asleep at Maria's bedside, and our Kathleen still not out of the woods. I know there's nothing we can do for either of them tonight. Tomorrow, that's another day of sticking to the hospital, spreading love and praying for Kat to be okay.

Chase's lips come down to my clavicle where he licks a slippery line. Instead of lifting the shirt off my head, he pushes the straps down my shoulders eager to get to more skin. "Everything about you turns me on," Chase says. "Your pearlescent skin." He licks a line down between my breasts, pushing the shirt as he goes. I'm not wearing a bra because it could rub against my tattoo, so when he pushes it over, the swells my breasts pop free. Instantly he takes one into his warm mouth. He swirls his tongue around the tight knot of flesh, biting enticingly into the erect tip, sending ripples through my body and making me wet.

I moan as he sucks hard. "I love how your pretty pink nipples get dark, turning into ripe berries when I suck on them." He proves his point by squeezing the round globes, pushing as much of my breast into his mouth as possible, and biting down. My back arches instinctively, and I fist my hands into his hair, holding him close, giving myself to his ministrations. He takes it, plucking and ripening each nipple until they are hot points of need. He grabs my camisole and slowly pulls it over my tattoo, my shoulders, and over my head where he tosses it aside.

Chase's gaze zeros in on my tattoo. With a featherlight touch, he traces the area and kisses it. It's still scabbing over, but it doesn't really hurt. "I love seeing this on your skin, baby. Knowing it's for me." He shakes his head. "I don't know that I'll ever be worthy of you, but I'm going to spend my life trying."

I cup both his cheeks. "You're more than worthy. Chase, you're my world. You, me, and now this baby. We're a family. A *real* family. You've given me something no one else could give me. Don't you see that?"

After that, all words are unnecessary because Chase makes it so, keeping my mouth busy on his. He kisses me with his whole being, and I feel it down to my toes where they curl at each swipe of his tongue. The minty taste of him calls to me. Speaks to a place deep inside where a woman knows her mate instinctively.

Kiss after drugging kiss, Chase and I reconnect, find that togetherness we had in Ireland, and bring it into this bed in our home. Chase's lips tear from mine as his hands slide over my thighs. "Need to be inside my wife."

He doesn't even take the time to remove my panties, just rips them at the side so they're out of the way. Chase holds my legs open wide, staring down at my arousal-slickened sex like he's ravenous, not sure whether he wants to put his mouth on me or plunge in. It's a difficult decision, I know, for I'm ready for either one, equally desiring both.

Ultimately, he ends up with his eyes on the prize. Lightning quick, his face is between my thighs, hovering over my center. He inhales fully. "Christ, that smell. There's nothing like the scent of your desire, baby. Makes my mouth water." He proves this by pushing my thighs wider and licking me from bottom to top, groaning in pleasure. Then he places his lips over my aching heat and sucks me hard, his thumbs keeping me open, his index fingers spinning circles around my clit so perfectly I skyrocket into orgasm. My body convulses against his working mouth, his tongue delving in and out of me. The sounds he's making are primal, lost to the moment, and I love every second of being the focus of his attention.

Once he licks every inch, his eyes come to mine. His face is coated in my essence as he drags his tongue all over his wet lips as if wanting to get every last drop of my pleasure. Those beautiful blue eyes of his are hot. "Will it hurt the baby to fuck you hard?" he asks, holding my thighs open at the knees.

I shake my head. "No. Baby is well protected and very, very small."

Chase's nostrils flare, and he pushes his boxers down. His dick is huge, thick and straining. The wide knob at the top weeps at the slit, and I moan, wanting nothing more than to lick it off, taste his desire for me.

"Let me have a taste," I beg, locking eyes with him. His eyes are swirling with heat.

"You want a taste of my cock."

I grin. "I want a taste of *my* cock." I bite down on my bottom lip and lift my chin.

Chase's smile is predatory and his eyes gleaming. His hand comes down and cups my entire center. "This pussy mine?"

I nod. "Always has been."

"Always fucking will be," he grates, pushing the heel of his palm into my clit, at the same time plunging two fingers deep.

My head falls back to the pillow on a moan. I move my head from side to side while swirling my hips, wanting more of him. I can't handle it. When he's touching me, he owns me, and the smug bastard knows it.

He removes his hand and straddles the top of the bed at my chest. "Put your mouth on my cock, wife." Chase is going to use that word until I detest hearing it, I just know it. But this time, it makes me fucking hot, and a fresh bout of moisture slickens my thighs.

I lick the tip of his dick and give it a welcoming kiss. He places a hand at the headboard, balancing himself above me. His head falls down to his chest, and he closes his eyes. Even though he's kneeling over me, I know it's me who owns him right now. His dick hovers over my lips, so I rub them all over, painting a wet trail down the side of his length and back up.

"You're teasing me," he warns, his voice strained just

the way I like it.

I place my lips just at the crown and lick a circle around the top before taking just the head in and giving it a good hard suck. Chase trembles and thrust his hips, wanting me to take him farther, but I pull back, preferring to tease. He groans and cups my jaw with his hand, his thumb pushing my bottom lip down, opening my mouth wide. "You're going to take it down your throat, baby, and then I'm going to plunge so deep into your pussy you'll forget where you end and I begin."

Now that sounds pretty fucking amazing. I nod, and he pushes his way down my throat.

Tight. So fucking tight.
Wet. So fucking wet.

Her perfect lips stretch wide over my cock as I push my way into her mouth until I reach that muscle and press past it. She swallows like the goddess she is, and I grind my teeth, enjoying the feeling of being all the way down her throat, feeling the puffs of air from her nose against my groin. Her eyes go wide, and I can tell she needs air so I pull back fast. She doesn't miss a beat, sucking in a breath and pulling me back down, deep-throating me like a professional. My girl, my wife, loves my cock, and the sweet woman has very little gag reflex. It's official. I married the perfect woman.

And now, she's going to have my baby.

Christ! That thought makes me painfully hard. Knowing she's got my child in her, growing something I planted inside of her, a piece of me. Stone. My dick is so rock hard I could chisel marble with it.

I pull out of her succulent mouth, but only because I know that her pussy is going to be just as hot and just as wet. She mewls in protest.

"Hungry for cock, baby?"

She moans, widening her legs, offering me entrance into the promised land.

Maneuvering her legs high and wide, I center my dick at her sopping entrance. I stir my hips, rubbing my cock all over her wet pussy, paying extra attention to rubbing against her little cherry clit that's peeking out of its hiding place. I'd like to run my tongue all over that hardened bud, but right now, we both need to be one. Joined.

I plunge into her heat, and she clamps down on my cock, making her deliciously tight cavern even more so with the effort of her muscles. "Fuck me! So good." I pull out and thrust back in. She moans, her hands coming to my biceps where her nails dig in. Repositioning us, I pull her legs wide and push them up to her armpits. "This okay?" I groan, the top of my dick pressing into that spot within her that makes her stupid.

"Uh, uh, uh," she says, not making any sense. I lean up on my knees, pull her sexy body onto my cock, and press home over and over. The nonsensical sounds start again, and I feel extreme pride, knowing I've reduced this intelligent woman to a babbling entity driven only by pleasure.

With my thumb, I caress the place where we're joined. Her eyes open like a shot. "Look down," I tell her, and like a good girl, she does. Following her gaze, I watch as I plunge my cock in and out of her impossibly tight pussy. I make sure to rub her red clit with my thumb and then down to where I'm taking her. "Feel us," I insist. She brings a shaky hand to the space between our bodies. I take her hand, press her fingers over her sweet clit where she moans, and then push farther down to where we're joined. Her eyes widen and her mouth opens as she feels me pumping in and out. "That's us, Gillian. We're connected." Her fingers play in the wetness between our bodies, sending jolts of pleasure through my cock and up my groin to spiral along my spine. "Feel it? That's me loving you."

She lets out a breath. Her head tips back, and her fingers glide up to her clit where she manipulates herself with two fingers in furiously fast circles. So fucking hot.

"That's it," I encourage, the muscles in her cunt fastening around my cock, her hips lifting to meet mine. She's incredible. Her entire body is strung tight like a drum. Sweat glistens on her skin, mingling with mine. Her nipples point in invitation to the sky. If I were in a different position, I'd be sucking those strawberry tips like a starving man.

"Harder," she begs. I planned to take her hard, but knowing my child is there makes me pause.

"Are you sure?"

She sucks in a breath. "Harder, Chase. Make me come."

That's all I need to hear. I lean over her body, her hand still working her clit while I pound into her. She screams in delight. "Yes, yes, more!" So I give it to her. Plunging in and out, growling with the need to mark my territory, fill her full.

Once I lean forward, I take a fat nipple into my mouth and suck hard. That's all it takes. Her body quivers, and her pussy gives my cock the lock-down. Straight up gripping me so hard it's almost painful. I fuck her through it, and when she spasms around me, her nails digging into my ass, I come and come, and come into her jerking body. She clings to me through it all until I collapse on top of her, completely destroyed in the best possible way.

I lean to the side, keeping her connected to me, wanting to stay inside her. Makes me feel closer to her. I wrap my arms around her, bringing her into the cavern of my arms. When I look down, I see she's passed out. I fucked her to sleep. A slow smile slips across my face, and I wedge her leg over mine, making sure that I'm still balls deep inside my woman. Me holding her close, protecting her and our child. Little puffs of air tickle the hair on my chest.

Feeling her in my arms, my dick still inside her, her breath on my chest, her arms around me, I can finally rest.

★ ★ ★ ★

I wake to the feeling of Gillian attempting to move out of my arms. Not an option. Without saying anything I roll over, my dick still nice and deep only now hard. She gasps, and I steal her breath, cover her mouth with mine, and thrust into her. Slowly I plunge in and out of her. Completely unhurried but still wanting her desperately.

Hands caressing one another, muscles softening, lips glued to each other, we make exceptionally slow love. I take her to the height of passion, bring her down, and take her there again. Over and over, I make love to her, whispering in her ear all that I couldn't say before.

"I'm happy about our baby," I tell her, thrusting deep.

"Me too," she whispers into my hairline.

"I want to be a good father. I *will* be a good father," I

promise, sucking on her neck, plunging into her.

"You will be. I know it. Our baby is going to be so loved," she says, lifting her hips, caressing my back.

"I'm going to love you both, give you everything…" I groan in between her breasts, taking a nipple and sucking. Her hand caresses my scalp as I worship her breasts.

"We only need you. You are everything," she says breathily, tipping her head back, offering her breasts to my greedy mouth.

I shake my head so she feels it in her hands. "You'll never want for anything." I thrust and suck hard at her at the same time.

"Only want you, just you." And that's when we come, both of us tumbling over the crest together, holding onto one another, my lips on hers taking her mouth the way I'm taking her body. She gives it all freely, willingly, beautifully. My wife. The mother of my child.

Once we're done, we lie there, holding onto one another in our dark bedroom. A million thoughts run through my mind about how I'm going to protect them, keep them safe from a man who's hurt so many, his twisted sights on Gillian.

My head is on her chest, my hand caressing her stomach. "Do you think he feels us? You know, when we make love?" I ask her, knowing absolutely nothing about a woman's pregnant body. A situation I'm going to rectify immediately. I'll be downloading whatever fucking guide to pregnancy books onto my iPad I can get my hands on. I need to know everything about our child, about what's happening to her body, and what I need to do and provide to make sure our baby comes into this world happy and healthy.

Gillian runs her fingers over my scalp, soothing the

anxiety that's building at the thought of how very little I know about being a dad. "I think our baby can feel love. But according to Bree, she's having regular wild monkey sex with Phil." Her face contorts, and I wonder if it's because she still has feelings for her first sexual partner. She looks down, and her brows furrow. "It's like talking about my brother and sister having sex. It kind of grosses me out."

I laugh and kiss her stomach, running my finger over the flat surface, imagining her growing bigger. It's going to be awesome to see.

She lets out a breath. "Anyway, her doctor said regular sex is totally fine as long as she feels fine."

"No restrictions?" I ask, very interested in this part.

Her shoulders go up and down. "I don't know."

"We need to get you in to see the doctor as soon as possible." I move to get up, but she holds me down.

"Where are you going? Chase, we need to sleep. We have a really long day in the hospital tomorrow." Her green eyes show concern, and I melt, giving her a kiss.

"I need to get my iPad. I want to download some books about pregnancy."

She looks over at the clock. "At two in the morning?" I can see why she'd think that was strange, but the need to know what's happening within her is nagging at my subconscious. "Chase, we don't even know how far along I am. And we can't tell anyone," she warns.

I sit up and look at her. My temperature rises. The relaxed feelings I just had leave me quickly. I hold her gaze, mine probably hard and unrelenting. "I'm fucking telling *everyone*. My wife is pregnant, and I want the goddamned world to know it."

She smiles and shakes her head. "Baby, we can't tell anyone until we know how far along I am and that the baby is okay. Plus, we haven't even told anyone we're married. I'd like to tell them when everything has calmed down, and we can celebrate. Maybe when Kat's out of the woods or out of the hospital."

I understand her point, but I don't like it. "I'll think about it."

"You do that. For now, can you please lie back down and hold me? I'm so tired," she whines, and I give in, pulling her into my arms, sliding the front of my naked body against hers. Once we're on our sides and intertwined, she releases a contented sigh. "You really okay with this?" she asks, her tone nervous.

I lay a hand over her where my child is nestled safely. "I'm very okay with this. We're just having our family a little sooner than we planned, but somehow, it makes it better because it just happened. And we have something to look forward to."

She places her hand over mine. "Yeah, something to look forward to. I like that, Chase. No, I *love* that."

Before long, her body gets heavy and her breath evens out in sleep. I lie there caressing her stomach in our dark room.

"I will protect you, little one. I will do whatever it takes. You will never know pain the way your mom and I did. I swear it."

I fall asleep imagining a dark-haired little boy with pale skin and his mother's bright green eyes.

X

DANIEL

CHAPTER SEVENTEEN

The alarm on my phone sounds, and I look down at the display. Looks like the blond bitch is taking a call from the rich fucker. I sit back on my bed at my adopted brother's place and click the phone. Stupid bitch never knew I put the device on her cell. It's a piece of technology that I, myself, invented. The device allows me to listen in to her calls while they are taking place with no one being the wiser. So when her phone rings, my display gives a special alarm, and I can see what she sees on her cell phone. In this instance, it says Chase Davis Calling.

Not that I especially want to hear the fucker's voice, but I do want to find out what's going on with my girl and glean any information possible on how I can once again take her from the prick and whisk her away to Canada where no one will ever be able to find her.

"Chase, I'm so sorry to hear about Kathleen and Maria," she says the moment she answers. Hearing about my latest victims and my girl in one call—damn, I'm a lucky man.

"Thank you, Dana. Maria is doing well. She'll be out of the hospital within the week. Kathleen's prognosis has yet to be determined." His voice sounds authoritative, and I want to reach into the phone and strangle him where he stands. Probably standing next to my perfect princess, the motherfucker.

"It's good that Maria is on the mend. I can't imagine how your fiancée must be taking this information right now."

"Wife." His tone is matter of fact, and I grind down on my teeth and grip my hand into a fist. I still cannot believe that she married him. How could she do that? I take several deep breaths, reminding myself that he had to have made her. It's the only reasonable explanation.

"Excuse me?" she says, her tone one of shock.

"We eloped. I took her to the home in Ireland I bought. Married her in a small church a few days ago. Just the two of us."

Dana doesn't speak for a moment, and finally she whispers, "I'm happy for you, Chase. I knew the day I met her she was going to change your life. And I'm sorry that my boyfriend hurt you guys so badly..." Her voice hitches even though she muffles the sound. If I can hear her crying, so can he. Me, it makes me fucking thrilled. Chase, on the other hand, is a wussy dick who will be sensitive about her feelings. I should have killed the bitch when I had the chance. Technically, I still can. Her boyfriend my red-blooded American ass. She was a hot piece of ass. A fucking whore I fucked to get what I wanted. Her boyfriend. I almost laugh out loud.

"Hush now. I didn't call you for that. I'm sorry I haven't been in touch, but Gillian and I didn't want anyone knowing about our plans to marry. Her friends still don't know, and now that tragedy has struck once again, they're not going to know for a while."

Her voice catches again, and I roll my eyes. Dumb bitch, put a lid on it already. He doesn't give a fuck about your tears. "Well, congratulations." She sniffs loudly. Probably wiping that shit on her sleeve. Disgusting cunt. That's why I always fucked her facing away from me. Couldn't stand to look into her weepy eyes all the time.

"Thank you," he says gruffly, as if he's not got a lot of time. Probably not. He's got the most beautiful woman alive in his bed. I wouldn't leave her to even make a phone call let alone call this stupid cunt. "Now, the reason for my call is twofold. One, Gillian needs to see an obstetric gynecologist immediately. I want an appointment as soon as possible, but any time within the week will be fine. The sooner the better."

"Everything okay?" Her voice is concerned, and I'm glad it is because my own anxiety has my gut clenching. He better not have given her an STD. I'll kill him. Technically, I plan on killing him anyway, but if he defiled her in an irreparable way, I'll make his death slow and immensely painful.

"Everything's great, actually." Chase's tone is jovial, practically laughing. "My wife is pregnant and needs to see a doctor to ensure our baby is safe." Pregnant. Gillian is pregnant with the rich fucker's baby? I could not have heard that right. Chase continues, "We gather she's closing in on six weeks along now, but we want to be certain, make sure the baby is okay after everything she's endured at the hands of that psycho."

Pregnant.

Psycho.

He stole my woman, stuck his filthy dick in her, and

put his bastard seed into her womb. The rage I'm usually able to control starts to rise up from deep within my soul. The darkness begins to swallow all light as my vision turns to tiny pinpoints of red. My body begins to sweat, giant fat drops beading on my forehead, my hairline, underarms, trickling down my back as the words penetrate. Pregnant. Psycho.

I can vaguely hear he's still talking. "I want to plan a dinner, just she and I. This is where you come in. I'd like for you to secure Coit Tower. Whatever the expense. Table, dinner catered, the works. And I want it to be completely private. The standard guards on duty will be enough. Gillian's favorite is Italian. Call a local place and have it delivered and set up."

"What about Bentley?" she asks, but I'm having trouble following. I'm still stuck on the fact that he impregnated my woman.

"He's feeding the family at the Davis Estate. Gillian and I need some time to be alone."

"Is that wise?" she asks, and I agree. Alone. He's more stupid than I thought. Not wise at all you stupid fucking bastard who impregnated my girl.

"McBride doesn't know where we are, and it will only be a few days. This Friday, I'm going to allow Jack to see his own family, and Gillian and I will be completely alone. I want to take her to one of San Francisco's most beautiful architectural buildings. When Gillian and I get back from the hospital, I want it all ready to go. I'm going to give her a night under the stars, an unobstructed 360-degree view of the city, and most of all, an evening she'll never forget."

"God, that's so romantic, Chase. But is Jack okay with

this?"

Her voice is warning, and I want to reach in and slap the fucking cunt. Tell her to shut the fuck up and let the ignorant fucker become a sitting duck.

"He doesn't know, and I don't want him knowing. As far as he's concerned, Gillian and I will be under heavy guard at the Davis Estate."

So they're going to be all alone in an old-ass building with lots of places to hide. That hatred in me starts to settle as a plan forms. It's too perfect. I'll sneak in that night before closing and hide out. Once I see the catering company leaving, it will just be the three of us—me, Gillian, and Chase. I'll kill him and then shoot her with enough drugs to force an abortion. If that doesn't work, I'll rip that devil spawn out of her with a wire hanger.

In a few more days, all of my problems will be over. Chase Davis will be dead, and Gillian will be mine, once and for all.

We're taken into a small white room. An examination table is covered in paper, and Gillian is stripping out of her clothes. All of them. I cringe, wondering why she needs to be completely naked for this. "Do you have to do this shit every time you visit the gynecologist?" I ask her. Her lips tip up into a smile as she closes the front of the paper gown. It's completely open in the front. One hundred percent of her body is stark naked and easily accessible. What. The. Fuck.

Gillian shimmies her heart-shaped ass on the table and sighs. "Yes, every time you go to the gyno it's like this. I don't know one woman in the universe who likes going to the gyno. I'd much rather go to the dentist."

I nod and scowl at her bare legs dangling over the edge of the table. Two long metal items stick out at the edge of the table. I touch one of them and tilt my head to examine it. "What's this?"

"Stirrups. You put your feet in them and push your bum all the way down to the end of the table."

"You have got to be kidding me?" My gaze locks on hers, hoping she's yanking my chain. Gillian often likes to joke, only this time her face doesn't hold even a hint of humor.

Her lips purse into a flat line. "Wish I were. It's very degrading, but at least Dana requested a female doctor."

The thought of her naked, even in a medical capacity, and her legs spread, her ass hanging off the edge of the table with another man's face between her thighs has me grinding my teeth so hard the sound reverberates through my eardrums.

She grabs my hand and leans up for a kiss. I give her what she wants as the door to the room opens.

"Mrs. Davis, Mr. Davis, I presume."

I nod as the small Asian doctor shakes Gillian's hand and then mine, introducing herself as Dr. Wong as she sticks her nose in a file. "I understand you have had a positive pregnancy test." She looks up over the rim of her glasses.

"Six," I say.

One sharp black brow rises to a point. "You took six tests?"

We both nod, neither of us commenting that by the time we'd figured out that all three tests we took first did, in fact, all come out positive, we thought it prudent to do three more. Okay, I found it prudent. Gillian just thought it was good fun.

"Okay," the doctor says. "Lie back, bring your bottom to the edge, and put your feet in the stirrups. Gillian follows her directions as the woman grabs a machine that has a keyboard and a giant wand attached to it. "When was your last period?" she asks while setting up the device that looks like a computer on a TV tray. Once she has it close, she walks around Gillian, blatantly opens the front of her gown, and manipulates her breasts. She rubs them everywhere.

I clear my throat, and Gillian's eyes cut to me. "Breast exam, babe," she says, like it's perfectly normal to have a woman fondling her tits.

It obviously bothers me more than it bothers her. She then answers the doctor's question. "I missed a full period, but there were extenuating circumstances. And I should have gotten my period again last week."

The doctor's eyes move to my wife's. "Extenuating circumstances?" she queries, and then palpates her stomach in a way that looks rather rough. Gillian clasps my hand tight. She either doesn't want to share this information with the doctor or she doesn't like what the doctor is doing. On top of that, I know this moment is important to her. She wants this to be a happy occasion, and we're both already filled with an enormous amount of anxiety over the fact that she was likely pregnant when she was drugged and kidnapped.

"Look, Dr. Wong, my wife was kidnapped almost six weeks ago on our wedding day. She was drugged, beaten, and held in a storm shelter for several days. We just found out that she's pregnant and are desperately in need of your medical expertise to tell us whether our unborn child is healthy and growing normally. She was tranquilized with Etorphine, given extremely high doses of antibiotics and painkillers in the hospital. Her medical files should have been faxed over by my assistant."

The doctor's cold gaze turns warm and concerned. I'm not sure if that's a good sign or bad. "They were, and now I understand why the drugs were there." Then she walks around and stands between Gillian's legs. She presses a dollop of what looks to be lubricant on her fingers and moves them between my wife's thighs. Gillian's entire body tenses, and I'm certain my eyes go wide.

"What the fuck are you doing?" I growl, but Gillian stops me with a hand to my stomach. "Internal exam, Chase," she says, breathless. Obviously, because a woman has her fingers in my wife's fucking pussy!

"Mr. Davis, I assure you, I'm checking her cervix, ovaries, and womb for cysts or textural abnormalities." She pulls her hand out. "Everything seems in order."

I want to bark that I could have told her that everything was "in order" as I'm very intimate with it.

"Well, let's take a look at the fetus, and I'll know more about what we're dealing with." She gives a small smile and lifts up the giant wand-like tool that's mysteriously covered in something achingly familiar to a condom. My eyes widen as the doctor, moves between Gillian's legs again. "You're going to feel some pressure and cold," she warns. Gillian's hand locks down on mine, and her eyes close.

Then all of a sudden the TV-like device shows some static-looking images. Then there's a black circle with blobs in the center.

For what seems like the longest time of our lives, the doctor clicks a bunch of buttons, writes notes on Gillian's file, but has yet to grace us with any feedback on her condition. I look down at my wife, and tears are slipping from her closed eyes. "Baby, don't cry. Does it hurt?" I can't imagine how a dildo-esque object pushed into my body by a stranger would feel. I crush my hands into fists at my sides and breathe deeply while lifting an arm to caress the top of her hand with my thumb, trying to sooth her.

She shakes her head. "It's not that. I'm... I'm so scared," she whispers, but the doctor, who is focused on the screen, finally realizes that living human beings are standing here, waiting to hear about the well-being of their child, while she efficiently makes notes.

"Sorry, Mrs. Davis." She turns the screen and points. "You see this bubble?" We both nod. "That's your baby. See that little flicker?" We both focus on the tiny spot of light that's blinking.

"Yes," we respond in unison.

"That's the heartbeat." She writes something more down on Gillian's sheet.

I look closely at the screen as Gillian strangles my hand. I cast a glance in her direction and see her beautiful face filled with joy. She's beaming so brightly it's as if her entire face is luminescent, lit up from within. As though her soul has come to the surface and is sharing its warmth. It's hard to look away, but I see something that I need clarified. "Dr. Wong, what's that bubble and that little blinking?" I use my nail to show the spot away from the first bubble.

"Very observant, Mr. Davis." I smile, and it instantly falls off my face when she responds, "That's your other baby."

Now my hand is positively about to break in half. I try to yank it out of Gillian's clawlike grasp to no avail. Her other hand comes up to her mouth and muffles a gasp–sob combination.

The doctor looks from me, to Gillian, and back. "Congratulations, Mr. and Mrs. Davis. In approximately seven and a half months, you're going to be the parents of fraternal twins."

Twins. With that, I back up a few steps, Gillian lets go of my hand, and when my knees hit the chair, I slump into it. "Twins."

"Twins," Gillian repeats, her green eyes filled to the brim with fear. I stare into her eyes, her lovely pale face—the one I go to bed to, dream of at night, and have the blessed privilege of waking up to every morning. My wife. My wife, who's pregnant with twins. My twins. Jesus Christ.

Two children. Our family of three just grew to our family of four.

"Chase…" Gillian whispers, her voice catching. Within two strides, I'm at her side. I've got her in my arms as she cries into my chest. Sobs rather. Loudly.

"Baby, it's going to be okay. We're okay. The babies are…fuck me, the babies are…" I look over at Dr. Wong. She's pushing the machine back to its corner and washing her hands.

Over her shoulder, she responds. "Babies are great. Heartbeats are strong, and size is perfect for two six-week-old fetuses. We'll do a blood panel on Mom to make sure, but I don't think whatever drugs she was exposed to could have done any damage as the embryos likely hadn't even implanted when the initial attack occurred.

The doctor stops in front of us, Gillian still teary, snuffling into my chest. "Here." She hands us both a snapshot of the two babies, one with a little A next to it and B next to the other. Our children, A and B. I stifle a laugh. It's honestly not that funny, but I need to see to my wife, get her out of here so the two of us can process this.

"Thank you," Gillian says, awe clearly controlling her emotions as she runs a finger over each blob.

"The nurses up front will set you up on a regular schedule with me. I'll see you once a month for the next five or so months, and then we'll determine the birthing plan. In the meantime, I suggest you read up on twins, what's happening to your body, and take your prenatal vitamins. The ladies will give you a packet of information to take home detailing the next steps. And just remember"—she sets a hand on Gillian's knee—"women have been having babies for centuries, and twins are not uncommon in my profession. I'm going to take good care of you."

We both nod. "Thank you, Dr. Wong. We appreciate you seeing us so quickly," I say.

The good doctor smiles kindly and leaves the room.

Gillian face-plants into my chest again. "What are we going to do?" she says, though her words are muffled lost within the confines of my shirt.

"We're going to take it one day at a time, baby."

"But twins... I'm going to be huge!" She scowls.

"More of you to love...and to fuck."

That last part got a full chuckle out of her. God, she could heal the world's problems with just her laugh.

"Pervert."

"With you...always." I wink and help her get up. She

247

dresses, and we get our packet from the front desk and set up a slew of appointments, which I request an additional copy of.

"Why do you need a copy?" Her lips come into a thoughtful pout.

I pull her into my side as Jack sees us from within the waiting room. He opens the door and leads us to the SUV.

"I need a copy to give to Dana so she can make sure I'm available for our appointments."

Gillian's eyes widen, and her mouth drops open. "You're going to come to all of them with me?"

I narrow my gaze. "Of course. You're my wife. These are my children. Does it not involve me?" I'm not sure where she's going with this line of questioning, and frankly I find it off-putting. What kind of man impregnates his wife and then leaves her to the wolves to go through it alone?

She clasps her hands in front of her lap. "I guess I just thought men didn't go to things like that. Phillip hasn't gone to all of Bree's appointments."

"I'm not Phillip." She frowns, but even the mention of Phillip has me clenching my jaw. She pets the hammering muscle, and one of her eyebrows rises along with a smirk of her lips. "Gillian, I plan to be a part of every single moment of your pregnancy, even if it's just to see Dr. Wong stick a plastic dick-shaped camera up your pussy. My wife, *my* pussy, I want be there. Is that okay with you?" I ask, my tone making it clear that any answer other than a resounding "yes" will *not* do.

"Baby, you want to trample all over our doctor already?" She laughs. "I'm going to be dealing with a crazy, unreasonable, overprotective daddy-to-be, aren't I?" She sighs, and my hackles rise.

I huff. "I don't think it's unreasonable to ensure that my wife and my babies are getting the best possible care."

"That's a lot of 'my's' since we left the doctor's office, Chase. You think you can tone it down a little?" Her tone is sarcastic, and I don't care for it.

I shake my head. "Absolutely not." I pull her close with one arm around her back, and with the other I manage to check that her safety belt is firmly fastened. She rolls her eyes and makes no bones about ensuring that I see it.

"This is going to be a fun seven and a half months," she grumbles.

I think about her rounding out with child, her hips becoming insanely soft, her breasts hopefully growing along with her. I grin and imagine how incredibly beautiful she's going to be. "I can't wait," I say out loud, not really meaning to.

"You can't wait? For our children?"

I look down into her soft features, that light that shines so brightly behind her eyes. "Yes. You're going to be the best mother, and with you by my side, I have an excellent chance of doing okay myself."

She lifts my hand and places it over her flat stomach. "As long as we're together, we'll get through anything. We'll give them two parents, a wonderful home, and most importantly, a lot of love."

I tip up her chin with my fingertips. "In the span of a week, our family went from two, to three, and now to four. Thank you." Leaning down, I plant my lips over hers and kiss her silly. She accepts it and more, and then gives it back tenfold.

"I love you," she whispers into my mouth before sealing her lips over mine. We spend the next thirty minutes in rush hour downtown San Francisco traffic, making out like a couple of teenagers in the back of the family SUV.

GILLIAN

CHAPTER EIGHTEEN

Her face is deathly pale in sleep, but the monitors bleeping next to her prove she's stable. Her heart rate is where it should be, and the same with her blood pressure. She's been in and out of consciousness since she was moved to the Bothin Burn Center at St. Francis Memorial Hospital over a week ago. I finally got Carson to leave her side to catch a shower and some sleep. Promised him I wouldn't move from this chair until his return, and I meant that. There's nowhere I'd rather be than here with my Kat.

I push a stray lock of golden hair away from her face. Her eyes flicker open. They're glassy and unfocused, but she smiles anyway.

"Hey, Kat, there you are," I say soothingly, making sure I'm close to her. I'm holding her uninjured hand. She has light bandages covering the first skin grafting over her arm, the worst of the burned area. The neck is second, and then down the side of her ribs. We were informed she'll undergo a series of grafting and surgeries over the next year. Chase, of course, is making sure she receives the best possible care and has informed the board of directors of his interest and considerable donations he foresees in their organization's future. Again, I don't care if Chase throws his money around like a hammer as long as Kat gets what she needs to heal. Phillip did and is almost in perfect condition. I want that for Kat.

I look at Kat's face, the bandages surrounding the upper half of the right side of her body, and the tears I've been holding back fall. This is my fault. "I'm sorry," I choke out and hold her hand to my face, kissing the top of her hand repeatedly.

"Did you hurt me?" she asks in a low tone, her voice rough, as though she hasn't spoken in a month.

I shake my head while the tears fall to her hand.

"Then stop acting like you did," she warns. "Now, tell me what the doctors say?" Her eyes become harsh. "They keep sugar coating my prognosis and doping me full of drugs, so I either fall asleep or I can't think straight. I need the truth."

Clearing my throat, I lean closer to her. "I think it would be better if Carson…" I start, and she shakes her head and then winces in pain. I stand up. "I'll get the doctor!" Again she stops me with a squeeze of my hand this time.

"You're my sister. Tell me. I want to hear it from you."

I close my eyes, let out a breath, and without looking at her, tell her what I know in a long rush.

"You're stable. They have the carbon monoxide poisoning under control. They're watching your lungs for any signs of pneumonia."

"Gigi…"

The tears slip down my cheeks, but this time I open my eyes and try to be strong, for her. "They said you will have little use of your right arm and minimal to no use of your hand. The nerve damage was too extreme."

"Go on." Tears fill her caramel-brown eyes and slide down her cheeks. I almost break down and sob, but I can do that later. Now is when I need to pull up my bootstraps and be strong for my girl.

"Okay...um...they harvested the grafts from your bum and both inner thighs, but there should be very little scarring. The grafts are doing their thing now. You will probably have to undergo a lot more surgeries down the road, but the hope is that most of this will be behind you within a year or so."

Kat nods, tears falling, and I wipe them away. "So my career is over."

"No, Kat. That's not true. There are ways..."

She shakes her head. "Not being able to sew or use my hands, especially my right hand. As it is I'm going to have to learn to be left-handed. It's over, the dream, and the sooner I accept that the better off I'll be."

"Kat, you don't know that. You have no idea what the use of your arm and hand are going to be like down the road. With physical therapy. Nerves regenerate. Muscles can be retrained. Don't give up. Just do everything the doctors say. All of us will help you through. Carson will help you..."

Her words are as cold as ice when she says, "Carson? You mean the man who has never once told me he loves me?"

Shit. I thought they were past that. Unfortunately, I've been so busy the past three months, focused on my own situation, I never even bothered to ask. I'm a shitty friend.

"He loves you, Kat," I say with as much conviction as I have in my heart, because I really do believe he does.

She brings her chin down, her eyes dark and hard.

"Really? You think through all of this and everything we've been through he could have maybe said it...maybe even once?"

"But he's been here with you every step."

Kat nods. "Yeah, he has, but that could just be to save face. And now that my arm, neck, and side are burned beyond recognition, my ass and thighs have been scalped, you think he's really going to want someone who looks like this?" She shakes her head, and I do not like where she's going. As a matter of fact, I can feel where she's about to go, and I hate it.

"Listen to me, Kat. He loves you. He'll be here for you."

With a cough and a wince, she lies back on the pillow. "But do I want someone who doesn't love me to be here?" Tears fill her eyes once again, and she moves to lift her bad arm to wipe them away and cries out. The pain must be excruciating, even with the painkillers. As it is, the smell of her wound, the dressing, whatever salve they've put on it is making my mouth water with the sour taste that occurs right before I hurl. I do everything I can to push the nausea down, but her temperament, where her head is right now is not helping. It's physically making the tension in my stomach feel like acid swirling around and around, ready to crawl up my throat.

"Look, Kat, I know Carson feels deeply for you." She lets out a puff of air between her dry lips. "He does, or he wouldn't have been here this whole time. As it is, the only reason he's gone is because I forced him to leave, to take a shower, and get some sleep so he could be fresh and ready to keep vigil over you. He's not left your side since you were brought in from the fire. If that's not love, I don't what is."

Kat purses her lips and closes her eyes. "Maybe. I guess time will tell." Her response is vague and delivered with absolutely no feeling. I have to just chalk it up to her being in a very emotional, vulnerable position right now and let it go. My job is to be here for her. That's all I can do. That's all any of us can do.

Everything is in place. Dana called and said the food is being set up at Coit Tower for my date night with Gillian. Pinpricks of anticipation mingle with tension while I peek into the room where my wife is holding hands with Kathleen. They are both talking so low I can't hear the words, but it's definitely a serious conversation. Slowly, I back away, pull out my phone, and text my woman.

To: Wife
From: Chase Davis
I'm going to be later than planned. Have Jack take you to Davis Estate after hospital. I love you. Kiss our babies.

That should do it. If something happens to me and this shit goes down badly, Gillian and our children will have that message. She'll always know that I love her and our children. If she knew what I was about to do, she'd lose her mind. As it is, I'm losing my mind worrying about her and the two children within her.

Desperate times call for desperate measures. This is our fucking Hail Mary. If it doesn't work, I fear this will never end. I won't be able to protect my wife or our children. We'll constantly be under watch, waiting for the next strike. Neither of us can live like that. It's wearing Gillian so thin, and after everything she's been through—Justin, losing her mother, her friends getting hurt, watching my mother die, being kidnapped and beaten—no, no more. I cannot stand by and wait for him to get his hands on her again. I'll die protecting her, and my only regret will be never having seen my children's faces. It's a risk I have to take.

The undercover cop is already in the blacked-out SUV when I arrive. The sun is just setting on the horizon darkening the sky. Agent Brennen was to have the team in place as of early this morning. We don't want to take any risks that they'll be clocked by McBride when he arrives. A couple are in the old heating and air ducts, another set on the buildings pretty far away, but the FBI assures us they're the best. And of course, Agent Brennen is close—where, I don't know. Detective Redding is inside the top of the tower, secured in a cutout in one of the stone pillars, fully loaded weapon ready to go.

Once I get into the car, I pull off my shirt and put the Kevlar vest on.

"You think he's going to fall for me?" the pretty redhead says. She looks nothing like Gillian normally, but she has very pale skin and is the same height and build aside from my girl's vivacious curves. When I met Detective White, I looked at her small tits and thought the first thing McBride would notice were the lack of Gillian's sizable attributes. Now, though, staring her up and down, she could easily be Gillian from a distance. She must be wearing a heavily padded bra. The wig she's sporting is almost frightening in similarity to Gillian's incredible locks, completely covering this woman's normal brunette hair.

I nod while buttoning up my shirt. Her normally blue

eyes have green contacts in them that do not hide the fact that she's checking me out. Well, at least the faking him out part will be easy. "You like what you see?" I grin, falling back on my old pre-wife flirting habits before mentally chastising myself for the poor behavior. If my wife finds out I am here with this woman, about to touch and kiss her, she'll tweeze the hair from around my cock one painful tug at a time.

"I'm sorry, Mr. Davis. That was incredibly unprofessional."

I shake my head and push my arms back through my suit coat. "No matter. We're here to do a job. It helps that you're not put off by me. If this is going to work, draw McBride out, he can't think it's a setup. We need to carry on as if you're my wife at a romantic dinner." I smile, and she takes a deep breath. I grab her hand and hold it. She instantly startles. "See, you can't push away from me. He'll be watching. God willing."

Her jaw is tight when she nods, but after a moment of holding hands, she softens and relaxes. I look down at my phone and check one last time to see if Gillian has texted. She hasn't. And the screen does not show that she's seen my message yet. Good. That just means I have more time before she suspects something is up. To make sure I'm not swayed or distracted, I power off my phone, taking one last look at her smiling face. Then I pull the picture out of my coat pocket and scan the two hazy white figures.

"What's that?" the nosey detective asks, leaning close to me. I want to snatch it from her view and hide it away, but I can't. This may be the last time I ever see them.

Gritting my teeth, I show her the image. She looks at it and smiles wide. "Twins?" she gasps.

How the fuck do women know that right off the bat? It's two blurry blobs, for crying out loud. These things must be in some type of health class when a girl is growing up. One that the boys aren't privy to. She looks at the photo. "Your wife?"

I nod but put the picture safely back in my breast pocket right over my heart.

"I am a twin." She shrugs. "Fraternal like yours." Again, she knows they are fraternal just by looking at the picture. "My sister and I are really close. Look nothing alike, but shared a room growing up and, then through college, and now we live next door to one another. She's married with a kid, no twins though. They say it can skip a generation. Any twins in your family?" she asks.

The last thing I want to talk about are my twins, but I also don't want to put her off. I need her to play along. The future of my twins and my wife hangs in the balance. "Not that I know of."

"Huh, well, possibly your wife's?"

I shrug. "I wouldn't know, but you're a wealth of information. Thank you," I offer. The detective smiles brightly and then remains quiet, thank God, for the rest of the journey to Coit Tower.

When we arrive, I have her place a pair of Gillian's glasses on her face. Our guard in front of us hands us two cordless ear mics. She puts one in, and I follow her lead.

"Mr. Davis, can you hear me?" Agent Brennen's voice comes through the tiny flesh-colored mic crystal clear.

"I do. Can you hear me?" I ask.

"Roger that. We have not seen the suspect, but that doesn't mean he won't show or isn't already here. Stay sharp.

It will be expected to have your bodyguard lead you through the building and then leave you alone. He'll be waiting for that. Detective White, you good?"

"Dandy," she says.

"Got your Kevlar and your piece on?"

"Yes, sir." She lifts her skirt and shows me the gun tucked into a holster at her thigh. It does give me relief aside from the fact that she flashed her lace panties too. That I did *not* need to see.

"Good," he rumbles through the mic, and she puts her skirt down. "Detective Redding is already in place. Sniper one, call out."

"Locked on," the first man says.

"Sniper two?"

"On point." The second man's voice is deep, much more so than the first.

"Sniper three?"

"Affirmative." This guy's voice sounds downright scary. A gravely rumble that reminds me of thunder.

Agent Brennen's tone changes and gets low. "Eyes on, be careful, and play it the exact way we planned. We'll get this bastard in cuffs by the end of the night." That's if he's actually still tracking Dana's phone where we planted the seed. "All right, let's make it good and head out."

Those last two words get both Detective White and me moving into action. Our bodyguard opens the car door. I get out and hold her hand. I pull her close, and she snuggles into my side, tipping her face toward my chest. Perfect. In case the fucker is watching, he won't get a good look at her face.

We make it into the building without any problems. As

if I'm really on a date with my wife, I lead Detective White through the catacomb of the tower's floors. She takes off her glasses and makes sure her hair is fluffed in front of her, covering as much of her face as possible. Christ, I sure hope this works.

The walls throughout the Coit Tower are painted in murals. Some are sports activities, like rowing and golf. Others show old-fashioned farmers picking oranges.

"So, baby, do you know much about the tower?" I ask, holding her close. She shakes her head. Smart girl.

"Well, Coit Tower, also known as the Lillian Coit Memorial Tower, stands approximately two hundred and ten feet tall. It was built in 1933 using Lillie Hitchcock Coit's bequest to beautify the city of San Francisco. When she died, she left a third of her estate to the city for civic beautification. It was designed by architects Arthur Brown, Jr. and Henry Howard, with fresco murals by twenty-seven different artists.

"Interesting," she says, low and thoughtful, as I lead her to another mural. Her eyes are not on the paintings but the surroundings. She seems to note every subtle nuance in the air as we move through the designs. When this is all over and done with, I'll bring Gillian here. She'll be in awe at the artwork and the magnificent design.

"Also, the story claims that the tower was designed to resemble a fire hose nozzle because of Lillie's affinity with the San Francisco firefighters." I waggle my eyebrows, and she rolls her eyes. Now see, if I'd made that joke to Gillian, her laughter would have filled this room and echoed off the walls. I already miss her, and it's only been a couple hours.

Again, I lead the fake Gillian through the rooms, pointing to each painting, trying to make it look like we're in love. I nuzzle her neck, hold her close, and she smiles. At one point, she nuzzles my neck, and I can feel her kissing along the skin. Even though it's what I want, it still doesn't feel right, and absolutely nothing is going on down below. Looks like my cock even knows the difference between Gillian's touch and someone else's.

After spending a good hour going through the rooms and traveling up a multitude of winding staircases, we make it to the top floor. The entire tower is in the shape of a sphere. Large concrete pillar-type walls that have half-moon-shaped arcs lead to the end of the expanse. Open cutouts shaped like small doors that start waist high give an unencumbered view of the city of San Francisco and the Bay. Every window-like shape is accessible and allows you to view the horizon without screens or panes. When you stick your head out, it is as if the horizon meets up on the other side like interlocking puzzle pieces.

The view from up here is beyond the view I have at the penthouse, and that is a top-notch view. I lead fake Gillian over to the table where champagne is chilling and pour her a glass. Once she takes it, I lift mine up in a toast.

"I hope our future is as beautiful as you are today."

She smiles, clinks glasses, and leans forward for a kiss. I pull her into my arms and look down at a face I don't recognize. I close my eyes and place my lips over hers. They are warm and tentative, nothing like the fire and passion I feel when I kiss my wife. While I am kissing her, I place my hands to her face, pull back, scan the area, and see out of the corner of my eye a dark figure just peeking out.

"He's here," I whisper against her lips, and then take her mouth in a crushing kiss.

From: Husband
To: Wife

I'm going to be later than planned. Have Jack take you to Davis Estate after hospital. I love you. Kiss our babies.

I look at the name over the text and laugh. Kat smiles, and for the first time, I feel like everything is going to be okay.

"What is it?" she asks, her voice even more hoarse after having spent the last couple hours talking to me.

I shake my head. I want to show her that Chase has changed his name in my phone to "husband," but then she'd know we are married, and I want to tell them all together about the wedding and the baby—shoot, I mean babies. That is the hardest secret to keep. I want to shout from the rooftops that I'm pregnant with Chase's children. Twins. I still can't believe it. "Nothing, honey," I say and am startled when Carson enters the room.

"Hey, our girl is doing much better today." I stand and give him a hug. He halfheartedly hugs me and then rushes over to Kat. Her face goes from happy to closed off instantly. I slump against the wall, watching what she's doing.

"Sweet cheeks, she's right. You've got some color back."

"Not sweet cheeks anymore since they cut off a layer from my ass to put over my arm." She sighs and looks away.

I know what she's doing and why, but it's the absolutely wrong way to handle this. I watch the sparkle in Carson's eyes dim, and his shoulders sag. Defeat is a tough thing to battle, especially when you're playing against someone who thinks she has nothing left to lose. She is so wrong, but it's going to take her figuring it out. The only thing that I or any of the girls can do for her right now is be here whenever she needs us. Whatever decisions she makes are hers. There's nothing we can do if she chooses to push Carson away. I can only hope they'll make it past this rough patch because I know he loves her, and she's head over heels in love with him.

I let out a slow breath and try to call Chase as I walk out. It goes right to voice mail. Huh. He said he was working late and to have Jack take me to the Davis Estate, but that's the last thing I want to do. I could surprise him at work.

Leaning against the waiting room chair, I can see Jack speaking to one of the other guards. He clocks me and dips his chin, making it obvious that he's aware of me and will join me shortly. I can't wait until I can walk around without a shadow. Though now that I'm pregnant, and we're not only dealing with a psycho, but also dealing with the paparazzi on a regular basis, the odds of me walking free are slim to none.

Pressing some buttons, I wait for the ring.

"Davis Industries, Dana Shepherd speaking," Dana answers from Chase's private line at his office. I narrow my gaze and look at the clock. It's after six.

"Hi, Dana, it's Gigi. I know Chase is going to be late—" I start, but she cuts me off.

"Gillian, why aren't you at the tower?"

Tower? "I'm afraid I don't know what you're talking about."

X

DANIEL

CHAPTER NINETEEN

It's like watching a mouse in a maze, tracking them as they take in the murals of the tower. It's easy to stay just out of view. Every moment that goes by, I want to storm over, blast his brains all over the shit they call art, hike Gillian over my shoulder, and take her away.

Seeing him touch her, hold her close, has the rage within simmering, buzzing just under the surface of my skin. I don't even attempt to calm down. No, I need this monster inside me to come out, to show Chase Fucking Davis exactly who's in charge and who's going to leave here with the girl. My princess. She's always been that way since the moment I saw her at the gym that first time. Her pale skin was glistening like a shining star, her bright hair a halo around her pretty face. I knew that day, close to two years ago, she was the woman for me. Then I found out about her history, about how a man beat her, and that was it. She had to be protected, cherished like the princess she is.

Only now, she's lost that status. No, the second she lay with the rich fucker, debased herself like a dirty whore, she lost a bit of herself. I'm going to bring it back. Even if I have to break her down first, she will eventually come back to the perfect woman I know her to be.

Over the next hour, they hold hands, touch, making their way up to the top of the tower where it will all end. I can taste how good revenge will be when I lock my pistol right in between the eyes of the man who dirtied up my girl and planted his seeds in her. A sort of cooling calm slides all over me from head to toe, easing the tension, the anticipation. Everywhere except for my hardening cock. Thinking about taking him out, that rich fucker leaving this world, makes me hard as granite. Maybe once I've killed Chase, I'll take her up against the wall. Yeah, that will be memorable. The first time I get my princess back, I'll stake my claim. Spill my cum all over her muddy cunt.

Leaving them at the last level, I snake my way through the inner workings of the tower to where I need to be on top. Before I find my spot, I hear the sound of heavy feet coming up the stairs. I look out the windows but don't see any cops. I do see one blacked-out SUV. Motherfucking Jack Porter. I wonder where he is. I hold back a groan, stand firm in my position just around the edge of one of the turns in the stairs, and wait for his ass to appear. The second I see the giant black block of man that is Jack Porter, I swing my gun directly into his face. He falls back a few steps, grasping for the wall. I use that opportunity to lift my leg and kick the fucker hard. His arms flail and his powerful form falls down the stairs, rolling, rolling, rolling, until it finally stops at one of the flat landings.

I wait several breaths to see if he moves. Nothing. I hope he broke his fucking neck. Stupid dick. Walking back up to my spot, I leave Jack the giant jock and hold my position off to the side. Quietly as possible, I remove the safety off my gun the moment I see them trail up the other side of the stairs, hand in hand like two love-sick teenagers. Chase brings Gillian over to one of the sides. The entire tower is surrounded by open windows built into the stone. Her hair blows as the wind streams through. Fuck, she's beautiful. I could cut a goddamned diamond with my dick looking at her like that. My girl is perfectly at ease, looking out the window, not a care in the world.

It changes the moment the prick puts his lips all over her neck. She returns the gesture, rubbing all over him like a slutty call girl in heat. My hand clenches around the gun weighing down my arm. The burn I sustained when I killed my parents left a scar, and that fucker still itches. It always does when it's time to right an injustice. Like blowing up that gym, taking out the yoga cunt, killing Chase's mother. That was the sweetest day of my fucking life. Seeing Gillian in her wedding dress, standing there, her mouth open in a silent scream as the blood poured down the chest of old hag Davis. I knew in that moment that she was proud of what I'd done. Once again, I proved I could protect her. Even from a nasty old woman who couldn't shut her fucking mouth. Thought she had the right to throw barbs and daggers at my girl. Well, I made sure she could never say a filthy fucking word again. And I know, I know deep down inside Gillian was relieved, happy I'd taken action in her honor, and I always will. Just like tonight when I rid the world of one snobby rich prick who thinks he can steal my girl away with his money, fancy houses, limos, and jet planes. He can't, because ultimately, my gun and I are going to have the last word.

I take my time, watch a few more seconds as he leads her over to the table, pours her a glass of champagne, and says something stupid about their future. Then she leans forward—my girl fucking leans toward him! Holding the gun supremely tight, I find my way out of the shadows as Chase pulls Gillian flat against his chest and kisses my woman. Fuck! The time is now.

"I just assumed you and Chase would arrive together, but you're seriously late!" Dana blows out a long frustrated breath into the receiver.

"Dana, hold on. I don't know what you're talking about. I've been at the hospital all day with Kat."

"I get that. What I don't get is why you aren't at the Coit Tower with Chase. He's planned this incredibly romantic dinner for the two of you." Her voice comes across panicked, and I can't for the life of me understand why.

None of this makes any sense. "Okay. And when did he plan this?"

"Days ago. It was supposed to be a celebration. Congratulations, by the way, on getting married and the baby!" she squeals into the phone.

Bastard! He told his assistant, but I can't tell my best friends. He is going to be in so much trouble when I get my hands on him. "Thank you, Dana. We're very excited about the twins."

"Twins!" she screams into the phone, and I have to wait until she calms down.

"Dana, where's Chase now?"

As if she's run out of breath, she says, "he's at the Tower. I sent a car with one of the other bodyguards. The entire thing is set up for dinner, so you'd better get down there fast."

"I don't understand. He sent me a text saying he had something to do late tonight, and he'd see me back at the Davis Estate."

Dana goes dead silent. "Why would he lie?"

Then it hits me. All the whispered conversations he's had before bed, off to the side of the hall at the hospital, first thing when he wakes up. I know he's been working with Thomas, Agent Brennen, and Jack, but honestly, would he put himself at risk?

I don't even need to think about it. He'd do just about anything, putting himself in the line of fire to ensure the babies and I are safe. "Fuck!" I roar into the phone.

"Jack!" I scream down the hall. He stops whatever he's doing and literally runs to me. If you've never seen a giant NFL-sized man run in a suit, you're missing out. It's extreme, it's lethal, and something I'll remember for the rest of my days. "Gotta go, Dana."

"Mrs. Davis." Jack clasps my shoulders, his dark eyes piercing mine.

"Chase is going after Danny alone. Probably working with Tommy and that agent. He's at Coit Tower now. He's going to do something stupid."

"Let's go." His voice comes out in a deep bark.

Jack and I race to the parking garage and to the car. Jack's flying out into traffic within minutes of my giving him the rundown. It takes twenty of the most intense moments of my life to get to the tower, only to have Jack stop at the front entrance loading zone like he was in a bad cop chase movie. Just when I grab the handle to get out, he locks the doors.

"Stay in the car," he growls.

"But..." I try.

"Stay in the fucking car!" He takes a tone with me that he never has before. It's scary, it's bad ass, and it actually frightens me a little. "This guy is after *you*. You go in there, he has you. I'll bring Chase out. Got me?"

Looking into the fierce eyes of one Jack Porter, I whisper, "I got you."

Then he's gone. Up the stairs and out of view. For five nail-biting minutes, I wait. Then I wait two more. Nothing. I can't handle it. The prickles are firing all up and down my scalp, the hair of my arms, and down my spine. Fear replaces the prickles. Not fear for me. Not for our unborn babies. Fear for Chase. The love of my life. This life isn't worth living if I don't have him to share it with.

I hit the unlock button and am running up the steps to the tower in seconds. Once I get to the top, I can't see anyone through the glass doors but am supremely thankful to find them still unlocked.

If I were Chase or Daniel or even Jack for that matter, I'd sneak up the stairs, find every dark corner possible, and hide in it. Only I'm not them. I'm me. So I'm going to take the path more often traveled. And if I know my husband, and I'm pretty sure I do, if he was going to make a romantic gesture, even a fake one to ferret out Daniel, he'd go big. So the top of the tower it is. I hit the button for the elevator, and it opens with a ding. The double blue doors shut, and then I see a set of metal gate-like doors. I push those closed, hoping I'm doing the right thing, and lock them into place. Now that I'm inside, I look around for a panel of buttons to get to the top and find there isn't one. However, on the back wall there is an old-fashioned lever with a ball at the end of it. Making a guess, I shift the lever from the left side to the right. Instantly the car starts to go up. I'm assuming it's going to take me to the tower level.

The elevator creaks and rumbles as it goes up the twenty-one floors. Eventually it stops, and it's so loud I'm afraid the entire building heard my arrival. Either way, I know my man is up here sacrificing himself for me, and I'm not letting him put himself into the frying pan alone. The blue doors open. After struggling with the metal door, I finally get them to unlock and open into place so I can walk through. A sign across the wall says "Top of Tower Use Stairs."

Now I'm scared. The hallway is dark, barely lit by a speck of light lining the floor every few feet. Fire lights probably. I reach the stairs and slowly make my way up. I hear the sound of wind screaming through an open space and brace myself for the chill.

I do not expect what I see when I arrive at the top stair. Chase, my husband, kissing another woman.

On instinct, I yell, "Chase!" The words come out of my mouth like a banshee wail, complete with the heartache it brings. He pulls back from the redhead who looks frighteningly like me. His head flips around behind him, and then I've got his eyes. Sadness, fear, love hit me like a wall of fiery heat as our gazes lock.

"No!" he yells, his face becoming hard. And that's when I see a dark figure behind Ms. Redhead. One holding up a gun. Aiming at Chase's back.

I scream, but it's not enough. The man fires twice.

Chase's body jerks midair, his body flying up, back arching as a roar leaves his lips before he falls into a heap on the floor. Oh my God! My feet move, and I run into the fray, not caring that someone has a gun.

It's as if everything happens in slow motion. The redheaded woman riffles under her skirt, pulls out a gun, and aims it across the way and fires. The shooter comes into the light of the moon, and I see Daniel, his blond hair now dark, his face covered in hair. He fires back two shots, pinning the woman right in the chest.

"No!" I scream, useless as she falls to the floor like a domino.

I almost make it to Chase when Danny grasps me around the waist. My feet go flying into the air as I struggle to get to my man.

"Leave him," Daniel growls, his voice filled with hatred.

"Danny, I need to get him help," I cry, kicking, my eyes focused on the lifeless bodies in front of me.

"Where they're going, they don't need help." His voice is a knife shredding my heart.

Danny moves us close enough to them that I can see Chase isn't moving. His face is looking away from me. The redhead's too, so I can't figure out who she is. But she had gun, so I'm guessing she's an undercover cop. Daniel stops all movement when he gets me into a position where his grip is around my chest and the steely cold of his metal gun is pressing into my temple. He pushes me away from their bodies, right against the flat wall of the tower next to a window. Out of nowhere, I see a single red dot glance off the wall next to my head. Danny sees it too and reacts lightning fast, swooping me into a more hidden location behind a pillar.

The wind is blowing viciously from the open spaces. He brings the gun up to my face and presses it under my chin. "Fucking snipers." He looks around and makes sure he's not vulnerable. One side of the tower faces the Bay, which means the snipers must be on the other side. This doesn't seem to faze him at all, because when I look into his eyes they are solid black, colder than I've ever seen before.

"Danny," I whisper, trying to appeal to the side I spent months with. The side I was extremely fond of for almost a year.

"How dare you let him marry you? Fuck you? Stick his bastard child inside you?" He presses the muzzle of the gun deep into my chin. I whimper, not knowing what to do or say that will help, and right now all I can think about is Chase lying unmoving ten feet away and I can't get to him.

"Daniel, I know you don't want to kill these people. Please, call for help. I'll go anywhere you want. Do whatever. Just don't let them die." The tears fall in a river down my cheeks.

He shakes his head. His light eyes are giant and black as night. "No fucking way. They can die right here, and you can watch. Maybe I'll turn you around, get you on your knees, and fuck you like the whore you are, the way you wanted me to fuck you when things went to shit. You know." He grips me painfully by the hair, pulling at the roots. I look everywhere, wondering where Jack is, why he hasn't intervened, and then worrying that maybe Daniel already got the lock on Jack.

"You looking for the fucking bodyguard?"

My eyes fly to his once more.

"Yeah, I knocked that fucker out nice and quiet so as to not interrupt the festivities. He took a tumble down a flight of stairs. Now that I know all this was a setup, all the better. I'll go back and shoot him in the face, and you and I will be off the grid. Of course, after I take you home so I can rid your body of the vile parasite."

"Not my babies." I hold a hand protectively over my stomach. My body goes frosty cold, and I pray. Pray to God to get me out of this, to save my children, to not take Chase away from this world.

"Babies? You mean there're two of those fucking disgusting things inside of you? Motherfucker!" he roars. He looks at my face, presses me harder into the wall, and gazes down my body, his lips a fierce scowl. "You're infested. And it's my job to clean you up. Make you pure again. Put my baby in you."

That's when the fire lights under my ass. He's going to kidnap me, use me for his personal fuck toy, and kill my children. Not going to happen. I look at his face, grind my teeth down, and snarl, "Over my dead body." I pull back a knee and slam it as hard as I can into his dick.

He lets out a pained cry and crouches as I push him back and start to run. If I can get outside, I can get help. He catches me right before I reach the stairs, swings me around, and punches me in the face so hard I see stars. Blood oozes out of my broken lip, and he wraps a hand around my neck, cutting off any air and slamming me back against a pillar again.

Just as I'm about to black out, I hear the click of a safety being removed from a gun. "Back away from her." Hearing Tommy's voice has never been more welcome.

Danny loosens the hold he has around my neck, allowing me to take in some blessed air. I suck in huge amounts before he locks the grip down again. I struggle and try to kick out, missing my target uselessly.

"Let her fucking go, McBride," Thomas screams.

"Okay, man, I will." But before I can warn Thomas, Danny crouches low and issues a leg sweep, knocking him off his feet. I slide down the wall to the ground. Thomas's gun goes clattering, but his hands are fast and he pulls Danny down. They wrestle for Danny's gun, and a shot goes off.

Blood instantly starts to spread from a wound in Danny's body. Thomas stands up, turns around, and is almost to me when I see his body fly forward. He slams into the wall where the large open window is. The force of the hit has his body toppling over the window ledge and out into the night sky. While in midair, Thomas turns his arm. I scream, and a shot rings out, but I don't see where it lands. All I can see is Thomas, his body floating in midair, arms flailing as he barrels twenty-one stories to the ground. I scramble for the window and see his mangled, lifeless body on the ground. Behind me, I hear a gurgle. I spin around and crouch down, protecting my stomach.

Danny is standing there swaying, a river of blood flowing down the front of his neck where the gunshot ripped open the tissue, making his head hang at an odd angle. His eyes roll back into his head, and his entire body falls face first onto the concrete floor in front of me.

The world around me goes pitch black. All I can feel is everything within me and around me is shaking, my teeth chattering so hard I can hear the noise like a woodpecker pounding on a tree, only the tree is my head. Then, a familiar warmth surrounds me. My body is being moved, adjusted, floating, and then nothing but love surrounds me. I'm suddenly encompassed by a cocoon of light and love. Arms around me, large chest plastered against my side until I'm in a seated position in someone's arms.

Citrus and sandalwood fill my nostrils, and I open my eyes. The blackness shrinks, the fuzzy edges sharpening until I see his face. The most beloved face I've ever known. The one I watched cry out in agony as two bullets pierced his back.

"I'm dreaming. You're dead." I let the words escape out my lips and into the wind.

My love shakes his head, holds my cheeks. "I'm here, baby."

I shake my head, tears trailing down my cheeks, drying as they fall, sticking against my skin. "I watched you die."

Chase leans back, rips open his shirt, and puts my hand on the hard material. "Kevlar."

"But, but he shot you in the back. I saw you go down," I hiccup and sob unbelievingly.

"Knocked me out. There's pain, but not enough to keep me from you."

"Oh my God, oh my God, oh my God," I chant into his neck over and over. He holds me close, filling me with life once again.

That's when things get crazy loud. Sirens blare, voices yell, the sound of feet hitting concrete at a run slamming into me. I hold Chase close and cower into him. If I'm in his arms, it will all go away.

"It's over, baby. He's dead."

I nod against his neck, but then remember why he's

dead. Thomas. "He pushed Tommy out the window."

Chase's entire body tenses, and he holds me close. "Fuck."

"He's dead," I say flatly, not even knowing how this will change the very threads of my world as I know it.

"Baby…" he whispers into my hair. "H-He died a hero," he offers in a raspy whisper, the emotion clogging his words.

Again, I breathe in his scent, trying to let it bring me back to the here and now. Just knowing that someone else I love is about to be destroyed breaks me half. Danny took one more person with him on his way out. Maria's Tommy. Our friend.

"Yeah, but now I have to tell my best friend that the man she loves is dead." My tears are coming so fast I don't even have the time to wipe them away. Instead, they soak Chase's shirt. He doesn't care, just wraps me in his embrace and gives me everything he is, everything I need.

★ ★ ★ ★

The nightmare is over, but not without heavy losses.

The men and women who died at the gym. Charity, the young twenty-year-old yogi look-alike to Bree. Phillip with his hospitalization, coma, and months of physical therapy. Dana being used like a pawn to the point where it's doubtful that she'll ever trust a man again. Austin, my southern bodyguard, who's still suffering the effects of being poisoned by Etorphine. Colleen, Chase's mother, who was a mean bitch, but she loved her son and wanted nothing but to protect him, was brutally murdered on our wedding day.

Kat, who's being treated in a special burn unit, will never sew again, and the beautiful light in her eyes is currently gone. Jack, who's in the hospital being treated for shattered hips, a broken clavicle, and a severe head injury. And last, our hero, Thomas Redding, the young hotshot detective who had a woman who loved him and a whole life to live, gone, after falling twenty-one stories to his death while protecting me. Now my soul sister Maria is left to pick up the pieces of her life after losing the one man she gave her heart to.

No, I'd say the nightmare is not over, but we're strong. Together we'll find a way to deal with the past, the present, and the future.

CHASE

EPILOGUE

Three years later...

"Take it, baby. You take my cock." I slam into her over and over. "Fuck, yeah." Gripping her hips tight, she mewls and presses back into me.

"Chase." The sound comes out soft, sweet, and the way I like it. Her head falls down in front of her as I power into her juicy cunt. The fiery curls of her hair skim the white sheets every time I thrust. Leaning forward, over her back, I roll her hair around my wrist, grip the roots, and lift her up and on my cock, her knees planted to the mattress.

"Gillian, baby, you like it when I fuck you hard?" I ask her, and then pull my cock out and slam home. She cries out.

"Oh, God, I'm gonna come again," she pants into our large room.

"Yes, you are. Over and over. Didn't I promise you that?" Stirring my hips, I can feel the moment when her pussy locks down on my cock. It takes all my effort not to come into her sweet cleft. She's so wet, her skin flushed from two orgasms. Once her body is a boneless heap, I pull her off my cock, turn her around, and take her mouth, pushing her down flat on her back. She opens her legs willingly, allowing me to fit in-between. She thinks I'm going to enter her again, and I will, after I've had a taste.

I slip my hands down and cup her sex. She's so wet I growl into her mouth. "You're dripping down your thighs, baby," I say, as I spin two fingers around her sensitive clit.

"I can't," slips out of her lips, but I know better. My wife can come over and over. I've clocked her at six times in an evening.

Kissing her long, full, and deep, I keep playing with the hard little button until she squirms beneath me. There it is. My woman is back in the game, ready to go for a third orgasm. It takes strength, but I pull away from her succulent mouth and kiss my way down her body, making sure to stop at her fucking perfect tits. I suck, bite, and nibble on the plump tissue until her hips are fucking air. Oh, yeah, my wife is ready.

I lick my way around her bare, flat stomach. Caressing the area with just my fingertips, I can imagine this area stretched wide with my children. She was a fucking goddess big and pregnant. Nibbling around her belly button, I span the area with my hands and move my face between her thighs. Her scent alone could make me shoot my load. Inhaling deep, I get comfortable and suck at her flesh. The second I touch down, she rocks up, reaching for more. "Greedy," I growl into her pussy, licking my way all over her drenched sex. Her taste cannot be compared to anything. She's sweet, yet salty, rich, musky all at the same time. Basically, the most decadent of desserts, one only I get to enjoy, and Christ, do I enjoy her. I eat her like a man who hasn't had a solid steak in a decade. I gorge on her until she gives me what I want, and that's her screaming out in release. I slurp and drink from her until every drop is gone. Until I'm filled with her everywhere—her taste, her touch, her arousal, her body open to me. She gives it all, and I take it as often as I can.

Soon she calms, and I crawl up her body, sink my dick as far into her as I can go. She groans and juts her head back, offering me her neck. That's when I take it slow. She's already had three orgasms, her cunt is raw, but I like fucking her into submission. It's the only time I can get my fiery redhead to do what I want.

She moans and sucks in a breath as I take her particularly deep, pressing high and hard into that spot within her that makes her gush. Her green eyes go wide and panicked. This is it, the moment I wait for. That moment where she looks lost and found at the same time. She's just come. She's so sated that I could ask her what her name is and she wouldn't be able to tell me. Then in a moment of surprise, I can see the second she realizes her pleasure was a lead-up to the big finale.

I press my cock deep and lock down. Her pussy spasms around me, squeezing my dick so tight I could lose my mind. It's like the sweetest, tightest glove. Almost like when I'm fucking her ass, only when I fuck her hard like this, I can see her face, and that's what I need. What I'm hungry for. I've had her ass, her tits, her pussy, her cum on my tongue all over me and around me, but nothing beats this. That split second of panic where her pleasure and the tiniest bit of pain coalesce and break her defenses down, leaving me with the barest version of her. She breaks down, and I put her back together, with my eyes, my words, my love. Fucking beautiful.

We come together, her entire body clenching around mine, her mouth open in a silent scream that rocks her to the core. Eventually, she either passes out or blacks out. It's not the first time, and I silently promise it won't be the last. While she's out, I get up, hit the bathroom, bring back a warm washcloth, and clean between her legs. The combined fluid has already started leaking out of her. Seeing me coming out of her gives me the biggest sense of pride. I know it's fucked up and twisted, but I love seeing a piece of me spilling out of her. Knowing I was there, that a portion of me will be in her for days, and keeping with that, I make sure to keep her full of me. I never felt this way with another woman, but my wife brings out the animal side in me. Especially after what she's survived. We've survived.

Pulling back the comforter, I tuck her back into bed. It's still early, but I'm sure Colin and Rebecca are entertaining the kids.

I toss a pair of pajama bottoms and a T-shirt on and make my way across the house. I look out the windows lining the hall and see the rolling landscapes of our home in Bantry, Ireland. The ocean has a fine mist, blocking a perfect view, but it will burn away when the sun is high.

As I approach the kitchen, I can hear giggling and banging noises. When I enter the kitchen, my children are playing on the floor with plastic bowls, wooden spoons, and cups.

Claire's fiery red hair is a wild mess of curls, her ocean-blue eyes sparkling in delight as she sees me. She lifts her chubby two-and-a-half-year-old hand up and waves the spoon in greeting. "Daddy!" she says clear as day. Claire has always been social, started talking very early, and never stops.

I walk over and scoop my girl into my arms, throwing her in the air and then nuzzling her sweet baby neck, giving her a set of raspberries. She howls with glee, and I set her back down to play with her utensils.

My son, Carter, is more pensive, thoughtful, exactly like me. He assesses every situation, considers his course of action, and then reacts. He never does anything on a whim, and I get that. The only thing I ever did on a whim was approach a redhead I didn't have the time for on a day I wasn't prepared to meet the woman of my dreams. I lift up my boy. His dark hair is rich, the color of a roasted coffee bean, but his eyes—they are like looking directly into my wife's emerald gaze. He's going to be a handsome young man.

"How's my boy today?"

Carter purses his little pink lips together, tilts his head, and thinks about it. "Good." His response is matter of fact before he adds, "better if we eat pancakes."

I laugh and snuggle into him. He's not the type to howl with glee like his free-spirited, whimsical sister. No, he just accepts the attention quietly and with a smile.

Setting him back down, I note that there's a steaming cup of coffee on the counter sitting next to two large chocolate chip homemade cookies. "Thanks, Rebecca," I tell the house help while munching on my first bite of chewy goodness. Colin and Rebecca have turned more into family than just the help. Rebecca feeds us and helps with the children and does the housework. Colin keeps the grounds and makes sure everything is in order. They've been fantastic, and the children adore them.

"Becca, pancakes?" Carter requests with a smirk.

Oh, I know that smirk. It's the same smirk I use on his mother. Works every fucking time. And of course, Rebecca melts and gets out the mix.

Claire leaves her household items in preference of coming over to me and lifting her hands. "Up, Daddy," she demands with absolutely no concern for whether or not I want to hold her. She knows I always want her in my arms. If I'm not holding my wife, I'm holding one of my children. I scoop her up, and she wraps her arms around my neck. Together we go out onto the patio, but not before she takes a monster-sized bite out of my cookie. I don't care. We share cookies every morning. At least when Mom's not awake to see it.

Our guests should arrive soon. The rooms have been made up, and I know Gillian is beyond excited to see them. It's been months, and we've taken the entire summer in Bantry. Now that it's coming to an end, we want to spend the last couple weeks with our friends and family.

A little hand smacks at my face. "Daddy?"

"Yes, sweetie?"

She holds my chin in her hand, her little face very serious. "I want a sister," she says definitively. I'm convinced these children are advanced. Gillian believes it's the *My Baby Can Read* series she's been doing with them, but whatever it is, it's working.

I scrunch my nose and kiss her cheek. "Now why would you want that?"

Her sweet blue eyes narrow, and the wild red curls glint in the sun. "Car-Car don't like dollies."

I nod. "You make a very good point, sweetheart. How about I talk to Mommy about it?"

She smiles one of her I-own-the-universe smiles, scrambles off my legs, and goes running into the house, screaming, "Sister, sister, sister."

"Planting ideas in our daughter's head again?" The voice within all of my sweetest dreams lays a hand to my shoulders. Gillian leans forward, and I'm instantly assaulted by the scent of vanilla and sex. She hasn't showered yet. Mmm, I love smelling me on her. I turn fast, pull her around the waist, plop her into my lap, and kiss her silly, her arms looping around my neck.

Gillian gives her all in every kiss, and this one is no different. When she pulls away, she's smiling as brightly as our daughter. "Claire decided she wants a sister," I announce. I'm greeted with a sharp pointed brow.

"And what did you tell her?"

I nudge my nose against hers, kiss her again, and say, "I told her I'd talk to you."

"Do you want more children?" Her gaze is guarded.

I slide a hand up to cup her cheek, not liking that she's hiding something in those emerald pools. "Hey, I didn't promise her anything."

"But do you want more kids?" she asks, biting her lip.

Looking deep into her eyes, I respond honestly and without hesitation, "Marrying you, having Claire and Carter has filled my life with reason and purpose. Making another baby with you could only make our lives more full."

She kisses me hard, wet, and deep, and then pulls away, gasping. She sits up, pulls her hand she's been hiding around my back, and shows me three sticks I'm very familiar with.

"I'm glad you think so, because it's time to pee on three sticks."

Her eyes are smiling, the sun is shining down on us, and the sound of our children playing in the kitchen doesn't prevent me from lifting her up, her legs wrapped around my waist, as I carry her into our bedroom.

The children squeal in delight seeing Daddy carrying Mommy through the kitchen. Rebecca just shakes her head and continues making pancakes.

"What are you doing?" My wife laughs into my neck, but I don't stop until I've led her through the house and to our master bath where I set her on the vanity.

"You need a glass of water?"

"I love you," she says, kissing me.

"I love you more. Now, woman, get down and pee on these three sticks. Can you do it all at once?" I ask with a heaping dose of déjà vu coming over me.

Her eyes quirk into a point. "Do you like having sex?" I look at her and laugh. "I told you once before don't ask me stupid questions." She shakes her head. "God, men. Dumb."

"Is there a test that tells you if we're having twins again?" I ask her while she proceeds to pee on the three sticks. Then her eyes come up, looking pained.

"Do you seriously think we'd have two again?"

I shrug. "Anything's possible."

"Fuck me," she cusses.

"I did. That's why we're here again."

We both laugh until we can't laugh anymore. She sets the sticks on the counter and jumps back into my arms. Instead of waiting the five excruciating minutes, I choose to undress her and fuck her up against the shower wall.

When we get out, happy, clean, and sated again, the three tests are there, our answer another blaring moment of déjà vu.

Two lines.

One plus symbol.

One electronic device clearly stating: PREGNANT

The girls arrive in one long limo. Bree steps out, her petite little body back in perfect shape. She steps aside, and her little mini-Bree they named Dannica toddles out. At three years old, she already has hair down to her shoulders, and it's the color of spun gold. Her blue eyes are soulful and happy. Her little legs bring her to me fast, and I lift her into my arms and hug her tight. "How's my precious girl?"

"Ire Land is forever away. That plane never stopped." Well it obviously did, but in her three-year-old mind it took a very long time.

"I know, precious, but Rebecca has treats waiting for you."

She runs off into the house. It's not her first time here. Our families have come here three and four times a year since we had the children. It's been a wonderful home away from home for all of us.

Bree embraces me, pulls back, and looks at me. "You're glowing." She squints and her lips twist into a pretty pout. "Shit. Again?" She shakes her head. "Just when you got that fine body back." She clucks her tongue. "How far?"

"Just found out for sure today." I watch as Phillip shuffles out of the limo.

"Crazy girl. I'm never having any more. My body is my temple, and after pushing out God's most perfect child, I am not risking a demon spawn. Besides, we have Anabelle too, so technically, I have two."

"Whatever. Rebecca has food out on the patio ready to go. She included all the healthy organic shit you like too."

"Excellent!" She smiles and heads into the house. Phillip gives me a teddy bear hug. "I need a beer." His face looks tired, and I know that look. It's the same one I have after a twelve-hour flight with my children.

"Where's Anabelle?" I look around and find her hiding behind her dad.

"Boo!" she screams, so I act frightened. Then I hunker down and hug her little body to mine. Her bright blond hair smells exactly like Bree's. It's refreshing and reminds me of the yoga studio.

After hugs from the Parks family, I turn back to see Maria stepping one long dancer's leg out of the limo. Damn, that girl has a great pair of legs. "*Cara bonita*, that is one long flight." She says this every time. "But thanks for flying us in one of the Davis jets. They treat us like royalty, *mi amiga*," she says happily, pulling me into her arms. Directly behind her is a giant of a man. Massive, with eyes so familiar I gasp. Every time I see him it takes me back there. Back to three years ago when we lost Tommy. It's hard to look into his face without remembering.

Chase places a hand to my shoulder and brings me into his arms when Maria locks one around her beau. I don't judge. I never have, and she's finally happier than she's ever been, and it took a really long three years to get to this point.

"Go on in. Soup's on," Chase says, and the two locked at the waist enter our home. I shiver against Chase. "It's okay. I know you miss Thomas. It's hard for me to see her with him too. It will get easier. Just takes time."

"Three years is a long time," I remind my husband.

"But it hasn't been that long seeing them as a couple."

"True."

"Speaking of couples, I wish Carson were here."

"Me too, babe, me too, but we can't get involved. It's her life. We just need to love and support her the way only you and your girls can. I'm here for backup," Chase whispers in my ear as Kat walks up the path alone.

She's wearing a long-sleeved shirt in the dead of summer, and seeing it hurts my heart. I'm sure she's dying of heat, but she refuses to show her scars. Says she gets too many questions or grossed out looks. As it is, she keeps her hand tight to her body so people don't comment on the mangled tissue. When it's just us girls, she'll remove her sweaters or allow the skin to be visible. It's not pretty, but the last reconstruction made her neck smooth as well as down her side. Her arm still looks like skin was wrapped around an abraded surface, so it's bumpy, different colors, blotchy, the skin pulled tight in some places and loose in others. The surgeons have done what they can, but she'll live most her life with a deformed-looking arm. She can now grip things in her hand but nothing with substantial weight.

Finally, she reaches me, and I lock my arms around her. She's like sunshine and love rolled into one, but a sadness fills her. One so deep we've tried for the last three years to heal it, but it hasn't left her. I know only one person who can fix her, but he's tried over and over. Still, she refuses to let him back in. I fear he'll move on. No man is strong enough to be turned down for three years and continue waiting. Last I heard, he was finally dating someone else. It nearly broke her.

Now she seems okay. Every time we're in Bantry, it's as if the entire crew can breathe again.

I lock my arm around her waist and lead her to the patio. We all sit down, and drinks are passed around, food is hefted onto plates, and the four children run around at the landing below the first deck. Chase had Colin put up a small fence so the kids wouldn't run off toward the ocean cliffs. We also added a swing set and toys to keep them occupied.

Once everyone's sitting, Chase brings out two bottles of pink champagne. The same we drank on our wedding night, here in Bantry, three years ago today. Once all the glasses are poured, he grabs my hand and walks me to the edge of the table where all eyes are on us.

"Three years ago today, my wife and I eloped. At the time, it was what we needed to do to be together. Though we wish you could have all been there, you were definitely there with us in spirit.

"I'd like to start the next two weeks of celebration by reminding my wife of the promise I made to her three years ago today." Chase picks up my hands turns me to look into my eyes. "Gillian Grace Davis, I promise to love, cherish, and worship the ground you walk on every day of my life. I'll strive every day to be the man who's good enough for a woman like you." Just like when he said these words to me three years ago, my eyes fill with tears. He smiles wide when he sees them fall. "When you cry"—he moves forward and kisses each cheek—"I'll kiss away your tears. When you love, I'll love you in return. I will never forsake you, and I'll always make you and our children..." He looks over his shoulder at Claire and Carter running around with Anabelle and Dannica, and then he puts a hand over my stomach. Half of the table gasps, our secret fully out. He grins. "I'll always make you and our children," he repeats, "priority number one. Today is the first day of the rest of our lives as one whole family. Three years ago, I found my other half. Through infinity."

I look deep into his Caribbean-blue eyes so he can see how much he means to me, how important this moment is surrounded by the people we love, the family we chose, our children, and a baby on the way. "Infinity," I repeat and then kiss him. When he pulls away, I whisper the words I said to him and meant with my whole heart. "Chase William Davis…"

He holds my gaze, and I see the moisture there, the same way I did on our wedding day. Then I say the exact words he wants to hear.

"I give you me. Body. Mind. Soul."

TO THE READER

I want to thank you for taking this journey with me. Sometimes it was gut-wrenching, other times filled with laughter, a lot of heat, and mostly heaping bouts of love.

My mother was a victim of domestic violence for ten years. In the Trinity Trilogy, I wanted to bring light to a very difficult subject but also to show that with the right support, women who have been in a violent relationship can make it through that time in their lives and come out strong to live healthy, beautiful, fulfilling lives. Of course I've taken liberties with the rich billionaire, but that part is fiction. <wink>

If you are a woman being emotionally or physically abused, I encourage you to seek help. Tell a friend, call a battered woman's shelter or a domestic violence hotline. If you type the words "DOMESTIC VIOLENCE HOTLINE" into your internet browser, you will be given a wide variety of options to call and get immediate help in your area. *Taking that first step is the hardest.* Women everywhere are silently saluting you on making the first move. If you close your eyes and try really hard…you can feel us. Solidarity.

For the rest of the readers who were unhappy with Thomas Redding losing his life and Maria losing her man, there is a plan for her and a book with her story in it coming. Same for Kathleen and her time with Carson and her experiences recovering from her injuries. I promise... they will eventually get their happily ever after. For now though, I need to take a little time to write something less soul-altering.

Thanks again for being with me.

Namaste.

Audrey

ALSO BY AUDREY CARLAN

The Calendar Girl Series

January (Book 1)
February (Book 2)
March (Book 3)
April (Book 4)
May (Book 5)
June (Book 6)

July (Book 7)
August (Book 8)
September (Book 9)
October (Book 10)
November (Book 11)
December (Book 12)

The Falling Series

Angel Falling
London Falling
Justice Falling

The Trinity Trilogy

Body (Book 1)
Mind (Book 2)
Soul (Book 3)

ACKNOWLEDGEMENTS

For this one, I don't have to dig deep. It's important that I give credit to my real life soul sisters without whom I wouldn't have Maria, Kathleen, or Bree. Dyani Gingerich, Nikki Chiverrell, and Carolyn Beasley I love you. That deep, really intense kind of love, the kind that if I ever lost you my heart would break and my soul would shatter. This trilogy has been so much fun because the three of you allowed me to loosely base characters off of you, and I think the readers connected with the story more because of them. Thank you for being you so I could be me. BESOS.

To my PA Goddess, Heather, White, For making the most incredible teasers for this entire series…I give you one helluva Namaste my friend. Your art has brought attention to the series and there is no amount of thanks I can give for beauty like that. I think you're extremely talented and I'm so thankful to have you in my corner, on my team, supporting my work but most importantly believing in me and being my friend. I love you to the moon and back. One day we'll be signing in Europe my friend. You just wait!

To my critique partner, Sarah Saunders, for all the endless conversations about where the characters were going, letting me work the plot out with you, loving it maybe even more than me…I can only say I appreciate you more than I can ever give you credit for within these pages. If every author had a

critique partner like you, we'd all be best sellers!
To my editor Ekatarina Sayanova with Red Quill Editing,
LLC, I like to joke that you're smarter than a dictionary but
I honestly believe it. You're FREAKY smart. I like freaky.
<wink> All joking aside, I came to you with this book
knowing I was begging for your team to do it in one week.
Three to four times less than the norm. I applaud YOU for
meeting that challenge and doing a damn fine job. Also thank
you to Tracy Roelle for aiding in the editing process.

Any author knows they aren't worth their weight unless their
story is backed by badass betas. I have the best!

Ginelle Blanch—I always say it, but I mean it with my whole
heart...you prevent me from looking like an idiot. That alone
makes you a rock star! Your betas are incredible, thoughtful,
and right on point. Always. You're someone I have come to
count on and have become instrumental to my review process.
I hope it always stays that way because I love you lady!

Jeananna Goodall—My number one fan, my pre-reader, my
beta reader, my friend. So many titles for one lovely lady. It must
be tiring being superwoman. You always cry over my characters
because you live them the way I do and that is something very
hard to define. Thank you for your unwavering commitment
to my work. I love you more than you know.

Anita Shofner—I shall bow down to the queen of tenses and
pass over the crown. You blow me away Anita. I don't know
how I got so damned lucky to score a chick with an uncanny
ability to find such unique errors but I did, and you do, and
I'm thankful. So humbled to have your talent on my team.
Love you.

Lindsay Bzoza—My wicked fast beta girl. I bet if there were a
race between you and speedy Gonzales, you'd win. My money
is on you girl. Thank you for taking this on last minute.

To my street team, Audrey's Angels I can hardly type these
words I'm so filled with love and emotion for you. Each and

every one of you gives me hope that one day my books will be read and enjoyed by the masses. You make me believe that one day my dream of being a New York Times bestselling author could come true. Thank YOU Angels for committing your time, energy, and effort into helping me succeed. BESOS Angels!

If you are interested in hanging out with the craziest, most loving, wild chicks in all the romance world, contact me via Facebook to get your wings and become and Angel.

Special Thanks:

To Give Me Books and Kylie McDermott for spreading this book far and wide into the virtual stratosphere through your release day blitz...I owe you! Thank you to you and all your girls but especially my dream team Beth Cranford, Missy Borucki, and Devlynn Ihlenfeld. You ladies read my books and share your honest opinions and always find beauty in them. BESOS ladies!

ABOUT AUDREY CARLAN

Audrey Carlan lives in the sunny California Valley two hours away from the city, the beach, the mountains and the precious...the vineyards. She has been married to the love of her life for over a decade and has two young children that live up to their title of "Monster Madness" on a daily basis. When she's not writing wickedly hot romances, doing yoga, or sipping wine with her "soul sisters," three incredibly different and unique voices in her life, she can be found with her nose stuck in book or her Kindle. A hot, smutty, romantic book to be exact!

Any and all feedback is greatly appreciated and feeds the soul. You can contact Audrey below:

E-mail: carlan.audrey@gmail.com
Facebook: facebook.com/AudreyCarlan
Website: www.audreycarlan.com